Books by Laura Levine

THIS PEN FOR HIRE

LAST WRITES

KILLER BLONDE

SHOES TO DIE FOR

THE PMS MURDER

DEATH BY PANTYHOSE

CANDY CANE MURDER

KILLING BRIDEZILLA

KILLER CRUISE

DEATH OF A TROPHY WIFE

GINGERBREAD COOKIE MURDER

PAMPERED TO DEATH

DEATH OF A NEIGHBORHOOD WITCH

KILLING CUPID

DEATH BY TIARA

MURDER HAS NINE LIVES

DEATH OF A BACHELORETTE

DEATH OF A NEIGHBORHOOD SCROOGE

Published by Kensington Publishing Corporation

A Jaine Austen Mystery

DEATH OF A BACHELORETTE

LAURA LEVINE

KENSINGTON BOOKS
www.kensingtonbooks.com

KENSINGTON BOOKS are published by

Kensington Publishing Corp.
119 West 40th Street
New York, NY 10018

All Kensington titles, imprints, and distributed lines are available at special quantity discounts for bulk purchases for sales promotion, premiums, fund-raising, educational, or institutional use. Special book excerpts or customized printings can also be created to fit specific needs. For details, write or phone the office of the Kensington Special Sales Manager: Attn. Special Sales Department. Kensington Publishing Corp., 119 West 40th Street, New York, NY 10018. Phone: 1-800-221-2647.

Kensington and the K logo Reg. U.S. Pat. & TM Off.

ISBN-13: 978-1-4967-0847-2
ISBN-10: 1-4967-0847-4
First Kensington Hardcover Edition: July 2017
First Kensington Mass Market Edition: June 2018

eISBN-13: 978-1-4967-0848-9
eISBN-10: 1-4967-0848-2

10 9 8 7 6 5 4 3 2 1

Printed in the United States of America

For Frank Mula
The funniest (and kindest) man I know

ACKNOWLEDGMENTS

As always, a big thank you to my editor extraordinaire, John Scognamiglio, for his unwavering faith in Jaine—and for his never-ending supply of terrific story ideas. (Honestly, the man is a walking plot machine.)

And kudos to my rock of an agent, Evan Marshall, for always being there for me with his heartfelt guidance and support.

Thanks to Hiro Kimura, who so brilliantly brings Prozac to life on my book covers each year. To Lou Malcangi for another outstanding dust jacket design. And to the rest of the gang at Kensington who keep Jaine and Prozac coming back for murder and minced mackerel guts.

Special thanks to Frank Mula, man of a thousand jokes. To Mara and Lisa Lideks, authors of the very funny Forrest Sisters mysteries. And to Jan Wallis and Nick Roulakis for graciously allowing me to use their names. (Blessings, Jan!)

Hugs to Joanne Fluke, author of the bestselling Hannah Swensen mysteries, for her many kindnesses—not to mention a cover blurb to die for.

Thanks to John Fluke at Placed for Success. To Mark Baker, who's been there from the beginning. And to Drucilla and the friendly folks at Skydive Santa Barbara (www.skydivesanta barbara.com) for cluing me in on a murder that was simply too good to pass up.

XOXO to my family and friends—both old and new—for your much-appreciated love and encouragement.

And finally, a heartfelt thank you to all my readers and Facebook friends. I've said it before, and I'm saying it again: I wouldn't be here without you.

Prologue

I swear, it was a miracle. Okay, maybe not as big as the parting of the Red Sea. Or Daniel surviving that lion's den. Or how M&M's melt in your mouth, not in your hand.

But a miracle nonetheless.

I watched in disbelief as my cat, Prozac, lay snoozing on my bed in her spiffy new cat carrier. Yes, Prozac, the cat whose longest record for staying silent in her carrier was about thirteen and a half seconds, had been napping for a whole twenty minutes without a peep.

And I owed it all to my good buddies at Wiki-How, who'd given me some much-needed tips on how to prepare my kitty for an overseas airplane flight.

I'd been feeding her in her carrier for the last several days, getting her used to her plush new accommodations, throwing in one of my old cashmere sweaters for good measure. Now the place was like a second home to her, a kitty pied-à-terre.

And Prozac's exemplary behavior was only one of the many miracles that seemed to be floating my way.

Just last week, after answering an ad in *Variety*, I'd been hired as a writer on a TV show shooting on a Pacific island off the coast of Tahiti.

The show in question, called *Some Day My Prince Will Come*, was a *Bachelor* type rip-off, where a gaggle of gorgeous young bachelorettes gathered together to vie for the hand of a handsome European nobleman.

Wait. Did you actually think people on reality shows just say what comes out of their mouths without any help? That enemy housewives just happen to be seated across from to each other at parties in the Hamptons? That drunken catfights erupt out of sheer chance? I hate to be the one to disillusion you, but the shows' producers are the ones plotting all these lively stories, and, at least on *Some Day My Prince Will Come*, there was a writer on hand churning out bon mots for the characters to say other than, "Eat dirt, you bitch/skank/ho!"

And I, Jaine Austen—ordinarily a writer of ads and brochures for small businesses like Toiletmasters Plumbers (*In a Rush to Flush? Call Toiletmasters!*)—had been hired to write said bon mots.

Can you believe it? I was getting paid real money to jet off to be a TV writer in a tropical paradise!

And not only was the show's producer letting me bring Prozac; but for once in her feisty life, my feline significant other was cooperating with me, hanging out in her new cat carrier without the slightest yip of protest.

How lucky could one gal get?

Of course, there's always a fly in the ointment, and the fly at that particular moment was my neighbor, Lance Venable.

That day, Lance was sitting on my bed, helping me pack. And by helping me, I mean driving me crazy.

With each item I tossed into my suitcase, he wailed stuff like:

My God! Elastic-waist pants? Are you insane?

Who was the last person to wear that bathing suit? Ma Kettle?

Yuck!! Where'd you get that dowdy top? Forever 71?

Lance, who fondles the feet of the rich and famous at Neiman Marcus's shoe department, fancies himself a fashion guru and is forever bombarding me with unwanted advice.

"How do you expect to meet the handsome show biz exec of your dreams if you show up in these ghastly outfits? Don't you have anything more sexy? A flirty little sundress?"

Somehow I resisted the urge to strangle him with my Ma Kettle bathing suit.

"The closest I've got to flirty is this," I said, holding up my prized I'M OUT OF ESTROGEN AND I'VE GOT A GUN t-shirt.

"Whatever you do," he said, blathering on, "promise me you won't wear any of your pathetic elastic-waist capris."

"Yeah, right," I said, shoving in another pair when he wasn't looking.

"I'm so sorry I can't keep Prozac while you're gone," he said, making a tsking noise at Pro's carrier. "But you know how it is when she and Mamie get together. Like Thelma and Louise on steroids."

Only too true. Prozac has been known to lead Lance's adorable pooch Mamie on all sorts of daring escapades, including but not limited to chewing on electrical wiring, gnawing at baseboards, and a little game they've invented called Bowling with Houseplants.

"Not a problem," I assured him. "The show's producer has pulled some strings with the locals in Tahiti so Prozac won't have to be quarantined."

"Isn't bribery wonderful?" Lance gushed. "If you ask me, it's the bulwark of a civilized society."

"And besides," I said, "I don't think it's a good idea for Prozac and me to be apart. Too much separation anxiety. All that yowling and screaming and crying."

"True," Lance nodded. "And Prozac gets sort of upset, too."

At which point, my pampered princess awoke from her slumber and sauntered out onto the bedspread, yawning a yawn the size of a sinkhole.

My, that nap was refreshing!

And with that, she promptly curled up into a ball and began another one.

"This is so darn exciting!" Lance said, scratching Pro behind her ears as she dozed. "Just think what this job could mean!"

"I know. Maybe I can make the transition from small-time ad copywriter to big time TV writer! Maybe I'll never have to write another ad for Toiletmasters ever again."

"There's that, of course, and your chance to meet that European nobleman. The prince of *Some Day My Prince Will Come*. Promise me you'll find out if he has a cute available brother. I've always wanted to date nobility."

"Got it, Lance. My top priority will be finding you a noble boyfriend. I'll get to work on it as soon as my plane lands."

"Aren't you an angel," he said, my sarcasm whizzing past him undetected.

"I hope you haven't forgotten," I said. "When I'm gone, I need you to take in my mail and mist my Boston fern."

"No problemo, honey. It's as good as done. Which one's the Boston fern?"

"The green thing with leaves."

I led him into the living room and pointed out a delicate fern I'd recently bought and had been nursing tenderly.

"Got it," he said. "Mist Boston fern."

"Every day."

"Every day. Just call me Mr. Greenthumbs."

"Thanks so much, Lance. I really appreciate it."

"Don't be silly, hon. That's what friends are for. Well, must run and feed Mamie. I'll pick you up bright and early tomorrow to take you to the airport. Just remember—"

"I know. I know. No elastic-waist pants."

And off he zoomed to his apartment.

I ordered Chinese food for dinner that night and ate it in bed, Prozac chowing down on bits of shrimp from my shrimp with lobster sauce, a cool breeze wafting in from my bedroom window. I didn't know it then, but I was to think of that breeze longingly in the days to come.

Hours later, I settled down to go to sleep, thrilled about my exciting new job, certain I was jetting off to paradise.

Little did I realize I was heading straight for the jaws of hell.

Chapter 1

It took about nine hours to fly from L.A. to Tahiti—nine of the most harrowing hours of my life.

All that training I'd done with Prozac, getting her used to her carrier, keeping her calm and relaxed, worked like a dream—until we actually boarded the plane.

After which she began yowling at the top of her lungs, a cry so piercing, so decibel-shattering in the narrow confines of our crowded coach cabin, even the cranky toddler across the aisle was giving me the stink eye—pissed, no doubt, that Prozac had robbed him of his title as the Most Aggravating Passenger on board.

The whole plane was buzzing with annoyance as Prozac's shrieks ricocheted around the cabin.

I even heard one of the flight attendants mum-

ble to her partner as they rolled the drink cart
down the aisle, "It's days like this I wish I'd kept
my job at KFC. Those paper hats weren't so bad
after all."

Prozac's nonstop wails were silenced only by a
steady succession of kitty treats and, as it turned
out, a good portion of my in-flight meal. Finally,
when my eardrums could stand it no longer, I
fell back on the pet owner's last resort in times
of crisis: a healthy dose of valium.

And I'm happy to report it put me down for
two hours.

When I woke, I discovered Prozac and her cat
carrier were gone.

Oh, heavens. Had some furious passenger spir-
ited her off to the lav and done away with her?

No, it turned out that the coach passengers
had taken up a collection to move Prozac to first
class, where I found her sprawled out on a plush
leather seat, nibbling at a plate of caviar.

Desperate to shut her up, the flight attendants had taken her out of her carrier and given
her what she'd wanted all along: a nice comfy
chair all to herself, away from the plebes in
coach.

At which point, she'd apparently switched to
full-tilt Adorable Mode, cocking her head at a
rakish angle, purring happily, and batting her
baby greens.

At least that's how I found her when I came
bursting through the curtain to first class.

"Prozac!" I cried. "I was worried sick. I thought
someone had kidnapped you."

She looked up at me lazily.

Oh, hello there. Don't you belong in coach?

"I hope she hasn't been any trouble," I said to the aristocratic lady sitting next to her.

"No, no trouble at all," the grand dame replied, cheekbones sharp as Ginsu knives. "Bad behavior is never the fault of the cat. It's always the owner."

From her lap of luxury, Prozac gave an appreciative meow.

How true. How true.

Eventually, we began our descent to Tahiti, and Prozac was returned to coach and placed in her carrier, howling every minute of the way.

When we finally taxied up to the gate at around noon Tahiti time, Prozac and I were the first to leave the plane, escorted by the captain with a cordial warning to never again step foot in his aircraft.

After bidding him a hasty toodle-oo, I hurried off to the gate, where I was greeted by a burly islander with gold front teeth and muscles the size of rump roasts.

And, as promised by the producer of *Some Day My Prince Will Come*, I was whisked past customs and their animal quarantine department straight out to the tarmac and into a golf cart that zipped us over to a small airplane hangar.

At first, I thought we were at some sort of aeronautical graveyard where ancient aircraft came to die.

The plane standing before us in front of the hangar was old. Really old. Amelia Earhart and goggles old.

"Here you go, missy," my gold-toothed guide said, pointing to a rusty set of steps leading up to the decrepit plane.

Seeing the fear in my eyes, my rump-roast guide assured me, "Plane very safe, missy. Made by Boeing Corporation."

No doubt in their Popsicle stick division.

Taking a deep breath, I climbed on board to meet the pilot, a doddering fellow with a matchstick dangling from his lips and a disconcertingly rheumy look in his eyes.

It was a half-hour trip to our destination, Paratito Island, and once again there was nonstop howling. This time from me.

Never had I experienced a more bumpy flight.

Honestly, I felt like I was in the spin cycle of my washer.

But at last we landed, and I climbed down the rickety steps, thrilled to have survived the flight.

The first thing that greeted me when I stepped on terra firma was a blast of furnace-hot humid air. I'd gone from the spin cycle straight to the dryer.

Already I could feel my hair frizzing like an overfertilized Chia Pet.

Looking around, all I could see was a small shack, a few dusty palms, and floating clouds of gnats. Then suddenly a lanky, twentysomething guy came charging out of the shack, whooshing past me onto the steps of the plane, a feverish look in his eyes.

He stopped halfway up and turned to me.

"So you're the patsy they roped into the job," he said, staring at me with unabashed pity.

"Patsy?"

"You're the new writer, right?"

"Guilty as charged," I nodded.

"They hired you to take my place. The show's already chewed up three writers. If you know what's good for you, you'll get back on this plane and get the heck out of here."

Of course, if I knew then what I know now, I would've hustled up those steps ipso pronto.

But at the time I thought he was just a Negative Nelly. Surely the job couldn't be that bad. He was probably one of those writers with a giant ego, who got all hot and bothered if a single syllable of his lines was rewritten.

No way was I about to pass up a TV writer's salary.

And besides, I simply couldn't face another nine-hour plane trip with Prozac.

"Thanks, but I think I'll stay."

"Then take this," he said, tossing me a can of bug spray. "You're going to need it."

With that, he hustled off into the plane.

Minutes later, the plane took off with a sputtering roar, leaving me alone on the tarmac with my suitcase and Prozac, who, exhausted from her in-flight wailathon, was at last asleep in her carrier.

My gold-toothed guide in Tahiti had told me someone would be picking me up at the airport, but so far, my only greeters had been these damn gnats. I was beginning to feel a bit like

Cary Grant stranded in the cornfields in *North by Northwest*, when suddenly a Jeep came roaring onto the tarmac.

And things brightened considerably when I checked out the guy behind the wheel—a handsome native dude with rippling muscles, jet black hair, and amazing brown eyes.

"Jaine Austen?" he asked, hopping down from the Jeep in shorts and tank top, exposing thighs to die for. "I'm Tai, your driver."

He flashed me a megawatt smile, almost blinding me in the process.

"So nice to meet you," I managed to sputter, sucking drool back into my mouth.

"Let me get your things," he said, hoisting my suitcase onto the backseat of the Jeep.

"And who's this?" he asked, gazing at Prozac, still snoring and barely visible behind the mesh in her carrier.

"It's my cat. She's exhausted after the flight."

"Poor little thing," he tsked.

Save your pity for me, I felt like saying, but instead offered up what I hoped was an incandescent smile.

"Well, hop in," he said, opening the passenger door of the Jeep for me.

Oh, lord. Is there anything more awkward, more tush-exposing, than climbing into the front seat of a Jeep? Honestly, I bet pole dancers show less tush in their routines.

I only hoped my fanny didn't look too ginormous as I climbed on board.

Tai handed me Prozac in her carrier, then hopped in beside me and took off.

"How interesting that you have a cat," he said as Prozac's snores filled the air. "Cats have played a large part in my tribe's cultural mythology."

"Is that so?" I said, eyeing his thighs and hoping my hair hadn't mushroomed into too much of a frizzfest.

"You must be a noble person to keep such a treasured animal in your life."

"Kinda sorta," I said.

After what I'd just been through on that plane, I was ready to nominate myself for sainthood.

"Anyhow, welcome to Paratito Island," Tai grinned. "Did you know that Paratito is Tahitian for 'paradise'?"

And indeed, as the roads wound away from the airport, the scenery had become lush and verdant, with swaying palms and bushes laden with a riot of brightly colored blossoms.

"Yes," I said, sneaking a peek at the muscles popping out from under Tai's tank top. "It sure looks like paradise to me."

We rode along for a while, me admiring the view, sometimes even the one out the window.

"So do you work on *Some Day My Prince Will Come*?" I asked.

"Part-time," Tai replied. "I drop off and pick up things from the airport. Mainly I'm in charge of picking up Manny's pastrami."

"Manny's pastrami?"

"Manny Kaminsky. The show's executive producer. He has pastrami flown in fresh from New York every week."

"Wow, that must cost a fortune."

"Manny can afford it. Wait'll you see his mansion where the show's being shot. What a palace. We're almost there now."

He turned off onto a pitted dirt road and began an ascent through dense brush dotted with run-down wooden cottages. I didn't know what Tai's idea of a mansion was, but these sure weren't it.

Then at the crest of the road, the mansion appeared—a sprawling extravaganza studded with Moorish archways, room-sized balconies, and a wide verandah—all set on a sea of velvet green grass.

Tai drove up a circular driveway to the mansion's front entrance and then hopped out from the Jeep, retrieving my suitcase from the backseat.

"Well, it's been fun talking," he said, flashing me another toe-tingling grin. "Hope I'll see you around."

With my usual cool and collected sangfroid, I shrieked, "Heck, yes! Me, too!"

Then Tai hopped back in the Jeep, muscles rippling, and tore off down the driveway.

And I couldn't help thinking about that foolish writer urging me to go back to the States. What a ridiculous idea. If Tai was any indication of the working conditions here on Paratito Island, I was clearly in for the job of my dreams.

I was standing there watching a butterfly flit from one hibiscus blossom to another, dreaming of moonlit kisses with my colorful native driver, when I heard:

"You must be Jaine. Thank goodness you arrived in one piece!"

I turned to see a wiry slip of a thing, her brown hair swept up in a ponytail, black-framed glasses slipping down the bridge of nose, her forehead obscured by a carpet of shaggy bangs.

"I'm always afraid that codger of a pilot is going to crash the plane smack into the Pacific!"

Clad in jeans and a T-shirt, she carried a clipboard clutched to her flat chest.

"I'm Polly Reilly," she said with a welcoming grin. "The show's production assistant/slave laborer. Come on in."

I followed her onto the mansion's verandah and past a massive front door into an open foyer with a view clear through to the other end of the house. Beyond the foyer was a spectacular living room furnished with designer sofas, island-themed knickknacks, and what looked like a couple of genuine Gauguins on the wall.

Sliding glass doors at the far end of the living room revealed a patio, pool, and another vast green carpet of grass beyond. I stood there, gaping at the wonderfulness of it all.

"It's quite a place, isn't it?" said Polly. "What God would build if He owned a hedge fund."

No doubt sensing she had arrived at deluxe accommodations, Prozac began meowing in her carrier, demanding to be set free.

"This must be your cat," Polly said. "Manny

told me you'd be bringing her. Let's get her out of that icky-smelling carrier."

So much for the Triple Strength Odor Eater potty liners I'd spent a fortune on.

"Aren't you the cutest thing ever?" Polly said, taking my pampered princess from her carrier.

Prozac purred in ecstasy.

I like to think so.

"C'mon," Polly said, handing Prozac to me and grabbing my suitcase. "Let me take you to your room."

With that, she led me to a grand staircase at the far end of the foyer.

"It's so sweet of you to carry my suitcase," I said. "You sure you don't mind?"

"Not a problem, hon. You must be exhausted from your flight."

"Yes, it was a bit trying," I said, glaring down at Prozac.

Who just glared right back up at me.

I'll say. I can't take her anywhere.

"There are only three bachelorettes left on the show," Polly said as we started up the stairs. "All the others have been eliminated. You should have seen those gals go at each other. It was like World War III with push-up bras."

Following Polly, I came puffing up to the second floor, which seemed to stretch out as long as a hotel corridor, lined with rooms on each side and huge double doors at each end.

"That's Manny's suite," Polly said, pointing to the doors at the far end of the corridor. "And this suite," she said, pointing to the double doors near us, belongs to the prince of *Some Day*

My Prince Will Come. Who, by the way, isn't really a prince. Spencer Dalworth VII is an earl from some county deep in the backwoods of Great Britain. But he's eighty-seventh in line to inherit the throne, so I guess you could say he's a prince-in-waiting.

"The rest of the bedrooms belong to the bitch-lorettes. I mean, bachelorettes. Now that the others have gone, they each have a room to themselves. As long as we're here, you may as well meet them.

"Here's Brianna's room," she said, turning into the first room along the corridor, a large bedroom with four single beds, bare mattresses on three of them. Only one of them was made up, and a statuesque redhead in a tank top and leggings sat on it, polishing her toenails. A tall drink of estrogen, with volleyball boobs and legs that went on forever, the woman was a *Playboy* centerfold come to life.

A delicate blonde with her hair pulled back in a demure headband sat next to the redhead on the bed, an open yearbook between them. The blonde wore shorts and a halter top. Not a speck of fat visible on her. Or cellulite. Heck, I was having a hard time even finding a mole.

I couldn't help hating them both just a tad.

"Hey, girls!" Polly said. "Say hello to Jaine Austen, the new writer. Jaine, this is Brianna Scott."

The redhead looked up from her toenails and lobbed me a weak smile.

"And I'm Hope Harper!" the blonde chirped. "Great to have you on board! Oh, look!" she said, catching sight of Prozac. "A kitty! Isn't she adorable!"

Her little pink ears always on the alert for praise, Prozac preened in my arms.

So I've been told.

"I was just showing Brianna my yearbook," Hope babbled on. "I was voted class president, treasurer, and the girl most likely to succeed!"

She whipped her yearbook off the bed and proudly showed me her "Girl Most Likely to Succeed" photo. It was a younger version of her current self, but the eager smile and determined thrust of her pointy chin was still the same.

"Very impressive," I said.

Brianna stifled a yawn.

"Well, I'd better show Jaine to her room," Polly broke in, cutting short our trip down high school memory lane.

"I hope you brought plenty of bug spray" were Brianna's parting words to me as we started for the door.

How odd. First the fleeing writer. Now Brianna. Why were they warning me about bugs? It was delightfully air-conditioned here in the mansion, not a bug in sight.

But before I got a chance to ask exactly why I'd need bug spray, all hell broke loose.

A stunning brunette with lush chestnut hair cascading down her back came storming into the room, oozing fury from every pore.

"Which one of you bitches stole my hair extensions?" she shrieked in a heavy Texan drawl.

Why on earth this woman with a head full of

shampoo-commercial hair would need hair extensions was beyond me. But apparently she needed them, and felt their absence strongly.

"Jaine," Polly broke in, eager to staunch any possible flow of blood, "meet Dallas, our third remaining bachelorette."

The brunette took a break to flash me a smile almost as dazzling as Tai's, after which she returned to her tirade.

"So who's got my hair?" she demanded of her fellow contestants.

"I have no idea what happened to your stupid extensions," Brianna said, sploshing polish on her big toe.

Dallas whirled on Hope.

"I bet it was you, you calculating little twerp. You'd do anything to lure Spencer away from me. But it won't work," she added with a confident grin. "He already told me I'm the one he wants to marry."

A tremor of shock flitted across Hope's face.

"He did?" she asked.

"He did!" Dallas crowed in triumph. "And stealing my hair extensions isn't going to get him to change his mind. I'm beautiful with or without them."

Indeed she was.

"But I'm warning you guys. When I find out who took them, there'll be hell to pay."

Then she turned on her heel and marched out the door, her glossy hair bouncing with every angry stomp of her feet.

"And this," Polly whispered, "is one of the good days."

Chapter 2

Bidding Hope, Brianna, and her nail polish adieu, I followed Polly up another flight of stairs to my room on the third floor.

"Do you really think Spencer asked Dallas to marry him?" I asked, as we started up the steps.

"I wouldn't be surprised. He seems gaga over her. Can't say as I blame him. She's a spoiled brat, but she's the best of the lot. Hope is a conniving operator, and Brianna's one G-string away from being a stripper.

"Although why any of those gals would want Spencer," Polly added, as she trudged along with my suitcase, "I'll never know. From what I hear, he's stone broke and lives with his mom in some dilapidated estate in the middle of nowhere. And 'Mummy' seems quite the tyrant, always chasing him down on his cell phone. Something tells me he's a bit of a mama's boy."

By now we'd reached the top floor of the mansion. I blinked in disbelief. Suddenly we'd gone from mansion to flophouse. Gone were the deluxe finishes. The place was barely dry-walled, with water stains on the ceiling and gaping holes where electrical outlets were supposed to have been installed.

The first thing that greeted me when I set foot on the landing was an oppressive blast of heat. Holy mackerel. It was like a sauna up there.

"I'm afraid there's no air-conditioning on the third floor," Polly said with an apologetic shrug.

She led me along unfinished wood floors to a tiny cell of room whose décor I can only describe as Jailhouse Chic: Lumpy bed with a sliver of a pillow and ragged bedspread. Card table posing as a desk, accessorized with a gooseneck lamp and folding metal chair.

The only thing missing was a urinal in the corner.

But there was one bright spot. An overhead fan on the ceiling. With the window open and the fan running, maybe it wouldn't be too hellishly hot in there, after all.

"Thank goodness there's a fan!" I said. "I'm sure going to need it."

Another apologetic look from Polly.

"I'm afraid it doesn't work, hon," she said. "Manny never did finish the electrical work up here. But you've got an outlet for your gooseneck lamp," she added with a hopeful smile.

An electric lamp. Whoop dee doo.

In my arms, Prozac thumped her tail in disgust.

I demand an upgrade!

I put her down, and after an imperious sniff at the unfinished floorboards, she hopped up on the bed, sprawling out on the bedspread.

Wake me when it's time to eat.

She'd just assumed her perch there when I saw something big and black and shiny skittering out from under the bed. Yee-uck. A waterbug. On steroids. Never had I seen a bug that big. I swear, it was the size of a golf ball.

At last I understood why my predecessor had tossed me the bug spray.

But I wouldn't need any insecticide. Not with Pro around. She's a natural-born predator.

"Go get that waterbug, Pro!" I commanded. "Sic 'im!"

Pro looked at me with wide green eyes.

Are you nuts? Did you see the size of that thing?

By now she was practically hiding under the pillow.

So, without any further ado, I whipped the insecticide out of my purse and gave the bug a blast.

I waited for it to wither and die, but the darn critter just stood there, stunned for a beat, then trotted right off again. I could not believe my eyes. This thing was the Godzilla of waterbugs.

"I'll get it!" Polly said, running after it. She stomped at it with her foot, but missed, and Godzilla slithered away under a baseboard, disappearing without a trace.

"Welcome to paradise," Polly said, with a wry grin.

Seeing the stricken look on my face, she added, "You think this is bad? You should see the cabins where the rest of us are staying. I'm lucky if I don't wake up with a snake in my bed.

"Gotta run, hon. After you get settled in, stop off and see Manny. His office is downstairs off the foyer. He wants to meet you and fill you in on your writing assignment. Basically, they're hiring you to write chatter for Spencer. He's a sweet guy. But dumb as an ox. It's all that royal inbreeding, if you ask me.

"Well, see you later."

And off she went, ponytail swaying, leaving me to fry in hell.

I was putting my clothes away in my cubbyhole of a closet, Prozac clawing at my already thread-bare pillowcase, when I heard a soft knock on door.

I opened it to find a timid island woman in a maid's uniform. In her arms she carried a litter box and water bowl.

"Hello," she said with a shy smile. "I'm Akela, your maid."

A maid? For me? At last, a luxury!

"I'm supposed to bring you these." She held out Prozac's cat supplies.

"Thanks so much," I said, taking the pile from her. "I'm Jaine, and that's my cat, Prozac."

I pointed to Pro, who, having conquered my pillow, was now snoring on top of it.

The maid took one look at Prozac, and her eyes widened with fear.

"No kitty! No kitty!" she cried.

Oh, great. My maid was afraid of cats. Something told me that was the last I'd be seeing of her. So much for having my bed made in the morning. Or chocolates on my pillow at night.

She raced off, and I looked for a place to put the litter box.

When I opened what I thought was a closet door, I discovered a tiny en suite bathroom, consisting of a sink, commode, and a shower the size of a phone booth.

I set down the litter box in the cramped space between the toilet and the phone booth shower.

A small window above the sink let in the faintest waft of a breeze. I sucked at it eagerly, then turned on the water in the sink, desperate to splash my face and neck with cool water. But when I turned on the tap, all that came out was a blast of rust. Eventually it turned clear, and I started splashing. But the pipes must have been boiling. The water flowed out sluggish and tepid.

After a few splashes, I felt about as refreshed as the limp towel hanging from my towel rack.

Slapping on a bit of lipstick, I checked my hair in the tiny mirror above the sink and groaned to see that in this humidity it had now blossomed into the mother of all Brillo pads.

Oh, well. There was nothing to be done about it.

Gathering my courage and my laptop, I started off for my meeting with Manny.

I took one last look at poor Pro, still spread-eagled on my pillow, limp as a wet rag. I felt terrible about leaving her in my sauna of a bedroom. I opened the bedroom window as wide as possible to let in the maximum breeze, grateful it was firmly screened in.

"I'm so sorry I got us stuck in this horrible room," I said to her as I started out the door.

Stirring from her slumber, she looked up and shot me a baleful glare.

Not half as sorry as you're going to be.

Oh, dear. I didn't like that look in her eyes. Not one bit.

Chapter 3

The door to Manny Kaminsky's office was open when I got there, and he motioned me in as he talked on the phone.

A barrel-chested guy straining the seams of his loud Hawaiian shirt, he sat behind a massive teak desk, a cigar clamped in his hammy fist. His dyed black hair perched in a thinning nest on the top of his head, cemented in place by buckets of industrial-strength hair spray.

"I want that pastrami as lean possible!" he was barking into the phone. "No fat like the last time or I'm sending it back."

He gestured for me to sit down in a seat across from him as he wrapped up his pastrami negotiations.

Settling my tush into a down-filled cushion, I took a look around me.

The office was at least three times the size of my attic hovel, decorated in island-style teak furniture, with an impressive mini-fridge tucked in the corner, sweeping views of the front grounds, and A/C blasting from overhead vents.

The tile floors were polished to glossy perfection; no waterbug would dare make an appearance here.

But the undeniable centerpiece of the office was an elaborate aquarium on the far side of the room. Furnished with grottos and reefs, a rainbow of fish frolicked in its pristine aqua water.

I only wished my accommodations were half as nice.

Having issued his final order to his pastrami purveyor, Manny hung up and turned his attention to me.

"Welcome, my dear," he said, with an expansive wave of his cigar, "to Casa Kaminsky. You all settled in your cell?"

Okay, so he said "room," but I'm trying my best to stick to the truth here.

"Still haven't quite finished construction up there," he said. "People in Paratito work on 'island time.' Takes forever to get anything done. So there's no A/C up there yet, but if you open your window, you should get a delightful breeze."

"The room's lovely," I lied.

"Your cat settled in?"

"Absolutely," I assured him, my fake smile firmly in place.

"Hope you don't mind my cigar," he said, twirling the fat roll of tobacco lovingly with his fingers.

"Not at all," I said, trying not to choke on its foul smell.

"These babies cost fifty bucks a pop, straight from Havana."

Omigod. Fifty dollars for a cigar! Couldn't he have just traded in a few cases for A/C on the top floor?

"So glad you're able to join our little team!" he beamed.

"I'm thrilled to be here," I said. And I wasn't lying. In spite of my lousy accommodations, I was happy to be earning some decent bucks.

"I suppose you know about all the shows I've produced," he said, chest puffed with pride.

Indeed I did. First thing after I got the job, I'd raced to my computer and Googled Manny. (Technically, the second thing. First thing was to celebrate with a wee bit of Chunky Monkey.)

I'd soon discovered that Manny had produced a rash of low-rent reality shows—clunkers like *Ping Pong with the Stars*, *America's Funniest Instagrams*, and *Say Yes to the Muumuu*.

But I didn't care how crappy his shows were. If he was paying, I was on board.

"And if I do say so myself," he said, waving his stink bomb of a cigar, "I think I've outdone myself with *Some Day My Prince Will Come*. Thirteen gorgeous gals duke it out to win the hand of a charming British royal, Spencer Dalworth VII, Earl of Swampshire, eighty-seventh in line to be king of England."

(Before you go racing to Google it, there is no actual Swampshire. It's a name I made up to protect the innocent—namely moi—from a lawsuit.)

"Of course, as Polly has probably already told you," Manny was saying, "ten of the gals have already been eliminated, and we're down to the final three."

"Yes, I've already met them. They seemed quite nice."

"Bunch of raging bitches," he said, dismissing my lie with a flick of his cigar ash. "But the bitchier they are, the higher the ratings."

Alas, he spoke the truth.

"All you have to do is punch out some dialogue for Spencer and the gals on his three remaining dates. Tomorrow he's got a picnic with Dallas, then a romp in the Grand Paratito Waterfall with Brianna, and the next day a parachute jump with Hope.

"Get started on the picnic scene as soon as you can. We'll be shooting on the back lawn tomorrow morning, with a picnic basket of champagne and caviar.

"I'm afraid Spencer's not much of a talker. Most of his vocabulary seems to consist of 'eh, what?' and 'brilliant.' The other writers haven't had much luck with him, but I'm hoping you'll be able to do better."

"I'll certainly try, sir."

"I'd like to get him to say an actual sentence or two in these last pivotal scenes of the series. So just rough out some snappy patter for him. Anything, just so long as he doesn't come across as a prize idiot—

"Ah, Spencer my boy, we were just talking about you!"

I looked up and got my first glimpse of Spencer Dalworth VII. And I must admit, standing there in the doorway, he was quite a royal specimen. Tall and rangy, with deep blue eyes and a crop of thick tawny hair. Think early Hugh Grant, with a soupçon of Jude Law.

If he'd heard Manny calling him an idiot, Spencer gave no indication of it. In fact, one of the first things I noticed about him was the amazingly vacant look in his beautiful blue eyes.

"Come in, my boy!" Manny beamed. "This is our new writer, Jaine Austen."

"Brilliant!" Spencer said, his vocabulary living up to its reputation. "Love your books. Well, I haven't actually read them, but I've heard they're jolly good reads."

"I'm not that Jane Austen. She's been dead two hundred years."

"Good thing you're not her, then. Eh, what?"

He strolled into the room in miraculously unwrinkled linen trousers and Hawaiian shirt. Unlike Manny's seam-straining version, Spencer's shirt draped loosely on his slim frame.

Settling down into an easy chair, he crossed one long, linen-clad limb over the other, a man completely at ease, if not aware, in the world.

"So, Spencer," Manny asked, "have you decided who's going to get the royal lei tomorrow night?"

"The royal *what?*" I asked.

"Garland of flowers," Manny explained. "Every

elimination, Spencer hands out a lei to the bachelorettes he wants to keep on the show. The one who fails to get a lei goes home.

"So," he said, turning back to Spencer, "have you made up your mind?"

Spencer blinked a few times, letting the question register.

"The lei? Oh, right. First have to discuss it with Mummy, of course."

"Of course, of course," Manny said in the kind of soothing voice one hears in a kindergarten class. "You talk it over with Mummy and get back to me."

"Brilliant!" Spencer said, breaking out in what I must admit was a most engaging grin.

"See you later, Jaine," he said to me as he unwound himself from his easy chair. "Glad you're not the dead one."

And with those words of endearment, he loped out of the room.

Manny shook his head in disgust.

"The guy can't make a single decision without discussing it with his mummy. Talk about an umbilical cord that needs cutting.

"Well," he said, hauling himself up from behind his desk, "if you'll excuse me, it's time to feed my little darlings."

With that, he opened a flap on the top of his aquarium and sprinkled in some food.

"Such beautiful fish," I said, as they flocked to the food in a frenzy.

"You've got to be very careful with fish," Manny said. "Some of the most beautiful fish in the world are predators. You put them in your tank, and before you know it, your other fish are dead and gone.

"Yep," he said, taking a pensive puff of his cigar, "you gotta watch out for the predators."

Words to live by, as I would soon discover, here on Paratito Island.

YOU'VE GOT MAIL!

To: Jausten
From: SirLancelot
Subject: A Fab Job

Hi, hon—

By now you must be in glorious Paratito, basking in the sun and the cool ocean breezes. And,
as promised, I'm doing a fab job of watching
your apartment. While taking in your mail this
morning, I discovered a coupon for Senor
Picasso's One-Day Auto Paint Job. Only $39.99,
plus free floor mats!

Nothing personal, sweetie, but your dumpmo-
bile could sure use a bit of freshening up. So I
drove it right over to Senor Picasso's. (What a
stroke of luck that you left me your car keys in
case of an emergency!) I'm having it painted a
glorious sunshine yellow. So bright and cheerful,
just what you need to liven up your drab little
life. No need to thank me. That's what friends
are for. You can pay me back when you get
home.

Ciao for now!
Lance

PS. Met the most adorable man, Brett, working
the reception desk at Senor Picasso's. Quel
cutie! I'm going to turn on the charm full force

when I go back to get your Corolla this afternoon. With any luck, I'll be picking up your car—and a hot date!

To: Jausten
From: Shoptillyoudrop
Subject: Evening in Paris

Hello, sweetheart!

Hope you and your precious Zoloft are having the best time ever at your fabulous new job in the South Pacific! I'm so proud of you, honey! My daughter, the TV writer!!

Meanwhile, everyone here in Tampa Vistas is all abuzz with preparations for our annual Evening in Paris gala. I'm sure I've told you about it. We take over the clubhouse dining room and turn it into a boulevard in Paris, complete with a seven-foot papier-mâché Eiffel Tower, lots of French flags, and Edna Lindstrom's magnificent replica of the Arch of Triumph made out of egg salad. The menu is all French, and so is the music. In other words, c'est magnifique! (Which I'm fairly certain means "magnificent" and not "magnifying glass," but I've never been good with languages, so I can't really be sure.)

Lydia Pinkus, our beloved president of the Tampa Vistas Homeowners Association, is in charge of the event, and with Lydia at the helm, it's sure to be a roaring success. She's always so good at organizing things.

And as if running the gala weren't enough, Lydia has been hard at work planning a trip to Colonial Williamsburg. She knows all about American history and has prepared several lectures to deliver. She's such a brilliant speaker; it should be absolutely fascinating! Edna Lindstrom and some of the other gals are going, and I'm going to try to talk Daddy into signing up, too.

XOXO,
Mom

To: Jausten
From: DaddyO
Subject: Dreaded Time of Year

Dearest Lambchop—

It's that dreaded time of year—time for the annual Tampa Vista's Evening in Paris gala. You wouldn't believe the fuss people make about having dinner with a papier-mâché Eiffel Tower and Edna Lindstrom's silly egg salad Arch of Triumph. What a snoozefest!

What's worse, Mom's trying to get me to go off on Lydia Pinkus's tour of Colonial Williamsburg. As if *that's* gonna happen. I may have to sit through the stupid Evening in Paris, but I'll be

damned if I'm going to listen to that gasbag
Pinkus yammer on about American history for
seven mind-numbing days.

Ooops. Gotta run. Someone's at the door.

Love 'n' hugs from
DaddyO

To: Jausten
From: Shoptillyoudrop
Subject: So Darn Excited!

Guess who just stopped by? Lydia Pinkus, with
the most wonderful news! She's hired a professional dancer to teach five lucky Tampa Vista
couples to dance the waltz to "I Love Paris" at
our Evening in Paris gala. And the best news of
all: she's chosen Daddy and me as one of the
couples! I'm so darn excited! I thought for sure
Daddy would be his usual grouchypants self
and nix the idea, but much to my surprise, he's
all for it.

XOXO,
Mom

To: Jausten
From: DaddyO
Subject: Dancing Feet

Good news, Lambchop. It looks like the Evening
in Paris gala won't be a total bust after all. Ap-

parently Lydia ("The Battleaxe") Pinkus has hired a dance instructor to teach us the waltz, and your mom and I have been tapped to perform at the gala. I'm not one to brag, Lambchop, but I happen to be a superb dancer. Did I ever tell you I once won a free case of beer in a limbo contest? It's true! Can't wait to wow the neighbors with my dancing feet!

Love 'n' cuddles from
DaddyO
(aka the Fred Astaire of Tampa Vistas)

To: Jausten
From: Shoptillyoudrop
Subject: The Fred Astaire of Tampa Vistas

Oh, brother! Now Daddy's running around the house calling himself the Fred Astaire of Tampa Vistas. All because he once won a limbo contest. Which, by the way, isn't even an actual dance. I've been dancing with Daddy for the past forty years, and I can assure you the only Fred he resembles is Flintstone. And he absolutely refuses to go on Lydia's tour of Colonial Williamsburg. For some reason, Daddy's always had it in for poor Lydia. I can't imagine why. She's such a delightful woman. Anyhow, I'm hoping if I leave a few tour brochures around the house, he might change his mind.

XOXO,
Mom

To: Jausten
From: SirLancelot
Subject: Minor Hiccup

Just got back from Senor Picasso's, and honestly, Jaine, I think I'm in love. Remember Brett, the cutie at the reception desk? Well, it turns out this auto-painting gig is only his day job; he's really a playwright. So intelligent, and sensitive, with biceps to die for. And the best news is: I'm pretty sure the feeling was mutual. I definitely felt sparks. Brett never did ask me out, but luckily I'll get another chance to work my magic charms when I go back to Senor Picasso's to get your car. It wasn't ready today. It seems the painters got a tiny spot of sunshine yellow paint on your windshield, and they've got to get rid of it. Just a minor hiccup. Nothing to worry about.

Chapter 4

Back in my room, which I'd now dubbed Sauna Central, I found Prozac sacked out, snoring on my bed. Oh, how I envied her, lost in oblivion.

I sat at my card-table desk and opened my laptop with every intention of working on Spencer's upcoming picnic scene with Dallas. But alas, I made the foolish mistake of reading my emails. Instantly my blood pressure shot up into the stratosphere. Can you believe Lance, having my car painted sunshine yellow? Who did he think I was—a taxi driver?

After dashing off three texts and an angry email, demanding he have the Corolla restored to its original grungy white and reminding him to mist my Boston fern, I perused the notes from my parents, always a source of mental indigestion. My parents are absolute angels, sweeties of the highest order, but somehow they have a knack for creating drama wherever they go. Daddy is the main culprit. The man attracts trouble like my thighs attract cellulite. Somehow Mom has managed to put up with his foibles all these years with strength, forbearance, and a healthy supply of Oreos. I just hoped Daddy would waltz through the Evening in Paris gala without stepping on too many toes.

As distracting as they were, I could not allow myself to fester over my emails, not with that picnic scene to write. I barely managed to open a "Picnic Scene" file on my laptop, however, when I felt my eyelids grow heavy. Exhausted from my long flight and the oppressive heat blanketing the air, I put my head down on the desk to close my eyes for just a few minutes.

The next thing I knew, I was awakened by the sound of knocking on my door.

Akela, the maid, poked her head in, eyeing Prozac with undisguised terror, and announced that dinner would be served on the back patio in five minutes.

I looked out the window and realized it was dark outside. I'd slept away the entire afternoon.

"Food for cat," Akela said, dropping a plate on the floor and scooting off.

I stumbled out of bed and checked out Prozac's dinner—chunks of moist, char-grilled white fish.

Normally I'm not much of a fish fan, but this stuff looked pretty darn delicious. I was tempted to grab a tidbit, but Prozac was already at my ankles, demanding to be fed. I didn't dare snitch a piece in front of her. Not unless I wanted a souvenir scar to mark the occasion.

Reluctantly abandoning the fish, I hurried to the bathroom and splashed tepid water on my face. Then I slapped on some lipstick and left Prozac inhaling her food.

They probably served all sorts of fresh fish and fruits here on the island, I thought, as I headed downstairs. What a wonderful health bonus. Thousands of miles away from the nearest Ben & Jerry's, I'd be sure to lose scads of weight in no time. Picturing myself frolicking in a bikini with nary a love handle in sight, I skipped out to the patio, my appestat set for a yummy seafood platter.

Two tables were set on the mansion's spacious patio, with lovely china and fine cutlery, under a night sky bedecked with stars, the air thick with the hum of cicadas and the lush scent of gardenias.

Talk about dinner in paradise.

Manny sat at the head of what was clearly the "A" table, his nest of hair firmly cemented in place. Spencer sat across from him down at the foot of the table, Dallas and Hope cozied up on either side of the would-be prince. Brianna was sitting next to a young guy with a headful of curls even sprongier than mine. And sitting across from them was Polly, who'd saved a seat for me between her and Manny.

As soon as she saw me, she waved me over to join them.

"So sorry I'm late," I said as I hurried to my seat.

"Think nothing of it," Manny replied. "Everyone, say hello to Jaine Austen, our new writer."

Everyone murmured hello, the gang at the other table gazing at me with undisguised pity.

"Congrats," Polly whispered as I sat down. "You're eating with the honchos. Manny makes the rest of the crew eat at the 'B' table."

Aloud, she said, "I think you've met everyone at our table, Jaine, except for Justin, our director."

The wiry-haired kid, in a T-shirt that said BUT WHAT I REALLY WANT TO DO IS DIRECT, tore his eyes from where they'd been lingering on Brianna's boobs to welcome me aboard.

"I hear this is your first reality-show gig," he said. "Me, too. Manny saw a student film I directed at USC and hired me on the spot. I can't tell you what a thrill it is to be here," he said, in the kind of voice one hears on the podium at the Academy Awards. Any minute now, I expected him to start thanking his agents, his parents, and his sixth-grade English teacher.

"I'm so darn grateful to Manny," he added, loud enough to be certain Manny heard him, "for giving me my big break."

He beamed a smile at his benefactor, who was otherwise occupied ogling Brianna's Double D's.

"Here's to Manny," Justin said, raising his wineglass in a toast.

Polly reached for a bottle of Pinot Grigio and poured some in my wineglass.

"I really shouldn't," I protested. "I've got a lot

of writing to do tonight, and I need to keep my head clear."

"Don't worry," Polly whispered. "Your head will be clear. Manny waters down the booze. There's not enough alcohol in this bottle to knock out a gnat."

Indeed, I took an eager sip, only to taste the faintest hint of Pinot Grigio.

At which point, Akela and another maid showed up to take our orders.

"Steak or pasta?" Akela asked when she got to me.

I thought for sure they'd be serving fish, but who was I to turn down a nice juicy steak? I could always start my healthy fish and fruit diet tomorrow.

"Steak, please," I said with a hungry smile.

After taking our orders, the maids trotted back to the kitchen to fetch our food.

Meanwhile at the other end of the table, Dallas and Hope were both cooing over Spencer, missing no opportunity to snipe at each other.

Dallas, like Brianna, was clad in a low-cut halter top, while Hope, going for the pristine look, wore a simple white blouse with her hair swept back in a headband.

Polly had said Dallas was the front runner in the Rope-A-Royal Sweepstakes, and it looked like she was right. Spencer kept gazing at the long-limbed Texan rapturously with his vacant blue eyes.

Hope, however, was not about to give up the battle.

"Gee, your hair looks nice," she said to Dallas

with a sly smile, "but not as full as usual. Guess it must be the weather, huh?"

I remembered the missing hair extensions Dallas had been so steamed about and watched her shoot Hope a death-ray glare.

"Love your hair, too, hon," she said. "Nothing says glam like an Amish headband."

"Ladies, you both look absolutely brilliant!" Spencer beamed, totally oblivious to the mounting hostilities. "Anyone care for a roll?" he asked, holding out a bread basket.

"I would!" I cried out, leaning over and grabbing one with impressive speed.

"Brilliant!" Spencer said. "I like to see a woman with a hearty appetite."

He eyed me appreciatively as I slathered butter on my roll.

"I'll have a roll, too!" Dallas said, not to be outdone in the hearty-eating department.

"Me, too!" echoed Hope.

"And me!" said Brianna.

"Looks like you've started a new precedent," Polly whispered in my ear. "Those're the first carbs that've passed their lips since they got here."

Dallas and Hope made an elaborate show of eating their rolls, taking the tiniest bites possible.

"I'm lucky," Hope said with a complacent nod of her shiny blond bob. "I can eat anything I want, and it never shows. I've got good genes, I guess."

"That, and bulimia," Dallas parried back with an evil grin.

"Look who's talking," Hope sneered. "The woman who chews diuretics like Tic Tacs."

Manny, meanwhile, had given the signal to two cameramen who'd stationed themselves behind the feuding beauties and were catching every syllable of their bitchfest on tape.

Soon to be seen on a cable station near you.

Brianna opted to stay out of the fray, occasionally shooting Spencer a dazzling smile and turning to give him a bird's-eye view of her boobage. But most of her time was spent oohing and aahing over Manny.

The other two bachelorettes may have had their eyes on a royal title, but it looked like Brianna was going for power and big bucks.

"I just love a man who smokes a cigar," she crooned at Manny. "It's so virile!"

"I've been thinking about taking up a pipe," Justin chimed in, eager to impress.

"That's nice," Brianna said, barely turning to look at him.

At which point, Akela and the other maid returned to the patio, wheeling food carts.

My last meal a distant memory, my taste buds now sprang into overdrive. I clutched my knife and fork eagerly, ready to dig into my thick, juicy steak.

You can only imagine my heartbreak when Akela handed me a plastic tray with a tiny lump of dried-out meat, a scoop of desiccated mashed potatoes (whose main ingredient, I am certain, was Elmer's Glue), accompanied by a salad of wilting greens smothered in gonky white dressing.

Polly leaned over to me and whispered, "Manny buys overstock airline meals at a discount. The guy has money up his wazoo, but he's cheap as they come."

Meanwhile, I couldn't help noticing that the steak on Manny's plate was an actual steak, prime all the way, charred on the outside, juicy on the inside, and thick as a copy of *War and Peace*.

It took every ounce of willpower I possessed not to reach over and cut myself a piece.

Instead, I dug into my hockey puck of a steak, struggling mightily to make a dent in it, wishing I'd remembered to pack a hacksaw.

Down at the other end of the table, Spencer, clearly a culinary space cadet, pronounced his steak "brilliant!" And his potatoes. And his second glass of wine water.

Dallas, eager to score points, offered him some of her Elmer's Glue taters, plopping a blob of them on his plate.

"How sweet of you," Hope simpered. "I just hope trench mouth isn't catching."

It looked like Dallas was on the verge of lobbing her buttered roll at Hope, but all hostilities came to a halt just then when a rugged young guy, unshaven and tousle-haired, came weaving out onto the patio in jeans and a T-shirt, clearly more than a little sloshed.

"Hey, everybody," he mumbled, his voice slurred with booze as he headed for the "B" table.

"That's Kirk," Polly whispered, "the company propmaster."

Manny slammed down his steak knife, disgusted.

"For crying out loud, Kirk," he said. "I can smell the gin on your breath from here."

Kirk muttered something unintelligible as he sat down.

"What's that?" Manny called out.

"It's bourbon," Kirk said. "Not gin."

"I don't care what the hell it is. I'm tired of you showing up drunk all the time. You keep this up, and you'll never work on another Manny Kaminsky production again. You got that, Kirk?"

Kirk nodded, slumped in his chair.

Next to me, Polly was gazing at him with unabashed sympathy and—if I wasn't mistaken—a bit of longing in her eyes.

"Poor guy," she sighed.

Was it possible, I wondered, that our plucky production assistant had fallen for the beleaguered propmaster?

Somehow, I managed to finish most of my steak and potatoes, my taste buds groaning in protest. I was hoping that Manny would make up for the crummy dinner with a yummy dessert— possibly cheesecake flown in from New York, along with his pastrami—but my hopes were dashed when he announced:

"Now, if you want, you can all adjourn to the basement for dessert."

Dessert, in the basement?

"He's got a vending machine down there," Polly informed me. "Factory-second Snickers."

So much for dinner in paradise.

* * *

The mansion's basement was little more than a glorified crawl space, furnished with only a washer, dryer, and the aforementioned vending machine.

"Can you believe it?" Polly said, as she led me down the basement steps. "Manny actually makes us pay for our desserts! He's got goodies galore for himself—all sorts of cakes and cookies, not to mention a boatload of Eskimo Pies and Dove Bars in his office mini-fridge—but he makes us fork over our hard-earned cash for his stale candy.

"Well, here it is," she said, pointing to an ancient vending machine.

I stared at it in disbelief.

"Five bucks for a Kit Kat bar? That's highway robbery."

"That's why nobody ever comes down here. But don't worry. I know a little trick."

A mischievous gleam in her eyes, she gave the vending machine a violent kick and out popped a bag of Cheetos.

"It's Vending Machine Roulette," she said, holding up the bag in victory. "You get whatever falls out."

Another kick, and the machine coughed up a pair of chocolate peanut butter cups. Which Polly was gracious enough to give to me.

"A dose of chocolate is just what I need right now!" I said, thanking her profusely.

"Don't get your hopes up," she warned. "That candy's probably as old as Manny."

And she was right. My peanut butter cups were chalky, stale, and hard as a rock.

Sad to say, they were the highlight of my dinner.

Polly and I ate our desserts out on the front verandah under a canopy of stars, Polly's fringe of bangs enviably straight in the humid night air.

"I swear," she said, popping a Cheeto in her mouth, "this is the last time I ever take a job on location. If I'm going to be miserable, I might as well be miserable in L.A.

"I thought being a production assistant would be a stepping-stone to becoming a producer, but I've been at it seven years, and I'm still running for coffee and Xeroxing scripts. There's got to be a better way to make a living than this."

Raking her fingers through those fabulous bangs, she got up with a sigh.

"Time to turn in. I'd ask you over to my cabin for a nightcap, but the snakes don't like it when I have company."

I watched her as she headed down the path to her cabin, shoulders slumped.

After gazing at the stars for a few minutes, praying my show biz experience would be a tad more fulfilling than Polly's, I got up from the verandah and made my way upstairs.

I had just reached the second floor when I saw someone dashing across the hallway into Spencer's suite. It was Hope, clad in nothing but a lace-trimmed white nightie.

Well, well. Maybe Miss Goody Two-Shoes was taking over the lead from Dallas in the Rope-A-Royal Sweepstakes.

But all thoughts of Hope's romantic tryst were forgotten when I returned to my room and found Prozac perched on the windowsill, clawing at the screen.

"Prozac! What're you're doing?" I said, swooping her in my arms and plopping her down on the bed.

She looked up at me with indignant green eyes, oozing misery and chewing the scenery for all it was worth, a proud graduate of the Feline Academy of Hammy Overacting.

What do you think I was doing? Breaking out of this hellhole! I can't take it anymore, I tell you. I can't take it!

"Don't even think of jumping from that window," I scolded, looking down at the grass below. "It's a three-story drop! I know you hate it here, sweetheart, but I promise I'll make things better."

With that, I went to the bathroom, wet a washrag, and sat down on the bed next to her, wiping her down with coolish water.

That seemed to soothe her a tad.

Grabbing an in-flight magazine I had taken from the plane, full of interesting articles about places I would never get to visit, I began fanning her.

I breathed a sigh of relief as she started to purr.

Aaah. Much better. Now do my belly. Now my legs. Now my left ear. Now my right ear. Now my belly again . . .

This was all very well and good for Prozac,

but eventually I had to quit my stint as a Nubian slave and get some pages written for tomorrow's picnic scene with Dallas and Spencer.

So, setting my laptop on the bed, I spent the rest of the evening writing picnic banter and periodically cooling Prozac with my copy of *Tahiti Today*.

After a few hours, I had some passable dialogue for tomorrow's picnic scene. And Prozac, thank heavens, had fallen into a deep slumber.

I collapsed into bed, on what little space my sprawled-out princess had left for me on the mattress. I didn't dare wake her to move over, afraid I'd be drafted for fanning duty.

Thoroughly exhausted and huddled on my sliver of the mattress, I was just about to drift off to slumberland, lulled to sleep by the rhythmic sounds of Prozac snoring, when suddenly I saw a black blur skittering across the floor, illuminated by the moonlight streaming in my window.

I told myself it was the shadow of a cloud passing by in the night or a palm frond rustling in the breeze. But deep in my heart I knew the truth:

It was Godzilla, the waterbug.

Too exhausted to get out of bed and do battle, I listlessly tossed my slipper at the black blob.

And much to my surprise, it hit him.

Just when I was congratulating myself on my skilled marksmanship, wondering if perhaps I had a future as a Navy Seal, I saw the slipper move ever so slightly. And there before my eyes was Godzilla, creeping out from under the shoe, unharmed.

Good heavens. That bug was indestructible.

And call me crazy, but I could swear I heard the little devil snicker as it scampered off under the baseboard.

Chapter 5

There was no sign of Godzilla when I woke up the next morning. Just my slipper, the failed murder weapon, in the middle of the floor, chilling evidence of Godzilla's superpowers.

The room had cooled down somewhat during the night, so it was only slightly hellish when I climbed out of bed. Prozac, still listless, lay sprawled out on the sheets. That is, until Akela showed up with her morning bowl of fish parts. One sniff and Prozac was up like a bullet, sending Akela scurrying away in fear.

Prozac was busy slurping up her breakfast, when there was another knock on the door.

This time, it was Polly.

"I managed to find this for you," she said, holding out a small room fan. "I hate to think of your poor cat stuck up here in this heat all day."

Talk about your angels of mercy!

We set the fan on my night table and plugged it in to an outlet that actually worked.

A lovely breeze wafted across the room.

"Thanks so much, Polly!"

"Think nothing of it, hon. Well, gotta run and make sure Manny's orange juice is fresh-squeezed. See you down at breakfast."

When Polly had gone, I picked up Prozac and held her in front of the fan.

"Doesn't the room feel so much better now, sweetheart?"

She shot me a jaundiced look.

Yeah. This joint's a regular Four Seasons.

Plopping her down on the bed, I headed for the bathroom, where I showered under a trickle of tepid water, then quickly slipped on some elastic-waist capris and an oversized T-shirt.

Then I gathered my script notes and left Pro lolling on the bed, hoping she'd be okay with the window open and the fan on full blast.

Outside on the patio, breakfast had been laid out on a buffet table, with coffee and orange juice, stale muffins, and plastic trays of airline scrambled eggs.

I took a seat at one of the two tables from last night and dug into my rubberized eggs, going over the dialogue I'd penned for Spencer's picnic with Dallas. Taking no chances, I'd given most of the lines to Dallas, who I was certain would have no trouble spilling them out, along with a good portion of her cleavage.

Across from me at the other table, Spencer was sipping tea in miraculously unwrinkled white linens, surrounded by the bachelorettes. Dallas and Brianna were dressed to seduce in short shorts and clinging tank tops, while Hope had opted for a perky floral sundress.

Spencer pronounced his airline eggs "brilliant!" as the girls took calorie-conscious sips of their orange juice.

With no time to waste, I rounded up Spencer and Dallas, and we adjourned to the pool area to go over their "suggested dialogue" for the upcoming picnic scene. Dallas had no trouble with her lines and soon scooted off to have her hair and makeup done, leaving me alone with Spencer to rehearse.

Spencer, while declaring my suggestions "brilliant!", had trouble memorizing the few paltry lines I had tossed his way.

"Not a very good student, I'm afraid," he said with an apologetic shrug.

After about his fifth try saying, "I think I may be falling in love with you," his cell phone rang.

"Oops," he said, checking the screen. "Mummy calling. Must take it."

I sat there as he chatted with Mummy—although Mummy did most of the talking, Spencer adding only the occasional "Yes, Mummy," "No, Mummy," and "Absolutely, Mummy!"

At last he managed to untangle himself from Mummy's apron strings and ended the call. We were just about to resume our rehearsal when his phone pinged again.

This time it was a text.

"Hold on a sec," he said, "while I check this out."

He glanced down at his phone, and for once his vacant blue eyes came alive—with fear. Beads of plebian sweat broke out on his noble brow.

"Something wrong?" I asked.

"No, no. Everything's fine," he replied with a frozen smile.

But I could tell things were far from fine. Something in that text had scared the royal stuffing out of him.

He looked over at the patio where some of the crew were still lingering over their breakfasts. Dallas was off to one side, having her hair done, and Brianna and Hope were still nursing their orange juices.

The girls noticed him staring at them.

Dallas blew him a kiss. Hope sent him a perky wave. And Brianna struck a boob-enhancing pose.

Spencer clicked off his phone and turned back to me with a determined smile.

"Shall we continue?"

We resumed our lessons, me pitching a few simple lines of dialogue, Spencer screwing them up each and every time. I'm guessing whatever mental facilities Spencer had to begin with had gone AWOL when he got that text.

Finally, when we'd gone over his lines about a zillion times and he still couldn't remember them, I figured out the answer to my problem:

Cue cards!

I raced over to where Polly was helping the crew set up the picnic scene and begged for her help.

Soon, working with cut-up cardboard from

Manny's pastrami cartons, she and I were writing out Spencer's lines on makeshift cue cards.

All the while I was writing out his lines, I kept thinking about Spencer's mystery text. What was in it that had frightened him so? And more important, who the heck had sent it?

In the annals of picnic history, I doubt there's ever been a bigger disaster than the one that took place on the rear grounds of the mansion that day.

It all started auspiciously enough.

A picnic blanket had been spread out in front of a charming thatched-roof gazebo, with pygmy palms at each side of the gazebo's entrance. Laid out on the blanket were an expensive wicker basket and an ice bucket sporting a bottle of chilled champagne.

Spencer and Dallas took their seats on the blanket, Spencer—in spite of his recent text scare—the very essence of Keep Calm and Carry On.

Dallas looked spectacularly lovely. Her long, tanned legs were set off by her white shorts, and a slouchy pink tee slouched just enough to reveal a nice hunk of boobage. Sitting next to Spencer, she fluffed at the sides of her lush chestnut hair, trying to induce some extra volume.

A result, I was guessing, of those missing hair extensions.

Manny stood near Justin and his crew as Justin called for quiet.

His wiry curls tamped down under a baseball

cap, Justin had been a ball of nervous energy, yakking to his cameramen about long shots, close-ups, and reverse angles, clearly fancying himself the next Steven Spielberg.

"Okay, let's roll 'em!" he called out.

"Wait a minute!" Dallas pouted. "I can't shoot this scene."

"Why not?" asked Justin, grinding his teeth.

"This palm frond keeps tickling my neck."

Indeed, Dallas was sitting in front of one of the pygmy palms, whose frond was brushing against her.

With a sigh, Justin crossed over to the blanket and whipped out a Swiss Army knife. With a few deft strokes, he hacked the palm frond off the tree.

"Happy now?" he asked, a stiff smile on his face.

"Delirious," Dallas replied, having caught the note of irritation in his voice.

Justin tossed aside the offending frond and returned to his crew.

"Action!" he shouted, and once again, filming began.

Dallas asked Spencer if he'd care for some champagne.

"Absolutely," Spencer replied, remembering his first line of dialogue.

Hallelujah.

But when it was time to open the bottle, try as he might, he couldn't seem to dislodge the cork.

"Probably because the bottle's been sitting in a factory-seconds warehouse for the past seventeen years," Polly muttered at my side.

Justin called "Cut!" and stomped over to the picnic blanket. For a skinny guy, he was pretty strong, and soon he'd loosened the cork enough for Spencer to give it the final shove.

The cameras started rolling again.

The champagne flowed, and Spencer, who was supposed to say, "To us!" instead relied on his old standby, "Brilliant!"

Frantically, I pointed to the cue cards, reminding him he had actual sentences to deliver.

And then I learned the true meaning of the words "Be careful what you wish for."

Because Spencer, squinting awkwardly at the cue cards, began to deliver those sentences. It was then, and only then, that I discovered that, in addition to his other shortcomings, Spencer was dyslexic.

I won't bore you with the gruesome details. It's all too cringeworthy.

Here's just a sample of the mangled words that came tumbling out of his mouth—with my delicate corrections whispered in parentheses:

I think I may be falling in vole with you. (Love, you idiot! Love!)

Never have I seen such beautiful lube eyes. (Blue! Not lube!)

Hold me, hug me, never let me og! (Go! Go! Go!)

And finally, the one that tugged at my heart strings—not to mention my ulcers:

I want you with ever hiber of my fart. (Fiber of my heart!!!)

Justin was calling "Cut!" every five seconds. Any minute now, I feared he would take his Swiss Army knife and start using it on Spencer.

Finally, everyone agreed to let Dallas do all the talking, with Spencer weighing in with an occasional "Brilliant!"

The cameras rolled, and we waited with bated breath as the scene continued.

Spencer somehow managed to get through the next few minutes without any major mishaps.

It was time, at last, for Spencer and Dallas to tuck into their picnic basket.

Spencer opened it.

"What have we here?" he said. And with that, he pulled out a hunk of glossy chestnut hair. Dallas's missing hair extensions!

Dallas's "lube" eyes burned with fury.

She leaped up from the picnic blanket and lunged at Hope, who was standing near me, smirking.

"You bitch!" Dallas cried. "You stole my hair extensions and put them in the picnic basket to sabotage me in front of Spencer."

"I have no idea what you're talking about," said Hope, her smirk firmly entrenched on her face. "But I got a great shot of you pulling them out of the picnic basket.

"Look," she said, holding out her cell phone. "Gosh, is your face red. Can't wait to post it on Instagram."

"Like hell you will," Dallas snarled, snatching the phone from Hope.

"There!" she said, acrylic nails clicking away. "It's deleted. Gone forever. So fooey on you!"

(Although *fooey* wasn't exactly the F word she used.)

As she stomped back to the picnic blanket,

Hope turned to me with a sly smile. "Dallas only thinks the picture's deleted," she said. "Most people don't realize that when they delete a photo, it's still in the phone, stored in their photo albums. Check it out."

And sure enough, with a few clicks, she'd located the picture of Dallas and her missing hair extensions.

"Oh, this will be on Instagram, all right," she crowed.

Meanwhile, back at the picnic blanket, it looked like the scene would finally get shot.

Dallas, having regained her composure, along with her missing hair, joined Spencer on the blanket as he once again offered her a flute of champagne.

They sipped and eyed each other with cloying smiles.

Then Spencer offered her some caviar on toast points.

And just when they were about to bite into their fishy treats, all hell broke loose—yet again—when a flying ball of fur came charging across the lawn and onto the picnic basket.

Damn! It was Prozac. Somehow she'd managed to escape from Sauna Central.

And now, she had her pink nose in the jar of caviar, lapping it up at lightning speed.

"What the hell is that cat doing eating my Beluga caviar?" Manny cried.

Pro looked up, oozing skepticism.

Beluga? Who're you kidding, buster? This stuff's domestic. Costco's finest.

At which point, after a delicate burp, Prozac

gazed up into Spencer's beautiful lube eyes and leapt into his lap, purring ecstatically.

Well, hello, handsome!

"Will someone get that cat off the set?" Manny bellowed, his face an alarming shade of puce.

My turn to rush over and pluck my shameless hussy from Spencer's lap, only to be rewarded with a nasty glare.

Party pooper.

Then she turned her attention back to her inamorata, giving him a blast of her bedroom eyes.

Call me later, big boy.

Oh, hell. It looked like a fourth bachelorette had just entered the competition.

Chapter 6

L eaving the cast and crew to finish shooting
what remained of the picnic scene, I carried
Prozac back up to my room.

Frankly, I wasn't the least bit surprised at what
had just happened.

Prozac is, after all, the Houdini of cats, and
had long mastered the art of jumping up and
opening doorknobs. I should've known it was
just a matter of time before she pulled her door-
knob stunt and broke out of Sauna Central.

So you can imagine my surprise when I trudged
the three flights of stairs back to my room and
found the door shut tight.

Prozac may have been a feline Houdini, but
there was no way on earth she could have clawed
the door open and then shut it behind her. Just
as I was pondering how she could have possibly

pulled the door shut, Akela the maid came up the steps with towels in her arms.

At the sight of Prozac, her eyes widened in fear.

"For you."

She thrust the towels at me and, quick as a bunny, started down the stairs again.

"Wait, Akela!" I called after her. "You didn't happen to come to my room earlier, did you?"

Maybe she'd stopped by and inadvertently left the door open, clearing the way for Prozac's escape.

"No! No! I no go in room. No kitty. No kitty!" she cried, careening down the steps.

That woman really ought to do something about her fear of cats, I thought, as I headed to my room.

Opening the door, I immediately felt a strong breeze blowing in through the window, bolstered by the air circulating from the fan.

So that was the answer!

The breeze from the window, combined with air from the fan, had probably blown the door shut behind Prozac.

Mystery solved.

Now all I had to do was make sure it didn't happen again.

That day at lunch (ham and Swiss on cardboard) I approached Manny, who was still glowering about Prozac's cameo appearance at the picnic scene.

"Do you have any idea how much your cat cost us this morning in unusable footage?"

"No," I confessed.

"Me, neither. But whatever it is, I've got a good mind to dock it from your pay."

Ouch.

I immediately launched into an apology, explaining Pro's past as an escape artist, and asked if it was possible to have a bolt installed on the exterior of my door, so I could lock her in when I left the room.

After a bit of grumbling, Manny assigned the task to Kirk, the propmaster.

And ten minutes later, Kirk was at my room with his tool kit, installing a bolt outside my door.

I remembered how Polly seemed attracted to Kirk last night at dinner. And I could see why. He was a handsome guy, with a bronze tan, thick surfer blond hair, and six-pack abs rippling beneath his skin-tight tank top. A few tats twined around his arms. (Definitely not my thing, but I knew it was a turn-on for some gals.)

He worked in silence, screwing the bolt in place.

"That ought to prevent any more escapes," he said when he was finished.

"Would you mind coming inside and checking the latch on the window screen?" I asked, just in case Prozac was plotting a three-story jump.

"Not a problem," he said, stepping into Sauna Central.

As he crossed the room, Prozac eyed him hungrily.

Hubba hubba, sweet cheeks!

First Spencer. Now Kirk. I tell you, that cat makes Lady Chatterley look like a nun.

Kirk took out a screwdriver from his tool kit and was just about to start tightening the latch when he became transfixed at the sight of something on the grounds below.

I followed his gaze and saw Hope in her pretty floral sundress, fiddling with her iPhone. No doubt posting the damning photo of Dallas and her hair extensions.

"She's really something, isn't she?" Kirk said, his eyes glazed over with longing. "Prettiest thing I've ever seen."

From the bed, Prozac flipped her tail in annoyance.

She's not so hot.

"And she's smart, too. Got her whole life figured out."

I sure hoped Polly wasn't too hung up on Kirk, because his heart clearly belonged to Hope.

Then, remembering the screwdriver in his hand, he said, "I'd better get this screen fixed, huh?"

Within minutes, he had the screen firmly fastened in place.

I looked over at Prozac, now sprawled out on the bed, belching caviar fumes.

With the new latch on the door, and the screen safely secured, there was no way she could possibly escape.

Right?

* * *

The next shoot of the day was Spencer's waterfall scene with Brianna. The rest of the crew had already left, so Kirk and I rode over with Polly, who had waited for us. And by us, I mean Kirk. Polly couldn't seem to take her eyes off him.

I sat in the back while Kirk drove, Polly in the passenger seat, sneaking covert glances at her tattooed heartthrob.

Life is so cruel, n'est-ce pas?

Here Polly was lusting after Kirk, while Kirk was lusting after Hope, who was no doubt lusting after Spencer. The old daisy chain of love, where someone is always bound to get hurt.

It's at times like this that I'm grateful for my own two longtime lovers: Ben and Jerry, whose happy smiles and high butterfat content never fail to warm my heart and clog my arteries.

We arrived at the base of the Grand Paratito Waterfall, a rather impressive natural wonder, where sheets of water cascaded down craggy rocks to a sparkling pool below.

When we showed up at the water hole, Justin and his crew were setting up the cameras. Off to the side, Spencer and Brianna, clad in terry bathrobes, were having waterproof makeup applied to their faces.

After this morning's angst, Manny had opted to remain behind at the mansion.

I approached Justin with trepidation.

"I'm so sorry about those cue cards," I said. "I had no idea Spencer was dyslexic."

"Not your fault, hon. None of us did."

"I don't know how much good it will do," I said, handing Justin a few hasty lines I'd dashed off, "but I wrote some dialogue for the waterfall scene."

"Thanks, Jaine, but we won't be recording dialogue today. The noise from the falls will drown out anything Spencer and Brianna say. We'll dub in their stuff later. Maybe even using an actor with a working brain to read Spencer's lines," he added with a wink.

By now, the crew was ready to shoot.

Spencer and Brianna stepped out of their bathrobes, Spencer in modest boxers and Brianna in a micro bikini so tiny, I'd seen more cotton on the swab of a Q-tip.

Brianna was really quite a specimen, with her flaming red hair and Barbie bod. Soon she and Spencer were frolicking in the pool, Brianna laughing gaily and practically smothering Spencer with her massive Double D's.

Never had I seen the cameramen look through their lenses with such avid interest.

Eventually, one might even say inevitably, Brianna was doing so much bouncing around, her bra top sprang loose and was floating around in the water.

The cameras stopped, all eyes (all male eyes, anyway) glued on Brianna's chest as she bobbled around trying to retrieve the top. Justin was standing there *thisclose* to drooling when his cell phone rang. Somehow he managed to tear himself away from Brianna and check his phone.

"It's my agent."

I could see an internal tug of war waging in

his brain. Take the call, and miss out on more boobage? Or ignore it, and miss out on what could be important career news?

His career won out.

"Hey, Jeff," he said into his Bluetooth. "What's up? . . . You're kidding? . . . Really? . . . That's fantastic! I'm over the moon, buddy. Over the moon!"

He clicked off with a whoop of joy.

"Guess what?" he said. "I just got offered a movie deal. From a major studio!" He threw his baseball cap in the air. "Yippee! No more schlock reality TV for me!"

Much to the crew's consternation, Brianna's bra had now been retrieved, and filming resumed. Justin continued to give directions to his cameramen, but I could tell his heart was no longer in it.

I remembered how grateful he'd been to Manny last night at dinner for giving him this directing gig, and what a kiss-up he'd been.

How quickly he was ready to jump ship to advance his career.

Happens all the time in Hollywood.

In fact, I think you can major in it at USC Film School.

As it happened, Justin's was not the only good news of the day.

Soon after Brianna and Spencer had resumed romping at the base of the falls, I looked up and saw Tai, my hunky native driver, getting out of his Jeep and walking over to me.

"Hey, there," he said, gracing me with his heart-melting smile.

"Hi," I managed to croak, longing to run my fingers through his black curls. "What brings you here?"

I couldn't get over how dazzling his teeth were next to his tan skin.

"I was making some deliveries and decided to stop by."

"You're absolutely gorgeous. You realize that, don't you?"

Okay, so what I really said was, "How nice."

But you know darn well what I was thinking.

"Actually," he added with a mischievous grin, "I lie. I had no deliveries to make. I stopped by hoping I'd run into you."

"Really?" I gushed, practically melting into a puddle of goo at his feet.

"Yes, I wanted to ask you to dinner."

A dinner date with my tanned Tahitian cutie! But I couldn't get too excited. Time to rein in my enthusiasm and play it cool. Give myself an air of unattainable mystery.

"Omigod, yes! I'd love it!" I squeaked.

What can I say? I'm hopeless.

"I thought you might come over and have dinner with my family."

Wait. Whoa. What? His family? I was hoping for a moonlight dinner for two, with lots of hugging and munching for dessert.

"Yes, you can stop by my village, and I can introduce you to the king of my tribe."

"You know the king?"

"Sorta," he grinned. "He's my dad."

"Really? Your dad's an actual king?? Does that mean you're a prince?"

"Yep," he said, with another dazzler of a smile.

How do you like that? It looked like Spencer wasn't the only royalty on the island.

"So what about dinner tomorrow tonight?" Tai asked.

True, I'd been hoping for that romantic twosome, but chowing down with the king wasn't too shabby.

"Sounds fab!"

"Great! I'll pick you up at six."

Can you believe it? I, Jaine Austen, freelance writer and commoner, had a date with an actual prince!

I watched Tai drive off in a haze, my imagination in overdrive, already picturing myself arm in arm with Tai, on the cover of *People*, Princess Jaine of Paratito.

YOU'VE GOT MAIL!

To: Jausten
From: Shoptillyoudrop
Subject: Zombie in a Hawaiian Shirt

Hi, sweetheart!

Today was our first lesson with Alonzo, Lydia's dance instructor. Such a charming young man. So handsome—and versatile, too! Would you believe he works part-time as a Ronald McDonald? Imagine! Clown by day, suave ballroom dancer by night. Talk about your Renaissance Man!

Frankly, honey, I was afraid I wasn't going to be able to keep up with the dance steps. I've never thought of myself as much of a dancer, but Alonzo said I had "the grace of a mariposa." (That's Spanish for "butterfly.")

Daddy, on the other hand, was shuffling around the floor doing his usual "zombie in a Hawaiian shirt" impersonation. He routinely ignored Alonzo's advice and actually had the nerve to give him pointers on doing the limbo, yapping about that case of beer he won hundreds of years ago!

But Alonzo was very patient with Daddy, thank goodness, and at some point Daddy started to pick up some of the steps.

All the others were quite nimble on the floor:
Edna Lindstrom and her new beau, Roger
Nordquist (she met him in water aerobics class
when their pool noodles collided; isn't that
the cutest thing ever?); Stan and Audrey Rothman (doing wonderfully well in spite of Stan's
recent hip surgery); and Nick and Gina Roulakis.
(Even though Nick, a former high school football
star, could stand to lose a few pounds, he was
impressively light on his feet.)

The only real shocker of the day was Lydia,
who'd partnered up with Ed Nevins, a recent
widower and newcomer to Tampa Vistas. So
adept in everything else she does, Lydia was
surprisingly awkward on the dance floor and insisted on taking the lead from Ed. Oh, well. At
least she wasn't as bad as Daddy!

XOXO,
Mom

PS. Guess what? Lydia wants us to wear gowns
and tuxes for our performance. Just like French
royalty! Won't that be fun?

To: Jausten
From: DaddyO
Subject: Quite an Impression

Just got back from our first dance lesson, Lambchop, and I'm proud to say I made quite an im-

pression on our dance instructor—a very nice fellow, who told me he'd never in all his life seen anyone dance like me.

And my stock rose even higher when I told him about that case of beer I won at the limbo contest. I even passed on a few tips on the art of doing the limbo. He kept pulling me aside to chat with me, perhaps hoping to glean some of my dancing secrets. Turns out the guy works part-time as a Ronald McDonald. And I could see how grateful he was when I told him a few knock knock jokes to share with the kiddies.

But the highlight of the day (and possibly my whole life) was seeing Lydia ("Anything You Can Do, I Can Do Better") Pinkus make a fool of herself on the dance floor. My god, the woman was like Frankenstein in support hose. My heart went out to Ed Nevins, the poor devil Lydia had roped in to be her partner. Ed just moved to Tampa Vistas a few weeks ago and clearly didn't know what he was getting into. By the end of our session, The Battleaxe had stomped on his feet so many times, I'm sure the poor guy needed toe surgery.

For once, I'm actually excited about this stupid Evening in Paris gala. Mom wants me to rent a tux to wear for our waltz, but there's no way I'm throwing away good money on a tux rental, when I've got a perfectly fine tux sitting right in my closet—the very same tux I wore when I married your mom thirty-nine years ago. I'm proud to say I've still got the same boyish figure I had back then.

Well, gotta go and practice my dance moves.

Love 'n' cuddles from
DaddyO

PS. Mom has been leaving brochures about Colonial Williamsburg all over the house, in a blatant attempt to lure me into taking a vacation with Lydia Pinkus. What a waste of time and brochures. I wouldn't go to a Starbucks with that woman, let alone Colonial Virginia!

**To: Jausten
From: Shoptillyoudrop
Subject: Of All the Ridiculous Ideas!**

Your father absolutely refuses to rent a tux for the Evening in Paris gala, insisting he can still fit into his wedding tux. Of all the ridiculous ideas! Daddy actually believes he has the same body he had as a twenty-four-year-old. He just tried on his wedding tux and could barely get the darn jacket closed. One deep breath and the button at his tummy will go flying. I swear, he's going to poke somebody's eye out.

XOXO
from your very irritated
Mom

PS. On the plus side, I ordered the most fabulous robin's-egg-blue sequined gown from the Home Shopping Channel. Only $129, plus expedited shipping and handling! I can't wait to see those sequins twinkling under the fluorescent lights of the clubhouse! And I ordered one for you, too, sweetheart, in Fabulous Fuchsia—perfect for one of your trendy L.A. cocktail parties. Oh, darling, what an exciting life you're going to lead now that you're a genuine TV writer. I can just imagine what a gay whirl you must be having in your South Seas paradise!

To: Jausten
From: DaddyO
Subject: Fits Like a Glove

Just tried on my tux, Lambchop, and it fits like a glove!

Love 'n' snuggles from your dapper
DaddyO

To: Jausten
From: SirLancelot
Subject: Best News Ever!

Alert the media! All my frantic flirting finally paid off. I've got a date with Brett! Dinner at the beach. Isn't that the best news ever?

Ciao for now!

Lance

PS. Tiny glitch with the Corolla. While they were trying to get rid of the paint spot on the windshield one of the workers accidentally gouged a scratch on the glass. When they tried to buff it out, there was some sort of mishap with the buffing machine. The bottom line is they cracked your windshield, and now it's going to have to be replaced. But no worries, hon. They promised they'd have it as good as new in no time.

PPS. For some strange reason your texts and emails are coming in garbled. Can't understand a word you're writing. Must be something wrong with the South Pacific satellite systems.

Chapter 7

The rest of the day passed by in a hazy blur, me lost in thoughts of my future life as Tai's princess bride. So swept away was I that I didn't even blink an eye when later that night in my bedroom I saw Godzilla scuttling off with a crumb of the peanut butter crackers I'd scored in Vending Machine Roulette.

I came crashing back to reality the next morning, however, when I read that infuriating email from Lance, pretending my messages to him were coming in garbled. I knew darn well he'd read my emails and texts, demanding that he repaint my Corolla white, but that pigheaded know-it-all was pretending not to be able to understand them. The nerve of that man! And to top things off, those bozos at Senor Picasso's had actually cracked my windshield.

As for poor Mom, I only hoped she'd convince Daddy to rent a tux so he wouldn't show up at the gala in his ancient tux looking like a refugee from *Saturday Night Fever*.

And as it turned out, I wasn't the only one feeling miffed that morning.

When I showed up for breakfast, I found myself right in the middle of an eruption from Mount Manny.

Our cigar-chewing, pastrami-eating producer was on a tear, ranting and raving about "those idiots" at the airport.

Apparently the plane scheduled to be used in Spencer and Hope's upcoming parachute jump scene was having mechanical difficulties and, according to the airport mechanics, would not be up and running until tomorrow.

Furious at the delay, Manny was hardly able to wolf down his mushroom and truffle omelet. (The rest of us got our usual rubber eggs and cement muffins.)

Eventually, his venom spent and his omelet demolished, our fearless leader headed for his office, chomping on a cigar.

Meanwhile, Spencer and Hope met with Kirk to learn how to use the parachutes for the parachute jump. According to the script notes I'd read, Hope and Spencer would fly up in the about-to-be-repaired plane, making love chat (or, as Spencer would say, "vole chat") and then jump from the plane in their chutes.

Having retrieved the chutes from the prop shed, Kirk gathered Spencer and Hope by the pool and was showing them how to use the contraptions—which cord to pull to release the canopy, and which cord to pull in case of emergency.

As he explained the workings of the chute, Kirk gazed worshipfully at Hope. But the perky bachelorette, looking particularly adorable in shorts and a floral tank, her hair caught up in a loose ponytail, was utterly oblivious to Kirk, her sharp eyes riveted on the cords of the chute.

All the while, I was seated on a nearby chaise, ostensibly writing witty banter for the parachuting duo. But now, fully aware of Spencer's limitations, I settled for coming up with synonyms for "brilliant," trying to limit each of his royal lamebrain's lines to three syllables or less.

And I have to confess I was having a hard time concentrating. By now I'd forgotten about my worrisome emails. Instead my mind kept wandering back to my hunkalicious suitor, Prince Tai. Or, as I had come to think of him, "My Tai."

What if the two of us hit it off and fell in love under the tropical stars? What if I wound up an actual princess, like Grace Kelly or Queen Noor?

True, Paratito Island wasn't exactly the cosmopolitan center of the universe, but who cared? I was sick of big city living, anyway. All the traffic in L.A. was enough to give the Dalai Lama ulcers. (Especially driving around in a neon-yellow Corolla!)

How lovely it would be to live in a charming cottage by the sea, with a wraparound verandah, and banana trees in the yard. At last I'd get to dine on fresh fish and island fruits and drop twenty pounds in no time.

Before long I'd be frolicking along the beach in my string bikini, holding hands with My Tai, taking time out to toss off a novel or two while my bronzed god of a hubby did whatever Paratitan princes did. (Hopefully, topless.)

I was just settling into a particularly yummy fantasy of me and Tai lying side by side on the sand, the sea lapping at our feet, the sun warming our bodies, caressed by cool ocean breezes. Tai was running his finger along my washboard-flat tummy and up to my chin, turning my face to his for a whopper of a kiss, when suddenly I was yanked back to reality.

Oh, crud. It was Mount Manny, erupting again.

"Are you crazy?" I heard him shout. "No way are you leaving this show."

He and Justin had joined us poolside, Manny in a terry robe and flip-flops, his face flushed with anger.

"I give you your first big break in show biz, hire you on the basis of that crummy little student film—"

"Crummy?" Justin cried, indignant. "*Casserole of Broken Dreams* just happened to win first prize at the West Covina Film Festival!"

"I hire you on the basis of that crummy little film," Manny steamrollered ahead, "and now you want to bail out for a movie deal. Forget about it, kid. It's not gonna happen. I've got it on good authority that *Some Day My Prince Will Come* is going to be picked up for a second season, and as long as this show is in production, you're not going anywhere."

Justin tried to plaster a conciliatory smile on his face.

"But, Manny. It's the career break of a lifetime. Surely you can understand."

Manny squashed out his cigar onto an unlucky ashtray.

"All I understand is you're under contract to me. Try to break it, and I'll sue you big-time. Trust me. It won't be a pretty picture."

With that, he whipped off his robe to reveal his big-bellied body in an eeny-weeny Speedo. (A sight, I can assure you, high up on the Not a Pretty Picture list.)

Then he dove into the pool, creating a tsunami of a splash.

I jumped up just in time to avoid the downpour.

Justin stalked off, fuming, steam practically oozing out from under his baseball cap.

And over by the parachutes, I could hear Spencer saying: "So which cord do I pull in an emergency? Don't know why, but I keep forgetting."

Oh, man.

With this guy in line to inherit the throne of England, all I could think was, "God save the queen!"

Chapter 8

That afternoon I got to see Manny's pride and joy—"the most thrilling moment of the show"—the Royal Lei Ceremony.

In this scene, shot on the mansion's gazebo, Spencer would place orchid leis around the neck of two lucky bachelorettes, while the third would be sent home packing.

Polly and I wandered over to the gazebo together.

Bursting with excitement, I told her about my upcoming date with Tai.

"I can't believe I'm going out with a real live prince!"

Polly gasped from under her fringe of bangs.

"Way to go, girl! Every woman on the set has had her eye on Tai. Not to mention a few of the guys."

"To think," I sighed, sailing along on Cloud Nine, "he picked me!"

"And unlike the dimwit Brit," Polly said, "Tai's an actual prince. Of all the gals on Paratito Island, you're the one who hit the jackpot, honey."

"Whoa, hold on. We haven't even gone on our first date yet. Let's not get ahead of ourselves."

Yeah, right. I was already planning the honeymoon. (Venice. Two weeks. Moonlight kisses in a gondola.)

When we arrived at the gazebo, the crew was busy setting up for the shoot—Justin giving orders, but clearly phoning it in. His stock response to any question from the crew seemed to be, "Sure, fine, whatever."

Periodically he shot filthy looks at Manny, who was lounging in a director's chair reading the latest edition of *Cigar Aficionado*.

The bachelorettes showed up, fresh from hair and make-up, Brianna's boobs making a spectacular appearance in a skin-tight spandex affair. Dallas sported a slinky white satin gown, setting off her creamy olive complexion, and Hope looked surprisingly sophisticated in a simple black column dress, her blond hair pulled up in a svelte chignon.

A table with a floor-length tablecloth had been set up in the center of the gazebo, with two leis lying in wait for their lucky recipients.

Thank heavens, I didn't have to write any new dialogue for this scene.

All Spencer had to say was, "Will you accept

this royal lei?" And after all these weeks of production, Polly assured me, he'd finally got that line down pat.

The would-be prince was looking quite the English aristo in a white linen suit, his tawny hair slicked back with gel.

I had to admit he was one hunk of a dyslexic mama's boy.

By now the lights were set, the cameras ready to roll.

Justin, with a bored sigh, called for action.

Spencer picked up one of the leis on the table, strung with lush purple orchids, and held it out.

A moment of hushed anticipation before he said:

"Dallas, will you accept this royal lei?"

Dallas squealed with delight.

"Yes, yes! Of course!" she said, racing over to Spencer, who lovingly draped the lei around her neck. I remembered what Dallas said the other day, that Spencer had already asked her to marry him. From the way he was looking at her now, love shining in his eyes, I believed every word of her claim.

Beaming, Dallas threw her arms around the handsome Brit, planting a big wet smacker on his lips.

Now it was zero hour.

Only one lei left, and two bachelorettes.

Brianna winked at Spencer, breasts thrust out like fishing bait bobbing in a river. Hope smiled bravely, a tiny vein throbbing in her temple.

Spencer creased his brow, his idea of looking thoughtful, and waited several endless seconds—

seconds which in production would be filled in with tension-inducing drum beats—before he said:

"Hope, will you accept this royal lei?"

Hope jumped up and down like a kid who'd just got her first bicycle from Santa.

Dallas, I could not help but notice, gritted her teeth in annoyance.

"Oh, Spencer!" Hope gushed, as he placed the lei around her neck. "You've made me so very happy."

She stood there in a triumphant glow, when suddenly a look of disgust washed over her face.

"Eeew!" she cried. "What's this?"

Reaching into one of the orchids, she plucked out a matted ball of slimy fur.

I knew exactly what it was: A cat's hairball.

Could it be? Was it possible? Had Prozac escaped from Sauna Central *again*?

Indeed she had.

Because just then, before my horrified eyes, she came sauntering out from under the tablecloth and began rubbing herself shamelessly against Spencer's ankles, writhing and twisting like a pole dancer on overtime.

Gazing up at him languidly, she batted her big green eyes.

Where's my lei, big boy?

"It's that damn cat again!" cried Manny. "Get her out of here!"

At which point I glanced over at Justin and caught him grinning slyly.

Mumbling apologies, I grabbed Prozac and

headed back to the mansion, wondering how on earth she could have broken out of Sauna Central, what with the door bolted and the screen latched. Remembering Justin's sly grin, I wondered if he had somehow been involved. Had he gotten a copy of the key to my door and let her out?

Had he orchestrated her escape to sabotage the production?

Back in our room, I plopped Prozac down on the bed.

"What're you trying to do, Pro? Get me fired?"

She shot me a reproachful look.

I was just trying to make friends with His Royal Cuteness. A cat's gotta have some fun on this crappy island.

Soon she was sprawled out on the bed, snoring, no doubt dreaming of munching fish guts in the Cotswolds. I just prayed she would stay asleep for the next few hours. I simply could not afford another one of her cameo appearances.

With much trepidation, I made my way back to the gazebo, where the Royal Lei scene was being reshot. I got there just as Spencer was giving the second lei to Hope.

As Hope jumped up and down and donned her hairball-free lei and Brianna gulped back her disappointment at being dumped from the show, Justin called out a laconic final "Cut!" and the crew started back to the mansion to shoot a scene in Brianna's room while she packed up her things to go home.

Catching up with Justin, I pulled him aside.

"There's something I've got to ask you."

"Go ahead," he said. I looked for signs of guilt in his eyes but saw none. Just curiosity.

"Did you have anything to do with my cat showing up on the set today?"

"What do you mean?"

"I know you're angry with Manny, and I thought you might've used my cat to sabotage production on the show. Did Kirk give you a key to the bolt on my door?"

He shook his head.

"Don't get me wrong. I was happy it happened. I loved seeing the look of apoplexy on Manny's face. But I have no idea how your cat escaped. Really. Not a clue."

And I believed him.

Somehow my scheming furball had discovered another escape route, and I was determined to find it.

Chapter 9

I stood outside Brianna's bedroom as the camera crew shot her packing to go home. Good heavens. Was that a real tear I saw streaming down her cheek? Somehow I didn't think Brianna Barbie was the crying kind.

Tossing her clothes into her suitcase, she talked about how she and Spencer came from opposite ends of the world, "me from a small town in Iowa and him from that big estate in England. I thought we'd made a connection. I thought our opposites had attracted.

"Oh, well," she said, throwing a leopard-print thong onto the pile in her suitcase. "I'm sorry he didn't choose me, but I wish Spencer all the best."

The lone tear that had been coursing down her cheek now plopped onto her thong.

For a minute I feared she might actually break out sobbing, but when Justin called "Cut!" she turned to him, all business, and asked, "How was I? Need more tears? I can cry if you need me to."

"No," Justin said. "You were great, Brianna."

Hell, yes, she was great. I'd been practically ready to take her in my arms and offer her the Almond Joy I'd won in my latest round of Vending Machine Roulette.

As the crew started filing out of her room, I was surprised to see Brianna dump her packed clothing back into her dresser drawers.

"Don't you have to leave the island now?" I asked, stepping into the room.

"I can't leave, not until Manny's plane is fixed. Yuck," she said, checking herself out in the mirror, "I can't wait to scrape off all this makeup and give myself a facial. Redheads like me have such sensitive skin. Want me to give you a facial, too, hon? Your pores sure could use a little tightening."

I saw nothing wrong with my pores, thank you very much.

"You'll love it," she said. "It's a tofu ginger soy mudpack."

Gaak, I wouldn't eat that stuff, let alone put it on my face.

"Um, thanks. That's awfully sweet, but I think I'll pass."

"Suit yourself, hon," she said with a shrug.

"So you don't feel bad about being kicked off the show?" I asked as she wheeled her suitcase back into her closet.

"Heck, no," she replied. "I got lots of air time, and that's what really counts. Not only that, I think I made a very good impression on Manny. I'm hoping he'll use me again in one of his other shows."

Looked like Brianna Barbie was alive and well, after all.

I left her sloshing goo on her face and made my way down the corridor, where I saw Dallas standing in Hope's doorway, talking to Hope. The petite blonde was seated at her vanity, brushing her hair, no doubt doing her hundred strokes per day.

Eager to eavesdrop, I lingered at the landing, pretending to tie my shoelace.

Which would have been far more effective, I'm sure, if I hadn't been wearing flip-flops.

"Better start packing, hon," I could hear Dallas saying to Hope. "You'll be next."

"I wouldn't be so sure of that," Hope replied.

"No? Did you see the way Spencer looked at me when he handed me my lei? That's called love, sweetheart. We both love each other, something anybody but a narcissist like you would be able to see."

And I had to admit, Spencer had seemed rather gaga when he'd placed that lei around Dallas's neck. Far more enthusiastic than he'd been with Hope.

"I'll be the future Countess of Swampshire. You can bet on it," Dallas said as she traipsed back to her room.

"Not if I can stop you, you won't," I heard Hope say.

I got up from "tying my shoelaces" and caught a glimpse of Hope in her vanity mirror, methodically brushing her silky hair.

But it wasn't her hair that caught my attention.

It was her eyes: Tough as steel and utterly impenetrable.

Sort of like my Almond Joy from Manny's vending machine.

Back in Sauna Central, I quickly forgot about the warring bachelorettes, my mind occupied with something far more important.

Tonight, lest you forgot, was my dinner date with Tai, my handsome island prince, and I needed to get ready to meet the royal family.

After a quick shower under a tepid trickle of water, I stood in front of my closet, wrapped in a towel, trying to decide what to wear. I definitely needed to dress to impress. But, alas, all I'd packed for my trip were a bunch of boring capris and tees. Why the heck hadn't I listened to Lance and bought myself a flirty sundress?

"Oh, Pro," I sighed. "What am I going to do?"

She gazed up at me from where she was stretched out on the bed.

I find a nice refreshing belly rub always helpful in times of crisis.

And then, just when I'd given up all hope of looking cute, a miracle happened.

Polly showed up.

Apparently Akela, still mired in her cat phobia, had begged Polly to bring up Prozac's dinner.

When Pro had swan-dived into her fish guts, Polly turned to me, excited.

"You all set for your date with Tai tonight? What're you going to wear?"

"Nothing," I mumbled, dejected.

"The naked approach, huh? That should get things off to a spicy start."

"Seriously, Polly. I haven't got a thing to wear. All I brought are boring capris and tees."

"That's all?"

"Not unless you count my I ❤ MY CAT sleep shirt."

I plopped on the bed face down, burying my head in the pillow.

"I may as well cancel."

"Don't be silly!" Polly said, heading to my closet. "I'm sure we can find something in here that will work."

After a quick perusal of its contents, she shook her ponytail in dismay.

"Looks like you packed for an L. L. Bean convention."

"Tell me about it," I groaned.

"Wait a minute," she said, holding out a pair of white stretch capris. "These don't look too baggy. And I think I've got a top that'll look great with it. I'll go get it."

"But, Polly. You're a size four and I'm a size . . . well, not a four. How am I ever going to fit into one of your tops?"

"It's oversized on me. I'm sure it'll fit you just fine."

And before I knew it, she was whizzing out the door.

Sixteen tension-filled minutes later (I was counting every second), she was back swinging a tote bag.

"Voilà!" she said, reaching into the tote and pulling out a gorgeous silk turquoise top. It was a boxy, boatneck affair, with three-quarter sleeves, cut very generously.

I tried it on, and Polly was right: It fit me just fine.

"I brought these to go with it," she said, holding out a pair of fabulous dangly silver earrings.

"And these!"

Flip-flops with bright turquoise flowers at the toe thong.

I tried on everything with my white stretch capris, and I'm happy to report I looked good. More than good. I looked pretty darn terrific.

"Wait, I'm not done!"

With that, Polly whipped out a pair of scissors from the tote and began trimming my hair, still damp from my shower. When she was through, she took out a tube of some miracle styling product she'd borrowed from the makeup department and began shaping my mop until it was a nimbus of sexy, shiny curls.

My gosh, I felt like Cinderella getting ready for the ball with Polly as my ponytailed fairy godmother! Any minute now I expected her to turn Prozac into a Prada clutch.

"Polly, you're an angel!" I cried. "How can I ever thank you?"

"Just have a good time with Tai tonight."

Brimming with confidence in my fab new outfit, I intended to do just that.

Chapter 10

After Polly left, I slapped on some lipstick and mascara, then whirled in front of Pro for her approval.

"So? What do you think?"

She gazed up at me through slitted eyes.

I think I'd still like that belly rub.

Fat chance. I was busy admiring myself in my closet mirror, striking poses and turning pirouettes, when suddenly my little lovefest was disrupted by the sound of a car horn honking.

Hurrying to the window, I saw Tai parked in front of the mansion in his Jeep.

Even from three stories up, he was a stunner.

After my heart stopped fibrillating, I blew Pro a kiss good-bye and sailed out the door, making sure to bolt the outside lock. Then I scurried down the stairs, Polly's flip-flops slapping against my heels.

Out on the verandah, I sighed in delight.

What a beautiful night. The sky was lit up with a gazillion stars. And balmy breezes wafted in the air, bearing the heady scent of gardenias.

But the most beautiful sight of all was Tai behind the wheel of his Jeep, looking particularly yummy in cutoffs and a tank top, the moonlight glistening off his sculpted bod.

"Hey, Jaine," he said, gracing me with a dazzling smile.

Was it my imagination, or was he looking at me with unabashed approval?

"You look terrific!" he beamed.

"Thanks," I said, sending silent blessings to my fairy godmother, Polly.

"Hop in," Tai said, and I climbed on board the Jeep, ever so grateful Tai couldn't see my tush as I hoisted it up to the passenger seat.

"For you," he said, handing me a gorgeous gardenia.

So that's where the delicious scent had been coming from.

"How beautiful!"

"Let me put it in your hair."

As he put the flower in my hair, his fingers grazed my neck, and I repressed a shiver of excitement.

"I just know my dad's going to love you," he said, staring deeply into my eyes.

Omigosh, did this mean what I thought it meant? Was he going to ask his father's approval to marry me? Wow, even me and my overactive imagination hadn't planned on things going this fast.

Tearing his eyes away from me, Tai put the Jeep in gear, and we set off for his tribal village.

"I can't wait for you and Dad to meet," he was saying.

I nodded absently, wondering if after we were married we could have a little pied-à-terre in the States. Maybe even in Manhattan. I'd always wanted to live in the Big Apple.

Tai kept telling me how pretty I looked, while I mentally chose silverware for our bridal registry. Something in a bamboo pattern would be perfect for island life.

"I'm so happy I got to pick you up at the airport the other day," Tai said, his hand perilously close to my knee. "What a lucky break that was."

"Absolutely," I gushed, barely restraining myself from running my fingers through his fabulous curls.

"Well, here we are!"

Snapping out of my reverie, I realized we had arrived at Tai's village—a barren stretch of land with primitive thatched huts built in a circle around what looked like a large fire pit.

Oh, dear. It was a lot less glam than I'd expected.

Where were all the lanais and swaying palms and waves lapping against the shore?

Tai parked the Jeep and led me past the thatched huts.

In vain I looked for a hammock swinging between two palms, but all I saw was underwear drying on clotheslines.

As we walked through the village, I noticed that one hut was larger than the others, with a verandah and an ancient TV antenna perched on the thatched roof.

"This is my dad's house," Tai said with pride as we approached it.

Whoa. I realized this wasn't Versailles, but wasn't a king supposed to live in a palace? Or at least a really nice house? With guards out front? And maybe a flag?

But all that graced the king's lawn was a pink plastic flamingo.

And a grunting pig.

"That's Ava Gardner," Tai said, pointing to the mud-spattered animal. "My dad's pet pig."

Tai led me past the pig up the front steps to the verandah, where a spectacularly lovely young native gal was standing, clad in a slinky sarong, her lush mane of wavy black hair flowing all the way down to her tush.

And before I knew what was happening, she was throwing her arms around Tai and planting a wet smacker on his lips.

Wait a minute! Who was this hussy, and why was she sucking face with my future husband?

Unwrapping himself from her clutches, Tai turned to me and said, "Jaine, I'd like you to meet my girlfriend, Leilani."

What the what? If Tai had a girlfriend, then what on earth was I doing here?

I was about to find out.

Leaving Leilani out on the verandah, Tai opened a tattered screen door and ushered me into the "palace" living room.

There I saw a squat sixtysomething dude leaning back in a cracked vinyl recliner watching a rerun of *I Love Lucy*.

"Hi, Dad!" Tai called out. "Jaine's here. The girl I was telling you about."

The old guy muted the TV and heaved himself up from the recliner.

He was a short, potbellied geezer with approximately three strands of hair clinging desperately to his scalp. Sporting a sarong type skirt which I prayed would not flap open, he was naked from the waist up, affording me an up close and personal view of his pot belly.

"Jaine Austen, I'd like you to meet my father, King Konga of Paratito."

"Er . . . hello," I managed to choke out.

"Welcome, my dearest Jaine," the geezer said, gracing me with the royal smile.

Which happened to be pretty much devoid of royal teeth.

As far as I could tell, he had about six remaining stumps. Which beat out the number of hairs on his head but still made for a fairly appalling first impression.

"I was just watching an episode of the venerated American TV show *I Love Lucy*." He stared in awe at the screen as Ethel traded zingers with Fred.

"Isn't she beautiful?" he said, staring lovestruck at Lucy's sidekick.

Wait. He thought *Ethel* was the pretty one?

"So what do you think, Dad?" Tai asked. "Isn't Jaine great?"

The old man looked me up and down, a naughty glint in his eye.

"Just what I've been looking for, son!"

"Then I guess I'll leave you two alone," Tai said.

And with that, the little rat scooted out the door.

"I suppose Tai's told you I'm looking to get married," Konga said when we were alone.

"No, as a matter of fact, he neglected to point that out to me."

I only wish Tai had been there to hear the frost in my voice.

"Indeed. I'm looking for another wife."

"*Another* wife?"

"I've already got eleven lovely spouses, and now I want to make it an even dozen. Polygamy is legal here in Paratito. For the king, anyway. Tai told me he thought you'd be perfect for me, and he's absolutely right! You're magnificent!"

This from a guy who thought Ethel was the pretty one.

"Yes, indeedie, you are one groovy chick."

Groovy chick? Who taught him how to speak English? Austin Powers?

"So how about it? Will you marry me and become Queen Number Twelve of Paratito?"

"It's awfully tempting," I said, at my diplomatic best, "but I'm afraid not."

"Why not?" His belly shook in indignation.

"I'll be a wonderful husband. I'll feed you good, give you all the coconuts you can eat, and you get to sleep with me every twelve days!"

"Once again, it's mighty tempting, but I think I'll pass."

"I understand," he nodded. "My fault. I'm rushing you. Get to know me, and you will love me. Just wait till we spend some time together. Come. Let me give you a tour of the palace living room."

He began leading me around the room, which was curtained off on one end from the room behind it.

Along with the recliner, there were about a dozen bean bag pillows (seating, I assumed, for his eleven wives) and an étagère full of what my mom likes to call "junque."

"You've already seen the television. Isn't it magnificent?"

Maybe, back in 1979 when it was no doubt originally built.

"We get all the best shows here on Paratito Island: *Hawaii Five-O. Gilligan's Island. Laugh In. The Golden Girls.* And my favorite, *The Dean Martin Variety Hour.* Love Deano and his buddy Frank. Such cool cats."

So that's where he learned his "groovy" English. From Deano and the rat pack.

"And look," he said, pointing proudly to a bunch of knickknacks on a shelf. "The royal collectibles: my dancing Santa, my Veg-O-Matic, my Elvis bobblehead. And my proudest possession— an autographed photo of the Golden Girls. Groovy, no?"

"A regular treasure trove."

"Right on!" he agreed, gracing me with a tooth-less grin.

"And now, on to dinner!"

With that, he pushed open the curtain at the far end of the living room, revealing a dining room with a long wooden table and picnic-like benches. The only actual chair was at the head of the table, a comfy padded affair that I bet my bottom Pop-Tart was reserved for King Konga.

Seated on both sides of the table were eleven native women, ranging in age from the mid-twenties to one rather large woman about Konga's age.

Not one of them looked the least bit happy to see me.

Indeed, a skilled doctor could have performed Lasik surgery with the dagger glares they were shooting me.

Konga introduced me to them one by one. To my amazement, he did not refer to them by name, but rather by number. Only did his Number One Wife, the large sixty-something gal, seem to have a name.

"And finally," Konga said, when he got to her (he'd worked his way up from Wife Number Eleven), "I'd like you to meet my Number One Wife, Suma."

A boulder-like woman, with cowhide skin and angry slits for eyes, Suma grunted a grudging hello.

As I'd suspected, Konga took the comfy chair at the head of the table, leaving the hard benches for his beloved wives.

I was seated at his right, across from Suma.

At the last minute, Tai and Leilani ambled in to join us, all happy and giggling.

I felt like strangling them with the WHATEVER HAPPENS IN PARATITO STAYS IN PARATITO scarf draped over Konga's vinyl recliner.

Once we were all settled, Konga struck a large gong at his side, and several of the wives scurried to the kitchen and started bringing out food. Apparently, when you married Konga you not only got to be queen of Paratito, you also got to be a part-time waitress.

If truth be told, though, I was looking forward to the dinner. It had to be better than Manny's airline food. At least it would be fresh.

Oh, it was fresh all right.

Fresh snake fricassee. Fresh octopus glands. And something else fresh from the sea whose glassy eye stared up at me dolefully throughout the meal.

As I was about to discover, the Paratito Islanders had a penchant for delicacies most Americans dissect in biology class.

While I industriously shoved food around on my plate, avoiding the death-ray glares from the other wives, Konga kept telling me what a "groovy chick" I was and urging me to eat more. He liked his wives with a little meat on their bones.

"Don't forget to eat the eyeball!" he said, eyeing the uneaten fish on my plate. "It's the best part."

Oh, glug.

Throughout the meal, he regaled me with tales of his favorite hobbies—harpoon fishing, crocodile hunting, flossing his six teeth, and grooming his pet pig, Ava Gardner.

Finally, our dishes were cleared away—Wife Number Seven happily munching on my fish eyeball as she took my plate—and it was time for dessert.

Suma stood up to make an announcement:

"Tonight, in honor of our special guest," she said, shooting me a filthy look, "we eat monkey chunks for dessert."

Omigod. Monkey? This was simply too much.

I was seriously considering getting up and bolting from the table when one of the wives set down a bowl of ice cream in front of me. And not just any ice cream. Chunky Monkey!

"Omigosh!" I cried, in my first and only moment of unalloyed joy. "Chunky Monkey. It's my favorite!"

"Mine, too," Konga assured me, love light shining in his eyes. "I have it flown in from Tahiti along with Manny's pastrami whenever Manny is on the island.

"See?" he said, with a most unsettling wink. "We have something in common!"

Actually, he had a point. I had yet to find a man who liked Chunky Monkey quite as much as I did.

I took another look at him, slurping his ice cream, his three hairs plastered across his scalp, and thought maybe he wasn't so bad after all. But I quickly came to my senses when he put his hammy hand on my wrist and suggested we go on a moonlight walk together.

Minutes later we were outside strolling around the dusty fire pit.

Konga tried to hold my hand, but I quickly yanked it away.

"Sorry," I said. "Can't hold hands. Bad case of eczema. Extremely contagious."

"I hope you will change your mind about marrying me," Konga said, kicking a dead iguana out of our path. "I will make all your dreams come true. I will even let you have an upper bunk in the wives' dormitory."

"How very enticing." I managed a weak smile.

"I know what you're thinking. That our ages are not compatible. That one of us belongs with a much younger partner. But don't worry, Jaine. For you, I'm prepared to make an exception and marry someone older than twenty-five."

I was too old for *him*?

Now he was smiling at me, his six teeth glistening in the moonlight, and holy mackerel, he was zeroing in for a kiss!

No way could this happen.

"It's been swell," I said, breaking away, "but I've got to run. Early day tomorrow. Thanks so much for the snake fricassee."

With that I sprinted back to the "palace," Konga huffing in my wake.

"I like a gal who plays hard to get!" he called out from behind.

Tai was waiting for us out on the verandah.

"Take me home," I snapped.

"Now? Don't you want to meet Ava Gardner?"

"No, I don't want to meet your father's pig. Just take me home."

"Okay," he shrugged.

I scurried back to the Jeep faster than a speeding gecko and practically dived into the car when I got there.

Tai got in next to me and started the engine.

The last thing I heard as we drove away was Konga calling out:

"Ava Gardner, my princess, come give Daddy a kiss!"

The ride back to the mansion was rife with icy silence. On my part, anyway. Tai seemed unaware of the chill in the air.

"That went great," he said. "I think Pop really likes you!"

"You never told me you wanted to fix me up with your father."

"Didn't I?" He didn't even have the grace to look embarrassed. "Gee, I thought I had. But it sure went great. Pop said if I found him another wife, he'd buy me a new sound system for the Jeep."

"How lucky for you."

"Isn't it?" he said, oblivious to the sarcasm oozing from my every pore.

At last we arrived back at the mansion.

By now the gardenia in my hair was as wilted as my dreams of royal glory.

Without a word, I opened the passenger door

and hopped off, not even caring if my tush looked big.

"See you soon, *Mom*," Tai called after me with a moronic grin.

Oh, man. If only I had Konga's Dancing Santa with me. I knew exactly where I'd like to shove it.

Chapter 11

Stomping up to the mansion, I read myself the riot act.

How could I have been such an idiot, thinking Tai wanted to marry me when we hadn't even gone out on a first date? It had to be a case of temporary insanity, brought on by extreme heat, humidity, and pizza deprivation.

Oh, well. At least my dinner from hell was over. I'd never have to go back to that stupid tribal village ever again.

I was just about to let myself into the mansion when I heard voices coming from the side of the house.

One of them was raised in anger. Snoop that I am, I couldn't resist a bit of eavesdropping. So I tiptoed over and peeked around the corner of the house, where I saw Kirk and Hope standing near some hibiscus bushes.

Kirk raked his fingers through his hair, distraught.

"I can't believe you're dumping me for that British dope! I was the one who got you a part on the show in the first place. You promised me you had no intention of going after Spencer, that you only signed on to the project to be near me while we were shooting."

If he expected any contrition, he was in for a disappointment.

Hope, a porcelain doll in a white eyelet sundress, barely blinked an eye.

"You should know me by now, Kirk," she said. "We've been dating for two years. I'm nothing if not practical. We've had some good times together, but you can't expect me to pass up British royalty. With Spencer's name, and my smarts, we'll be unstoppable."

She smiled at the thought of her future as a British royal.

"But how can you be so sure Spencer will choose you over Dallas?"

"I just know he will," Hope replied, her pointy chin thrust out with confidence.

Frankly, I thought she was being a tad delusional, but there wasn't an iota of doubt in her voice.

"You mustn't be a poor sport, Kirk. If you were in my shoes, you'd do the same thing."

"No, I wouldn't," Kirk said, blinking back what looked like tears. "I love you."

"Oh, sweetheart." Hope shook her head

sadly. "That's where you made your big mistake."

Wow. Talk about cold. Why did I get the feeling that Freon ran in her veins?

And with the precision of a military drill sergeant, she turned abruptly toward the mansion.

Oops. My cue to skedaddle.

I raced into the house, taking the stairs two at a time.

When I finally made it up to the top floor, I groaned to see Prozac perched on the landing.

She glared at me with an impatient thump of her tail.

What took you so long? You haven't scratched my belly in over an hour!

What with all the hooha of my almost becoming King Konga's Wife Number Twelve, I'd forgotten about my feline Houdini.

Once again, she'd escaped from Sauna Central!

I really had to put a stop to it. But until I figured out how she was making her daring escapes, I did the only sensible thing possible:

I let myself into my room, lay naked on my bed, and polished off the Dove Bar I'd nabbed from Manny's mini-fridge on a tiny detour I'd taken on my way up the stairs.

Chapter 12

As it turned out, I stumbled onto Prozac's escape route the very next morning.

I was standing at my bathroom sink, washing a snake fricassee stain from my capris, when I happened to glance over at my tiny bathroom window. And suddenly it occurred to me: I'd secured the window in the bedroom but had forgotten all about the one in the bathroom. What if Prozac had been using it to stage her Great Escapes?

I peered closely at the screen. Was that a rip along the bottom? Running my finger along the base of the screen, I realized that indeed it was. What's more, when I looked out the window, I saw a narrow ledge running under the window to the room next door.

Wasting no time, I dashed out of Sauna Central and burst into the room next to mine. As far as I knew, no one was using it. And I was right. When I opened the door, I saw no furniture except for a stripped bed. Racing into the room's en suite bathroom, I checked the bathroom window and discovered it was wide open—with no screen!

So that's how Prozac had been escaping! From my bathroom window, across the ledge, and in through this window.

I shuddered to think of my precious princess risking her life navigating that narrow ledge.

Immediately, I locked the window and returned to my room, where I did the same in my own bathroom.

Then I marched out to the bedroom where Prozac was sprawled out on the bed.

"I'm on to you, Pro," I said with an authoritative wag of my finger. "I've figured out how you've been breaking loose. No more roaming around the mansion getting into trouble, young lady. You have been outwitted by my superior brainpower once and for all!"

And I'm sure she would have felt the sharp sting of my words if she hadn't been so busy snoring at the time.

Flush from my bathroom window victory, I joined Polly for breakfast on the patio, both of us feasting on rubberized eggs and granite muffins.

Meanwhile, down at the other end of the table, Manny was scarfing down what looked like a fabulous fluffy omelet and a giant bagel smeared with cream cheese.

How very aggravating. I only hope he choked on his cream cheese.

Sitting next to Manny were Hope and Spencer, Spencer having a go at a muffin, while Hope sipped at some orange juice.

Justin, our disgruntled director, was at the "B" table with his crew—as far away from Manny as possible—yakking into his cell phone, presumably trashing Manny to everyone on his contact list.

"So," Polly said, hacking at her eggs, "how was your date with Tai?"

I started to tell her about my date from hell, but I soon saw her eyes wander over to the buffet table, where Kirk had shown up, looking like death warmed over. Unwashed and unshaven, a thick layer of stubble on his face, his hands trembled as he poured himself some coffee.

"Poor Kirk!" Polly said. "He looks terrible."

Not for the first time, I noticed a moony, lovestruck look in her eyes.

"Did you know that he and Hope were an item?" I asked.

"No!" she said, gulping back her disappointment. "I had no idea."

"Apparently they've been dating for two years, and last night I overheard her dump him for Spencer."

Polly tsked in pity. "Men are such idiots, aren't they?"

She wasn't going to get an argument from me on that one.

"Imagine a sweet guy like Kirk falling for an opportunistic twit like Hope. Oh, well. He's better off without her."

"He sure doesn't seem to think so," I said as Kirk staggered over to the pool and collapsed onto one of the chaises.

Down at the end of the table, Manny glared at Kirk in disgust.

"I swear," he said, "that's the last time I hire that alkie on one of my shows."

To which I heard Justin mutter, "Lucky Kirk."

But Kirk was upstaged just then when Brianna came sauntering onto the patio in micro-mini hot pants and an X-rated halter top.

All eyes followed her as she sashayed past Spencer on her way to the buffet table.

"See what you're missing?" she said, with a wink, wagging her tush.

Spencer blushed a deep crimson, while at his side Hope sat gritting her teeth.

Brianna grabbed a petrified Danish and headed over to the pool, the guys in the crew gawking at her every step of the way.

When breakfast was over, the crew started setting up for the first shoot of the day, a scene in the pool where Hope and Dallas would discuss Brianna's departure from the show.

Thank goodness, I didn't have to write dialogue for Spencer for that one.

Polly and I lingered over the sludge posing as our coffee, while down at the other end of the table Manny lit up one of his fifty-dollar cigars.

For fifty bucks, you'd think they could invent

a cigar that didn't smell like the inside of an outhouse.

I was in the middle of telling Polly about King Konga's snake fricassee, when suddenly all hell broke loose.

Like a perfumed tornado, Dallas came stomping out of the mansion, making a beeline for Spencer.

"Look what I just found in Manny's office," she cried, eyes blazing, flushed with anger. She waved a piece of paper in Spencer's face. "A breakdown of the scenes for the rest of the show.

"What's this supposed to mean?" she asked Spencer. "*Spencer's Proposal to Hope*"?

Spencer squirmed in his seat and began stammering. But before he could fumpher a reply, Manny whipped the paper from Dallas's hand.

"What the hell were you doing in my office?"

"Looking for something decent to eat. You keep all the good food for yourself in your minifridge, you selfish bastard."

Then, whirling back to Spencer, she continued, "You're not really going to ask Hope to marry you, are you?"

And with that gift of gab he was so famous for, Spencer stammered:

"Well, um, er . . . that is to say, uh, yes."

"But how could you? You promised you'd marry me!"

A royal deer caught in the headlights, Spencer mumbled something about how he'd thought it over and decided he really liked Hope best, after all.

"You don't mean that," Dallas moaned. "You told me you loved me and wanted to marry me."

But Spencer just stared down at his plate, unable to meet her eyes.

Meanwhile, Hope, who was still sipping her orange juice (at this rate, she'd be through with it by dinner), took time out to lob Dallas a smug smile.

I could practically see the thought bubble over her head:

I won! I won! Eat dirt, Texas bimbo!

Dallas saw her smirking and went a tad ballistic.

"Wipe that smile off your face, bitch," she hissed. "If I can't have Spencer, I'll see to it you never will!"

"Now, Dallas," Manny said, taking a puff of his stink-bomb. "Be reasonable. Spencer's made up his mind, and there's nothing you can do. You know what they say. All's fair in love and war."

Dallas's eyes narrowed into angry slits.

"As far as I'm concerned, Manny, this is war. If you think I'm going to show up in front of your cameras after this, think again. I'm done. Finito. Outta here. I'm going to call my father and have him send one of his corporate jets to pick me up."

Manny jumped up in alarm.

"But you can't leave the show! You're under contract. I can sue you for walking out."

"Go ahead and sue," Dallas snapped back. "Daddy can afford it."

"Damn!" Manny muttered, stubbing out his cigar and racing after her.

Hope, meanwhile, was loving every minute of this.

"I'm glad she knows, darling," she said to Spencer. "I want everyone to know. I don't want to keep our love a secret anymore."

Now that Dallas had gone, Spencer seemed to have crept out from under his shell.

"Absolutely, darling," he said. And with that, he took her hand in his and kissed it.

"Well, whaddaya know," Polly said. "Looks like the royal Brit really has fallen for the obnoxious twit."

By now, the crew was all set up at the pool to shoot Hope's scene with Dallas. But production was called to a halt while Manny and Justin took turns standing outside Dallas's room, begging her to return to the show.

A good hour and a half passed as the negotiations waged on.

Polly and I used the time constructively, playing Vending Machine Roulette (peanut butter crackers for Polly, Cheetos for me) and then hanging out at the patio, rehashing the details of my date from hell with King Konga.

"My God!" she cried, as I described my dinner. "They actually expected you to eat the eyeball?"

Periodically she looked over at Kirk, who was still sacked out on the pool chaise.

Once again, I saw the longing in her eyes.

"You have a thing for him, don't you?" I asked.

"Is it that obvious?"

"Sort of."

"Well, there goes my career as an international spy," she said with a weak laugh. "We worked together on a couple of the earlier bachelorette dates, and he seemed like such a great guy. And it doesn't hurt that he's got a bod to die for. Have you seen his abs? The first time I saw them, I thought I'd died and gone to Calvin Klein Underwear Heaven."

And so we whiled away the time, eating stale junk food and discussing our anemic love lives.

Later I would kick myself for not paying closer attention, but at the time I was only vaguely aware of what was going on around me. I heard Spencer on the phone with his mummy, saw Hope strutting around in a short terry bathrobe, looking quite proud of herself, and Kirk snoring on the pool chaise.

All the while, Manny and Justin were taking turns cajoling Dallas out of her room.

Finally, wiping sweat from his brow, Justin walked out onto the patio, triumphant.

"Dallas says she'll finish the rest of the show. But she insists on real steak for dinner each night. Not the airline crap."

"Okay," Manny grudgingly conceded.

"She says she needs a half hour to fix herself up."

And, indeed, a half hour later, Dallas returned to the patio, looking spectacular in an eensy yellow bikini, her tan a luscious shade of mocha, her glossy chestnut hair trailing in her wake.

Hope took off the robe she had been wearing, revealing her tiny bod in a polka-dot bikini trimmed with ruffles. Her little chest was puffed up with so much pride, I almost expected her to be using it as a flotation device.

The girls got in the pool to shoot the scene.

But before the cameras started to roll, Justin told Dallas: "Remember, you've got to play this scene as if you don't know Spencer has chosen Hope. Like you still think you've got a chance."

"No problem," Dallas said, lying back in the water and spreading out her arms.

"Okay," Justin called out to his cameramen. "Action."

With the cameras rolling, Hope plastered on a mask of false pity.

"Poor Brianna," she tsked. "She was very sweet, but not exactly the brightest bulb on the Christmas tree."

Brianna, lolling in a chaise out of camera range, looked up, irritated.

"So I guess it's just between you and me," Hope said.

"May the best woman win," Dallas replied.

"Thanks," Hope smirked. "I'm sure I will."

"I wouldn't be too sure about that, honey."

With that, Dallas began flutter-kicking in the pool, making sure she doused Hope with her spray.

"I don't think Spencer's going to marry you, Hope. In fact, I know he won't."

Wow, Dallas was turning out to be quite the little actress. If I hadn't known that Spencer was slated to propose to Hope, I would've sworn Dallas still had a chance with the guy.

She stood up straight now and shot Hope a sly smile.

"Cancel the wedding bells, sweetie. It ain't gonna happen."

And for the first time all morning, I saw a spark of fear in Hope's eyes.

Was it possible that Dallas had figured out a way to reel in Spencer, after all?

Chapter 13

Manny's plane had at last been repaired, and as soon as Hope had changed out of her bikini into shorts and a T-shirt, we headed to the airport to shoot her skydiving scene with Spencer.

Leaving Brianna and Dallas to soothe their bruised egos at the mansion, the rest of us tooled off in a caravan of Jeeps and SUVs.

Polly and I rode with Manny in his monster van, Kirk at his side in the passenger seat with two parachutes in his lap. Spencer and Hope sat behind them in the second row, thighs welded together, with Polly and me bringing up the rear.

I couldn't decide which was worse, being trapped in the van with the fetid smell of Manny's cigar or having to listen to Hope blather about how she couldn't wait to visit jolly old England and wondering if maybe Spencer could arrange tea with the queen.

Did Hope have no empathy whatsoever? Didn't she realize how hurtful this must be for Kirk?

Apparently not, because she just kept on babbling.

It was a short ride to the airport, thank heavens, and when we got there, Spencer and Hope were hustled into hair and makeup and then fitted with unflattering puffy jumpsuits that would have made ordinary mortals look like the Michelin Man.

Hope and Spencer, however, actually managed to look good in them, their bodies annoyingly thin under all that fluff.

Manny, in a burst of The Cutesies, had ordered a baby blue chute for Spencer and a pink chute for Hope. Now, with gritted teeth, Kirk helped Spencer and Hope put on their chutes, strapping them onto their bodies like backpacks, avoiding all eye contact with Hope.

Hope had no trouble handling her chute, so Kirk's time with her was mercifully brief. Spencer, on the other hand, was taking forever.

Why did I get the feeling the guy was still figuring out how to brush his teeth?

Finally, Kirk got him strapped in and went over the instructions for deploying the chutes.

Given that I know absolutely nothing about the inner workings of parachutes, you'll have to forgive my lack of techno-talk here. All I can tell you is that there were a couple of doohickeys they had to pull on the front straps—one to de-

ploy the main chute, and another to deploy a re-
serve in case of an emergency.

"Understood?" Kirk asked, when he was finished explaining.

"Absolutely," Spencer nodded. "I pull on my
left for the main canopy and my right for the
emergency canopy."

"No, no! It's the other way around. Right for
main, left for emergency."

"Brilliant!" Spencer replied, with an idiotic
grin.

"My God," whispered Polly, who was standing
next to me. "The guy has the IQ of a turnip."

At last the lovebirds were all suited up, and
Kirk fitted them with their helmets. At which
point, Justin, who had been busy yakking on his
cell with his agent, reluctantly clicked his phone
shut and called for action.

The cameras started rolling as Spencer and
Hope made their way up the steps to the plane.

"Isn't this exciting?" Hope asked, her perky
smile firmly in place. "It's going to be so much
fun!"

Back in the van, I'd handed Spencer a list of
bon mots to use in the scene, little gems like,
"I'm already flying high with you, Hope. This is
just icing on the cake."

But naturally, all he said now was, "Brilliant!"

Once they'd boarded the plane and the door
slammed shut, Manny's ancient pilot, matchstick dangling from his mouth, gave a thumbs-
up from the cockpit and took off.

Minutes later, the plane was hovering in the
air above us.

Of course, on a quality shoot, they'd have a special aerial photographer shooting close-up footage of the jump, but on this Grade Z production, Manny had settled for having his ground cameramen use zoom lenses.

The plane door now opened, and Spencer appeared in the doorway, resplendent in his blue jumpsuit.

We watched with bated breath as he jumped. For a terrifying second, nothing happened. Had he pulled the wrong doohickey? Or had his mind simply gone blank?

But then, a collective sigh of relief could be heard among the crew as Spencer's baby blue canopy billowed open and he began floating to the ground.

Now it was Hope's turn.

Silhouetted in the doorway of the plane, she waved to the cameras below.

When she took her plunge, I felt no fear. If nothing else, Hope was a smart cookie. I was certain she knew which doohickey to pull, and that she'd operate the chute with the expertise of a pro.

Wrong. Major league wrong.

I stared up in the sky, waiting for the chute to open and a pink canopy to appear. Seconds passed. More seconds. And still no sign of the canopy.

"What the hell's going on?" Manny shouted.

"It looks like she's trying to pull the controls," one of the cameramen shouted, "but they're not working."

Indeed, Hope seemed to be writhing in mid-air.

And then, before our horrified eyes, the future Countess of Swampshire was hurtling through space, plummeting to her death.

Chapter 14

The entire Paratito Police Department (two guys in Bermuda shorts and Hawaiian-print shirts) showed up at the airport to investigate. They quickly determined that someone had tampered with Hope's pink parachute, cutting the cords to both the main chute and the emergency canopy.

Kirk, eyes wide with panic, swore that both chutes were in perfect working order when he checked them in his prop shed that morning at around 9:00 AM. So whoever tampered with the chutes had to have done it sometime between 9:00 AM and a little after 1:00 PM, when Kirk went to get them for the shoot.

We all returned to the mansion, where one of the cops, a skinny young guy with enormous brown doe eyes, headed off to the prop shed, a small building on the rear grounds of the mansion, to dust for fingerprints.

My estimation of the Paratito PD took a nosedive when I saw a pamphlet sticking out from his back pocket called *Fingerprinting for Dummies*.

Ouch. Not exactly the FBI, were they?

The other cop, Paratito's chief of police, a paunchy guy who looked vaguely familiar, commandeered Manny's office and called us in, one by one, for questioning.

When it was my turn to be grilled, I found him sitting behind Manny's desk, his gut pushing up against the drawers, his hairs plastered to his head in an inventive combover. And then I realized who he reminded me of: King Konga.

Indeed, he bore an uncanny resemblance to the octopus-eating king.

Across the room, Manny's tropical fish frolicked in their tank, and I wondered if he'd leap over and grab one to snack on.

"Ah, Ms. Austen," he said, getting up to shake my hand. "I am Tonga, the chief of police. What a pleasure it is," he added, "to meet my future sister-in-law."

Say what??

"My brother, King Konga, has told me all about you. And I see he did not exaggerate," he said, giving the me a none-too-subtle once-over. "You will make a perfect Wife Number Twelve."

Oh, for heaven's sakes. This had to stop.

"I'm afraid I won't be marrying your brother."

"That's what they all say," he said with a jolly

chortle. "But in the end, Konga always gets what he wants."

Yikes, I didn't like the sound of that.

"But, of course, before you can marry Konga, we have to rule you out as a suspect in this unfortunate murder."

And for a crazy instant, I had a hard time deciding which would be worse: being accused of murder or being shackled to Konga for the rest of my life.

Actually, that murder charge wasn't looking so bad.

"Where were you," he asked, "between nine this morning and one this afternoon?"

Thank heavens I had Polly as my alibi!

"I was on the patio and at the pool with Polly, the production assistant. We were together the whole time."

"That's what she told me," he said with a broad grin. "Which means you're in the clear. The engagement is still on!"

Engagement? What engagement?

"I must introduce you to my wife. She knows several excellent recipes for octopus glands."

"Sounds fab," I said, scooting out of the room, wondering how long it would take me to book a flight back to L.A.

Back in Sauna Central, I found Prozac stretched out in bed watching Godzilla the waterbug strolling across the room.

I blinked in disbelief. Back home, Prozac

hunted down anything that moved. Birds. Mice. Dustbunnies.

And now she was just sitting there, doing nothing.

"Why on earth aren't you chasing that awful bug, Prozac? What happened to your killer instinct?"

Prozac gazed up at me lazily.

It's back in L.A., with my bacon bits and decent living conditions.

If Prozac wasn't up for the job, I'd have to do it myself.

By now, Godzilla had come to a halt, standing in the middle of the room as if daring me to stomp on him.

I have to admit I was more than a tad squeamish at the thought of bug guts all over my floor. But I took a deep breath and forced myself to do it.

Wham went my foot.

Needless to say, I missed by a mile, and Godzilla scampered off under a nearby baseboard. If he had fingers, I'm sure he would have been giving me one.

It was all most annoying, and I was just about to console myself with a Mars bar I'd picked up in my latest round of Vending Machine Roulette, when Polly came bursting in my room.

"Did you hear the news?" she said, her ponytail aquiver with excitement. "They're taking Dallas down to police headquarters for further questioning! Omigosh," she cried, racing to my window, "there they go now!"

I hurried over to join her at the window. Down

on the grounds below, I watched as the skinny cop struggled to drag a handcuffed Dallas to the official police Jeep. Writhing and tossing her hair extensions, she screamed, "Wait till my daddy hears about this. He's going to sue you people for everything you're worth!"

Which, I guessed, was approximately five co-conut shells.

Finally, the police managed to get her into the backseat of the Jeep, the skinny cop at her side.

"I can't say I'm surprised," Polly said as they drove off. "Dallas practically announced she was going to kill Hope. Remember how she said, *If I can't have Spencer, you never will?*"

"I remember. But it doesn't make sense. If Dallas was the killer, why would she announce her plans to everyone? You'd think she'd be a lot smarter than that."

"Honey, Dallas is a bachelorette. Not an MIT grad. And besides, guess what they found shoved way back in her closet, wrapped in one of her teddies? A wire cutter! The police have bagged it as the possible murder weapon."

Once again, I had my doubts. Why wouldn't Dallas toss the wire cutter into the bushes? Why bring it back and hide it in her own closet?

I couldn't shake the feeling that she'd been framed.

Oh, well. There was nothing I could do about it. And on the plus side, at least this meant the production would be over and I could leave the island, thereby avoiding any future contact with my potbellied beau, King Konga.

"I guess this means the end for *Some Day My Prince Will Come*," I said.

"Yeah, and Manny's inconsolable. Keeps talking about how it was cut off before it even had a chance."

"Does that mean we can all go home?"

"Afraid not. The cops say we all have to stay here in Paratito until the case is officially solved."

Gaak.

That could take forever, I thought, remembering *Fingerprinting for Dummies*.

"Well, gotta go check on Manny's latest shipment of pastrami," Polly said, heading for the door. "There's been some sort of delay, and Manny's having a snit fit."

With that she scooted off, leaving me alone in my misery.

I could not possibly stay in this bug-infested hellhole one more day than necessary. And with my confidence in the Paratito PD being absolutely nil, I made up my mind then and there to snoop around on my own and speed up the murder-solving process.

In the meanwhile, I dug into my Mars bar, making sure to leave absolutely no chocolate bits on the floor to tempt Godzilla from his lair.

YOU'VE GOT MAIL!

To: Jausten
From: Shoptillyoudrop
Subject: Upsetting News!

It looks like our Evening in Paris waltz has hit a
bit of a speed bump, sweetheart. Poor Ed
Nivens's back has gone out, and he's had to
drop out of the performance. Which leaves Lydia
without a partner. We've posted a notice on
the club bulletin board, trying to get a replace-
ment, but so far no one has volunteered.

XOXO,
Mom

To: Jausten
From: DaddyO
Subject: Great News!

Great news, Lambchop. It seems The Battleaxe and her two left feet may not be dancing at
the Evening in Paris gala, after all. Her partner,
Ed Nivens, has dropped out of the performance.
Not that I'm surprised. One dance with Lydia,
and I'd go screaming into the night, too. Ed
claims his back has "gone out." Which is
a patent lie, of course. I saw him on the golf
course this morning, swinging like Jack Nick-
laus. The guy just couldn't stand to have

his feet stomped on one more time by The Battleaxe.

Your mom and the rest of the gals are trying to rope in another man to take Ed's place. All I can say is I pity the poor sucker who winds up dancing with Lydia.

Love 'n' snuggles from
DaddyO

**To: Jausten
From: Shoptillyoudrop
Subject: Still No Volunteers**

Still no volunteers to dance with Lydia. And I must admit I'm a bit surprised. I'd think it would be an honor to dance with such an accomplished woman. But no matter. Alonzo, our dance instructor, just called. He says he's thought of a way for Lydia to dance in the show, after all!

We're heading off to the clubhouse to meet with him right now.

XOXO,
Mom

To: Jausten
From: DaddyO
Subject: Outraged!

Lambchop, you will simply not believe what's happened.

It's turns out *I'm* the poor sucker who has to dance with Lydia!

Alonzo just announced that he'd fill in as the missing dancer. Only he'll be dancing with your mom. And I'll be stuck with The Battleaxe. He claims it's because he's too short to dance with Lydia. And while it's true that The Battleaxe does sort of tower over him, I know that's just an excuse. He's seen what she's like on the dance floor and doesn't want to get caught in the web of her two left feet.

Well, if he thinks I'm going to dance with Lydia, he's sadly mistaken. I'm quitting the show and absolutely nothing will get me to change my mind.

Love 'n' hugs from your
Outraged
DaddyO

To: Jausten
From: Shoptillyoudrop
Subject: The End of the World

What drama! You'd think the world had just
come to an end. All because Alonzo assigned
Daddy to dance with Lydia at the Evening in
Paris gala. Now Daddy's threatening to quit the
show. I told him if he did, he'd be making his
own dinners from now on. And that he could
certainly forget about the meat loaf I was planning to cook for dinner tonight.

XOXO,
Mom

To: Jausten
From: DaddyO
Subject: Base Extortion

Well, Lambchop, I must admit I'm very
disappointed in your mom. This normally honor-
able woman has resorted to base extortion to
keep me in the show.

She says if I don't dance with Lydia, she'll stop
cooking for me. And tonight she was going to
make meatloaf. I may have a will of iron, honey,
but even Superman himself would not be able to
resist the lure of your mom's meatloaf.

No doubt about it. Your mom's got me over a barrel. I'll dance with The Battle-axe. But I won't like it. Not one bit.

Love 'n' hugs from
Your downtrodden
DaddyO

To: Jausten
From: SirLancelot
Subject: Another Tiny Glitch

Dinner with Brett was divine. He told me all about the new play he's writing. I wish I could remember what it was about, but I was so busy staring at his biceps, I guess I wasn't really paying much attention. Honestly, Jaine. I know it was only one dinner date, but I think Brett may be The One.

Ciao for now!
Lance

PS. Another tiny glitch with the Corolla. When they pulled out your windshield, the darn thing shattered, and a giant shard of glass ripped your passenger seat wide open. But worry not. They're sewing it up at this very minute, and Senor Picasso promises me it'll be as good as new. You'll hardly even notice the seam.

Chapter 15

The cops decided to keep Dallas in jail.

According to Police Chief Tonga, she was their number one suspect, and they had no intention of letting her return to the mansion, lest she try to flee the island.

The next morning at breakfast, Manny got a frantic call from the prisoner, begging him to send over some vital supplies—her 100 percent down pillow, anti-frizz shampoo and conditioner, pore strips, and eyelash curler—items she simply could not live without.

I volunteered to take them to her. Still convinced Dallas was being framed, I wanted very much to talk to her.

Manny gave me the keys to one of the production company Jeeps, and after gathering Dallas's prized possessions, I set off.

It had been years since I'd driven a stick shift, and following a dog-eared map, I made my way to downtown Paratito, merrily stripping gears—and pondering the latest news from back home.

Poor Daddy, forced to dance with his arch nemesis, Lydia Pinkus. And my precious Corolla! I cringed to think of that gaping hole in the passenger seat. Damn Lance and his stupid coupon from Senor Picasso!

I was in the midst of muttering a slew of transcontinental curses at Lance when I arrived in downtown Paratito.

At first, I thought I'd driven onto a movie set ghost town. The only thing missing were tumbleweeds drifting across the unpaved roads.

The whole shebang consisted of a general store and post office, the jail, and a Starbucks. Yes, Starbucks. I kid you not. It was directly across from the jail, for Paratitans in desperate need of a chai latte.

Heading inside the jail, I saw that it was little more than a shack with a rotary phone and a WANTED: DEAD OR ALIVE poster of John Dillinger tacked up on the wall.

A lone jail cell sat at the far end of the room.

Nobody was there except for Dallas, stretched out on her cell cot, reading a copy of *Cosmo*. For a gal who'd just spent the night in jail, she looked pretty darn terrific, her long tanned legs stretched out on the cot, her face radiant without a smidge of makeup.

Remind me never again to hang around bachelorettes. It's way too depressing.

Now she looked up eagerly at the sight of me.

"Thank heavens you're here!" she said, eyeing her possessions heaped in my arms. "Let yourself in. The key's in the lock."

And, indeed, the keys to her cell were hanging right on the cell door. She could have let herself out any time she wanted.

"They're not very big on security around here, are they?" I asked. "Aren't they afraid you're going to try to escape?"

"Where would I escape to? I have no idea how to make it back to the mansion on foot. Besides, that ratfink Manny would probably just turn me back in again. He's very tight with the locals."

Juggling Dallas's goodies, most of which I'd thrown into a tote bag, I let myself into her cell.

"My down pillow!" Dallas grabbed it from me, burying her face in its feathery depths. "You can't imagine what hell it was like sleeping on this rock," she said, coming up for air and pointing to a bumpy lump of a pillow on her cot. "Like a boulder wrapped in sandpaper."

Then, rummaging in the tote, she cried, "Super! You brought my anti-frizz shampoo. The humidity here is awful. Ari said he'd get me a fan."

"Ari?"

"The assistant police chief."

Oh, yeah. The skinny kid with the doe eyes. Mr. *Fingerprinting for Dummies*.

"He already bought me this *Cosmo* from the general store, which was awfully sweet of him. Of course, it's six months old, and I'd already taken the quiz on how to keep your man happy in bed with just a smile and a pair of edible panties, but at least this time around, I knew all the answers."

"Where is he now?" I wondered.

"At Starbucks, getting me a Frappuccino."

It looked like the Paratito jail came with five-star room service.

"And Tonga. The police chief. Where's he?"

"He said he was going to the airport to check out the crime scene," Dallas said, flopping down on her cot, "but if you ask me, I think he went harpoon fishing.

"Honestly, Jaine," she said, gesturing for me to sit down next to her. "I'm afraid he won't even conduct a proper investigation. He's convinced I killed Hope."

I took a deep breath and plunged ahead with the question I had to ask.

"Did you?"

"No, of course not!" she cried, her eyes wide with dismay.

"But what about what you said to Hope? That you'd see to it she'd never wind up marrying Spencer."

"When I told Hope she wouldn't wind up with Spencer, I only meant that I was planning to file a breach of promise lawsuit, hoping to throw a monkey wrench in their wedding plans. That's all. I had no intention of killing her. And if I did, do you really think I'd announce my plans to the entire cast and crew of *Some Day My Prince Will Come*?"

No, I didn't.

"What about the wire cutter they found in your closet?"

"I have absolutely no idea how it got there. I swear I never saw it before in my life."

"Did they test it for fingerprints?"

"Yes, but there were none. Whoever used it must have wiped it clean."

More and more, I was convinced she was being framed.

"Do you have any idea who the killer really is?"

"Who knows? Hope was such a nasty piece of work, I'm sure if Tonga dug deep enough, he'd find lots of people who wanted her out of the way. I heard rumors she and Kirk were an item and she tossed him aside for Spencer. Maybe Kirk did it."

Indeed, I thought, maybe he did.

"I put in a call to my father, and he's got his lawyers on the case. He and Mom are coming straight to Paratito just as soon as they finish their African safari. Daddy doesn't want to miss the rhino hunt."

Good heavens. The man was letting his daughter fester in jail while he hunted rhinos?

Right then and there, I decided that I did not like Dallas's father.

"I'm sure Daddy will make this whole thing go away," Dallas was saying with a brave smile. "At least I hope so."

But then her smile crumbled at the edges, and she looked like a scared little kid, waiting for someone to pick her up at the lost and found.

My heart went out to her.

"Actually," I said, "I've done some private investigating in the past." (It's true. Just check out the titles at the front of this book.) "And I'd be happy to poke around and see what I can dig up."

"Would you?" Her face lit up. "Name your price. I'm sure Daddy will be happy to pay it."

"Let's see what I can find out first, and then we'll talk about money."

See? It's idiotic words like those that keep my bank balance mired in the double digits.

Just when I was kicking myself for not asking for a hefty retainer, Ari, the doe-eyed prison guard, came hurrying into the jailhouse.

"I brought you your Frappuccino!" he said to Dallas. "Just the way you like it, with extra whipped cream! And a copy of *Vogue*, too."

He handed her both with a worshipful look in those doe eyes of his.

Dallas may not have won over Spencer Dalworth, but she sure had conquered the heart of Paratito's assistant police chief.

I only hoped she wouldn't be spending the rest of her days stuck with him in this dusty jailhouse.

Chapter 16

Pulling into the courtyard outside Manny's massive garage, I saw Polly sitting in one of the company Jeeps, leaning back with her eyes closed.

I got out of my Jeep and hurried to her side, alarmed at the sight of her flushed face and bangs plastered to her forehead, wet with sweat. It looked like the heat was really getting to her.

"Polly?" I said softly. "Are you okay?"

Her eyes fluttered open.

"I'm fine," she said. "Taking a little break." Then she reached for a can of Coke in the cup holder. "Just won this fabulous lukewarm Coke in vending machine roulette," she said, popping it open.

"But why are you sitting out here in all this heat?"

"I'm hiding from Manny. Now that the show's been shut down, he's keeping me busier than ever. Doing his laundry. Ordering drapes for his Manhattan condo. Color-coding his boxer briefs."

Oh, gaak.

"Trust me, folding Manny's underpants may well be the low point in my already rock-bottom career."

"You poor thing," I said, trying not to picture Manny's undies. A sight like that could give a gal recurring nightmares for months to come.

"So how was Dallas?" she asked.

"She insists she's innocent and swears someone planted that wire cutter in her room."

"Poor kid." Polly shuddered. "I'd hate to be in her shoes. Thank God I've got you as my alibi."

"And vice versa," I assured her.

"Do you believe her? Do you really think she's innocent?"

"Yeah, actually, I do. But unfortunately the local cops have her pegged as the killer. So I told her I'd nose around and ask some questions."

"Ask questions? You mean, like a private detective?"

"Yes," I nodded. "I've actually solved a few murders in my day."

"You?" She blinked in disbelief.

I get that a lot. For some strange reason, people don't have much faith in the crime-solving abilities of a woman in elastic-waist pants and an I ❤ MY CAT T-shirt.

"Isn't that kind of work dangerous?" she asked.

"It can be."

"Wow, how very Sherlock Holmesian of you."
She beamed at me with newfound admiration.

"Well, I just want you to know that, seeing as how we've become buddies, if you should run into trouble or any dangerous situation, don't even think of asking me for help. Seriously," she said. "I'm a dyed-in-the-wool coward."

"Don't worry," I assured her. "I'll be fine. Just fine."

How the gods must have been laughing at that one.

"Just fine" was the very last thing I was destined to be.

Inside the mansion, I stopped off at Manny's office to return the keys to the Jeep and got the shock of my life.

There, bold as brass, was Prozac perched atop Manny's fish tank! Somehow she'd managed to pry open the feeding flap and had plunged her paw into the water, whipping it back and forth, trying to skewer a tasty tidbit.

At this stage of our relationship, I was used to Prozac pulling crazy stunts like this.

But the real stumper was: How had she possibly managed to break out of our room again? The door was locked from the outside, and both windows were sealed shut.

And yet, there she was, scaring the poop out of Manny's precious fish as they swam away, frantic, from her swishing paw.

Thank heavens Manny wasn't around to see any of this.

"Prozac, how on earth did you get out of our room?" I wailed.

Looking up from her fishing expedition, she shot me a sphinx-like stare.

That's for me to know and you to find out.

I raced over to the tank and was just about to grab her when the little devil slipped from my grasp and began leading me on a merry chase around Manny's office. Round and round his desk we ran, past a potted palm via his mini-fridge (where, if you must know, I stopped off and tossed an Eskimo Pie in my purse).

Finally, backed into a corner, Prozac darted behind Manny's sofa. I pulled it away from the wall to get at her, and as I did, I noticed a wadded-up piece of paper on the floor, clearly meant for a nearby wastebasket. Looking down, I saw that it was a fax from the cable network airing *Some Day My Prince Will Come.* Momentarily forgetting about Prozac, I snatched it up and was just about to read it when I heard footsteps clomping toward the room—accompanied by the obnoxious smell of rotting garbage. I'd know that smell anywhere. It was one of Manny's fifty-dollar cigars.

Quickly shoving the fax in my jeans pocket, I managed to grab Prozac just as Manny came waddling in.

He stopped in his tracks at the sight of me.

"What the hell are you doing behind my sofa?" he asked, shooting me a particularly aggravated glare.

"I was trying to catch Prozac," I said, holding her up for Manny to see. "I'm afraid she broke loose from our room again."

"For crying out loud," he said, stomping for his desk, "can't you keep that cat under control?"

Now his face blanched as he checked the remains of a sandwich on his desk. I'd noticed it on one of our several laps around his desk, and it had seemed awfully skimpy at the time.

Irritation seeping from every pore, he held up two slices of bread, with nothing in between.

"What happened to the ham in my ham sandwich?"

A delicate belch from Prozac.

It was yummy. A little on the salty side, though.

Manny chomped down furiously on his cigar.

"If that cat doesn't stop poking around where she doesn't belong, there's going to be another murder on this island."

"I'm so sorry, sir. I promise it won't happen again."

I started to beat a hasty retreat when Manny called out to me.

"Hold on a minute. Now that you're here, I need to talk to you.

"Sit," he said, gesturing to a chair across from his desk.

I plopped down with Pro in my lap, praying she wouldn't reach out and nab the kosher pickle on Manny's plate.

"I suppose you know that Hope's death means the end of *Some Day My Prince Will Come*," Manny said with a pained sigh.

"Yes, Polly told me."

"I still can't believe it," he said, shaking his head. "Everything was going so well. The network was even talking about picking up the show for another season. And now it's all over because that little idiot had to get herself killed."

"Do you have any idea who could have done it?" I asked.

"Why, Dallas, of course," he said, with a wave of his cigar. "Who else? She practically threatened to kill Hope in front of all of us."

"Did you actually see Dallas going over to the prop shed?" I asked.

"No, I didn't see her going to the prop shed. If you remember, I spent most of the morning trying to convince her to shoot that damn scene in the pool with Hope. But that doesn't mean she couldn't have done it after I left her. She was supposedly in her room for a half hour changing into her bikini for the pool scene. Maybe she raced out to the prop shed and cut the cords on the chute then.

"Oh, well," he sighed. "The show's over, and there's nothing to be done about it. Now I need you to write a press release about how devastated we all are at the loss of our beloved bachelorette. You know the drill. Some chatter about how Hope was a shining star, a ray of sunshine. How we all loved and respected her, blahbitty blah blah blah. Got it?"

"Yes," I nodded. Although it would take all the writing skills I possessed to turn Hope into a ray of sunshine.

"And one more thing," he said as I got up to

go. "I just got a message from King Konga. He wants you to go harpoon fishing with him tomorrow."

Harpoon fishing? With Konga? Was he nuts?

"I'm afraid I can't do that, sir."

"Why not?"

"Let's just say I had a very uncomfortable dinner with him the other night, and I don't want to see him again."

"But you've got to go!" Manny growled, taking an angry puff of his cigar. "I can't risk alienating the locals. Not in the middle of a murder investigation."

"Sorry, Manny. But I'm not about to endure one more minute with that paunchy polygamist. Never. Nada. Ain't gonna happen."

A calculating gleam shone in Manny's beady eyes.

"I'll pay you five hundred dollars."

Well! If he thought I was the kind woman who'd sacrifice her dating principles for filthy lucre . . . he was absolutely right.

"What time tomorrow?"

And so it was that I slunk out of Manny's office with absolutely no pride. No dignity. No principles whatsoever.

But on the plus side, at least I had that Eskimo Pie.

Chapter 17

Juggling Prozac in my arms, I fished the Eskimo Pie from my purse and somehow managed to unwrap it as I headed up the stairs.

Not an easy feat, but I'm always highly motivated when there's chocolate-covered ice cream at stake. And given my upcoming date with King Konga, I needed all the chocolate-covered ice cream I could get.

I looked down at Prozac, busy licking melted ice cream from my thumb.

I still couldn't get over her escape from Sauna Central. How the heck had she done it? The room was practically hermetically sealed.

But all thoughts of Prozac came to a halt when I reached the second-floor landing and heard voices coming from Brianna's room. Considering Hope was dead and Dallas was in jail, I wondered who Brianna could be talking to.

So I wandered over to her room to take a peek.

There she was, propped up in bed, her computer on her lap, skyping with someone who sounded like a news reporter.

"Yes, it's been quite a shock," Brianna was saying, with all the solemnity of a pallbearer. "Hope was such a beautiful person, inside and out; we're all grief-stricken by her loss."

Here she actually managed to work up a tear or two.

Of course, those tears were as phony as her boobs, but she was giving a very convincing performance of someone who actually gave a damn about Hope's death.

Major props to Brianna's acting coach.

The reporter was now asking about Dallas.

"It's true Dallas is being held by the police," Brianna said, "but as far as I know, she's not been formally charged with Hope's murder . . . Do I think she did it? I have no idea.

"In this country," she said, channeling Atticus Finch via Jayne Mansfield, "we're all presumed innocent until proven guilty—a theme I will be exploring in great depth in the Pomona Playhouse's upcoming interpretive production of *The Crucible*, where I'll be portraying Angry Townswoman Number Three. True, it's not a very big role, but to quote the late great Konstantin Stanislavski, 'There are no small parts. Only small actors.'"

Stanislavski? Brianna knew about Stanislavski? I figured the only Russian she knew was black, with an extra shot of vodka on the side.

She smiled modestly as the reporter wished her the best of luck.

"My pleasure," she said, managing to cram in the dates of her upcoming production of *The Crucible* before signing off.

If the bottom ever fell out of the acting market, she had it made as a PR lady.

"Oh, hi," she said, clicking off her computer and catching sight of me in the doorway. "Can you believe I was just skyping with *Access Hollywood?* I'm going to be on the news tonight!"

"Congratulations," I said.

"And I've got three hundred twenty-six new followers on Twitter!"

"Super."

"Oh, look," she said, noticing Prozac in my arms. "You brought your kitty! Isn't she the sweetest thing ever?"

At which point Prozac began doing a little acting of her own, purring and batting her baby greens, giving the impression that she was actually the sweetest thing ever.

Talk about a world-class performance. That cat could give lessons to Stanislavski.

"And you've got an Eskimo Pie!" Brianna exclaimed. "Mind if I have a bite? I'm starving!"

Of course I minded, but I had to play nice if I wanted to squeeze any info from her.

"Not at all," I said, handing it to her.

Would you believe she scarfed the whole thing down in two gulps?

I gritted my teeth in annoyance.

"Sorry," she said, with an apologetic smile. "Being on TV makes me hungry."

And the really aggravating thing was that she probably wouldn't gain an ounce.

"It's all so exciting!" she burbled, licking the ice cream from the wrapper. "My agent says the offers are rolling in! I've got auditions for two TV pilots. And a Wonderbra commercial!"

"So," I said, easing the conversation away from Brianna's Wonderbra gig and back to the murder, "do you think Dallas killed Hope?"

"Not really," she said. "Dallas is a spoiled brat, but I doubt she's a killer."

"Any idea who might have done it?"

"Maybe Justin," she said with a shrug. "Now that Hope's dead, he's free to take that movie directing gig that he wanted so much."

Point well taken.

"Sorry to cut this short," she said, picking up a dog-eared script. "But I've really got to learn my lines for *The Crucible*."

"Right. Sure. Of course."

"My agent's going to fax me the pilot scripts tomorrow. I can't get over how much media attention Hope's murder is getting. Of course, I'm sorry she's dead," she said, plastering on her pallbearer face for an appropriate nanosecond, "but things couldn't have worked out better if I'd won the contest myself!"

Yes, things were certainly working out well for Brianna.

Which made me wonder: Was it possible that Brianna had bumped off Hope as a career move?

Had the buxom bachelorette executed the ultimate Hollywood power play and actually killed for a part?

Chapter 18

I woke up the next morning, dreading my harpoon fishing date with Konga.

"Can you believe I sold my soul for five hundred bucks?" I asked Pro, who was busy clawing my chest.

Absolutely. When do we eat?

As if in answer to her command, I heard a timid knock on the door. I opened it to see Akela fleeing down the stairs, Prozac's bowl of fish on my doorstep.

With a leap worthy of Superman, Prozac zipped down from the bed and within seconds had her nose buried in the bowl.

Throwing on my jeans and a T-shirt, I left Prozac belching fish fumes and trudged down to the patio for breakfast, where I was so nervous about my upcoming date, I could barely finish my cardboard corn muffin.

I looked around the breakfast table—at Spencer sipping his tea, Justin on the phone with his agent, and Manny, surprisingly chipper for someone whose show had just gone down the drain, scarfing down real eggs and bacon.

Polly sat at my side, staring dreamily at Kirk, whose bloodshot eyes darted nervously around the patio as he glugged down some coffee.

For the most part, the crew was silent and edgy, the chatter subdued. I couldn't help but feel a twinge of tension in the air.

After all, if Dallas was innocent, there was a killer among us.

I'd been meaning to nose around and ask some questions yesterday afternoon, but Manny had kept me busy writing press releases, updating his Facebook page, tweeting about Hope's death, and penning an angry letter to his dry cleaners about some missing buttons on a Tommy Bahama shirt. Any minute now, I expected to be ghosting his memoirs.

"Why so glum, hon?" Polly asked, as I pecked at my cardboard muffin.

I told her how Manny had bribed me into going harpoon fishing with Konga.

"He's paying you five hundred bucks?" Polly said. "Heck, I'd go harpoon fishing with Konga for five hundred bucks."

"No, you wouldn't," I assured her. "Not if you'd seen him. Remember? The guy has six teeth and three hairs, and a belly the size of a beer barrel."

"He does sound pretty deadly," she conceded.

"Oh, well. Just wear plenty of sunscreen, and try to think of the payola at the end of your harpoon."

And bolstered by those words of encouragement, I headed up to my room to change for my date.

I decided to wear the grungiest capris and tee I'd brought on the trip, figuring if I looked bad enough, maybe Konga would dump me as Wife Number Twelve.

Luckily it was a soppingly humid day and my hair was a certified frizzfest. I would not even attempt to tame it, nor would I bother to put on makeup.

I was just stepping out of my jeans to change into my grungy capris when I felt the crackle of a piece of paper in one of my jeans pockets. Then I remembered the fax I'd filched from Manny's office yesterday—the one from the cable network producing *Some Day My Prince Will Come.*

Now I took it out and read it. To the best of my recollection, it went something like this:

> *Dear Mr. Kaminsky:*
> *Thank you for sending us footage from your proposed reality show, SOME DAY MY PRINCE WILL COME. Unfortunately, we've decided to pass on it, as it does not live up to our standards of watchable TV.*
> *Very sincerely yours,*
> *Amanda M. Washton*
> *Director of Development*

*PS. Thanks also for the box of Cuban cigars,
but because neither I nor anyone in my family smoke,
I will be returning it to you under separate cover.*

Holy mackerel! Manny had been lying all along! There was no network deal. He was shooting the show on spec, hoping someone out there would buy it. And yet he pretended it was already a done deal. Not only that, he'd gone on and on about how much the network had loved it.

Why had he told all those whoppers? To get the crew to do the show in first place? To pump his flagging ego?

How pathetic.

I checked and saw that the fax was dated a few days before Hope's murder. And yet he continued to shoot. I guess he planned to finish the show and shop it around to some other networks. But now that wouldn't be possible. Hope's death had killed any chance of his show getting picked up.

Which seemed to let him off the hook as a murder suspect.

And yet, I couldn't help thinking: If Manny had lied about the network, was he lying about Hope's murder, too? Was it possible he had a motive to kill her, after all?

If so, what on earth could it be?

Chapter 19

I don't know if you've ever read Dante's *Inferno*. (I haven't, but I've Googled it, which is practically the same thing, right?)

For those of you not in the know, it's a gruesome little tale about the Nine Circles of Hell, chock full of demons, torture, suffering, and pain.

I only bring it up because I'm certain that if Dante were alive today, he'd be whipping out his quill and writing about the Tenth Circle of Hell: Harpoon Fishing with King Konga.

Never in my life had I spent a more ghastly afternoon.

I drove over to the tribal village, where I was met by Konga, wearing nothing but a loincloth and a necklace strung with rotting teeth.

Suma, his Number One Wife, stood at his side, glowering.

It seemed she would be our chaperone on this date. Which, frankly, was a bit of a relief. At least Konga wouldn't be trying any hanky panky.

Suma had packed a picnic basket, which she shoved into my hand to carry as we headed down to the water. While I carried the basket, Suma hoisted three massive harpoons.

The only thing Konga had to carry was his pot belly.

Trekking down what seemed like miles on a rocky path, I happened to notice a tattoo of Konga's grinning face on Suma's upper arm.

Yikes. It was bad enough she had to look at the guy every day. To have to wear him, too, seemed like the ultimate punishment.

At last we reached the water.

"There's our boat," Suma said, pointing to a canoe resting up against a sand dune. "Now push!" she commanded me.

Together Suma and I shoved the canoe to the water, Konga not lifting a finger, just whistling a happy tune and fiddling with his tooth necklace.

After loading the picnic basket, the harpoons, and Konga onto the canoe, Suma and I climbed on board and shoved off—Konga sitting at the head of the canoe, me in the middle, facing him, and Suma bringing up the rear.

I assumed we'd all be rowing, but I assumed wrong.

Suma and I manned the oars, while Konga lounged up front, snacking on crunchy round things, which I prayed weren't eyeballs.

It was a blisteringly hot day, the temperature

and humidity in the high nineties, and not a hint of a breeze on the glassy blue sea.

Within seconds I was drenched in sweat.

My God. This was worse than Sauna Central.

All the while I rowed, sweat dripping from my every pore, Konga was lounging in his loincloth and tooth necklace, staring at me admiringly.

"I like my women strong," he said, chomping on one of his munchies.

Soon he was regaling me with highlights from one of his favorite TV series, *Gilligan's Island.*

"That Mary Ann, she is a groovy chick. Like you."

This accompanied by a most unsettling wink.

"One thing I do not understand, though," he mused, his brow wrinkled in thought. "It says in the theme song that the passengers set sail for a three-hour tour. Which means they couldn't have brought any luggage. So how," he asked, like Steven Hawking puzzling over a black hole, "did they have enough clothes to last for the three years they were stranded on the island?"

That was a mind bender, all right. I could just imagine the fun conversations I'd be having with this nincompoop once we were married.

"How?" Konga pondered. "How did they do it?"

"Black magic!" Suma muttered. "Evil Americans," she said, shooting me the stink eye. "They practice it all the time."

Oh, please. I only wished I practiced black magic. The first thing I'd ask for would be a margarita and a one-way ticket back to L.A.

At last we'd rowed out far enough to go fishing. But before we tossed any harpoons, it was time to break out our picnic lunch, lovingly prepared by Suma.

By now I was starving, and could not wait to chow down.

Suma passed out the food, handing me a banana leaf, inside of which I found a particularly noxious-looking fish, white and slimy, eyeballs still intact.

I waited for her to hand out forks and knives, but I waited in vain. She and Konga begin tearing into their fish with their bare hands.

"Eat hearty," Suma said to me, her leathery face wreathed in a wicked smile.

I bet she purposely chose this Quasimodo of fishes, knowing full well it would revolt me.

And it worked. One look at that fish, and I totally lost my appetite.

Somehow I summoned the courage to pick off a minuscule piece and pop it in my mouth. Oh, gaak. Talk about slimy. It was like mucus with bones.

"You no like your food?" Konga asked, staring at my uneaten fish.

"Oh, no! It's yummy. I'm just eating slowly to make it last."

How the heck was I going to get through this meal without eating this damn snotfish?

Then I got an idea.

"Look!" I cried, pointing at a spot off in the distance.

He and Suma turned to look, and as they did, I tossed my snotty lunch into the water.

"I don't see anything," Suma said, squinting off into the distance.

"Really?" I said. "I thought I saw dolphins."

"There are no dolphins in Paratito," Suma grunted.

"Gee, it must have been an optical illusion."

Now Konga and Suma had turned back in their seats to face me.

"You finished your fish," Konga said, looking at my empty banana leaf.

"Yes, it was dee-lish!"

Suma eyed me suspiciously. She knew something was up.

"Really yummy," I added, shooting her a wicked smile of my own.

Once the banana leaves had been cleared away, we got down to the main event: Harpoon Fishing.

Suma handed out the harpoons, which we were supposed to use to spear innocent little fishies.

While Suma and Konga began thrusting their spears with gusto, I—refusing to be an instrument of death—made only a few half-hearted stabs in the water.

Konga, his belly jiggling with the effort, managed to stab a fish or two.

At the other end of the canoe, Suma maneuvered her harpoon with impressive expertise, snapping up fish with the same lightning speed I snap up franks-in-a-blanket at a cocktail party.

We were drifting along, the sun searing our backs, depopulating the water of its piscine contents when suddenly, with a sickening sensation, I realized my spear had made contact with something. Oh, yuck. I'd killed a fish.

"It's about time," Suma sneered, watching me pull my harpoon out of the water. "You finally caught something."

"Groovy!" Konga said, beaming at me.

But then, when I pulled my catch out of the water, I realized I had not killed any living critter. The creature at the tip of my harpoon was none other than my lunch, the same ghastly snotfish I'd thrown overboard.

"Is that your lunch?" Konga asked

"Yes," I admitted. "I'm afraid I wasn't very hungry."

"But you must have something to eat," Konga said, eyes wide with concern. "Here," he said, holding out some of the crunchy round things he'd been munching on earlier. "Have some deep-fried octopus glands. They're very tasty."

"No, no," I said, fighting a rolling wave of nausea. "I'm fine.

If Suma was hoping Konga would be angry at me for tossing my food overboard, she was sadly mistaken. It only seemed to make him like me more.

"Sweet little Jaine," he said. "I've got to fatten you up."

I actually sort of treasured that moment, certain I'd never hear those words again in my lifetime.

My uneaten lunch crisis having passed, we picked up our harpoons and resumed fishing. I was standing there, idly swishing my harpoon in the water, when from the corner of my eye I saw Suma's arm reach out from behind and shove me. The next thing I knew, I was tumbling overboard and flailing about in the water with all those innocent little fishies.

On the plus side, the water was a few degrees cooler than the air.

But heaven only knew what kind of creatures were swimming alongside me. Maybe they weren't so innocent.

Images of crocodiles and electric eels suddenly flashed through my brain. And what if there were sharks in the water? Oh, God. Any minute now, some giant white shark would be snacking on my thighs!

Frantically, I dog paddled over to the canoe and hoisted myself back on board. With absolutely no help from Suma, I might add.

She was barely suppressing a round of giggles.

Konga, on the other hand, was staring at me open-mouthed.

And then I felt it—something crawling on my shoulder.

Oh, lord. It was probably a jellyfish or a venomous stingray. I stood totally rigid, waiting to be stung to oblivion.

But when seconds passed and nothing happened, I looked down and saw a giant turtle.

Konga's eyes were wide with awe.

"A sea turtle!" he cried, taking it in his hands. "And look how big it is!"

Indeed, the sucker was huge.

"Do you know, Jaine, that in the Paratitan culture, sea turtles are a sign of good luck? This creature is certain to bring us years and years of good fortune. What a wonderful gift you have given us! Isn't this wonderful news, Suma?"

Suma was fuming, her plan to humiliate me gone totally awry. I could tell she wanted nothing more than to whack me over the head with her harpoon.

But instead she forced a grim smile.

"Yes, Konga," she managed to choke out. "It is good news, indeed."

"And to show my gratitude," Konga said, "I give you this."

With that, he took off his rotting tooth necklace and put it around my neck. "A necklace made from my own teeth!"

"Those are *your* teeth?"

All along I'd just assumed they were from a dead animal.

"Yes," he nodded proudly. "All twenty-six of them."

Oh, hell. The last thing I needed was Konga's decayed teeth as a fashion accessory.

"I can't take your teeth," I said. "I wouldn't feel right about it."

"I insist," he said sternly.

"Well, in that case, thanks so much. I'll think of you whenever I wear it."

Which will be never in a zillion years were the words I judiciously did not add.

Our harpooning adventure having come to a close, Suma and I rowed back to shore and toted the fish back to the village.

Konga kissed my hand and wished me a fond farewell, urging me to wear his teeth in good health.

Wearily I made my way over to the company Jeep I'd used to drive over to the village. Just as I was approaching the car, I heard footsteps behind me. I turned and saw Suma, harpoon in her hand, no longer trying to hide her rage. She stomped to my side, grabbing me by the wrist.

"Give up Konga," she hissed in my ear, "or I'll make you wish you were never born."

With that, she took her harpoon and hurled it at a nearby tree, nearly splitting the trunk in half.

Holy Moses. This was one angry cookie.

"Honest, Suma," I assured her. "I'm not interested in Konga. I swear on a stack of octopus glands. You'll never see me here again."

"I'd better not," Suma said. "Or who knows where my harpoon will land next?"

And with those words of warning, she yanked her harpoon from the tree and waddled away.

Wasting no time, I jumped in the Jeep and drove off—with fear in my heart, sweat in my armpits, and Konga's teeth rotting around my neck.

Like I said, the Tenth Circle of Hell.

Chapter 20

I returned to the mansion reeking of snotfish and turtle. And although I desperately needed a shower, there was only one thing on my mind:

Food.

Lest you forget, I hadn't had a thing to eat since that cardboard corn muffin at breakfast.

Stomping into the house, I'd planned to head straight for the basement vending machine. But then I passed Manny's office and was thrilled to see he was nowhere in sight. Without thinking twice, I marched right in and made a beeline for his private fridge, where I helped myself to a Dove Bar. (Okay, two Dove Bars. And, if you must know, an onion bagel.)

As brazen as could be, I plopped down in Manny's office chair, my feet up on his desk, and began to eat.

For once, I wasn't my usual sniveling self, cowering at the thought of being caught trespassing. On the contrary. I was tough. I was fearless. I was totally unafraid. (Mainly because, as I was parking the Jeep, I'd seen Manny driving off in his monster van.)

The coast, for all intents and purposes, was clear.

So I ate with abandon.

Oh, lord, those Dove Bars were divine. As was the onion bagel. All washed down with a vintage bottle of chocolate Yoo-hoo.

Sheer heaven!

When I was licking the last of the bagel crumbs from my fingers, I began to idly glance through the papers on Manny's desk. I mean, what good was trespassing if I couldn't do a little snooping, too?

Riffling through the papers, I found receipts for cigars and pastrami, as well as a catalogue from the International Hair Club for Men.

But what really caught my eye were the letters I saw from Lifetime, Bravo, and the CW—all rejecting *Some Day My Prince Will Come.*

Wow. Manny sure was a master of hype. From the way he'd been talking about *Some Day My Prince Will Come,* no one would ever have guessed it had been rejected all over Hollywood.

And then, among the rejection letters, I noticed a thick sheaf of papers. Pulling it out to examine it, I realized it was an insurance policy.

Quickly I scanned it and saw that Manny had insured the production of *Some Day My Prince*

Will Come for two million dollars! According to this document, if anything should happen to shut down production of the show, Manny had a two-million-dollar payday waiting in the wings.

Which meant Manny had a very powerful motive to kill Hope.

The most powerful motive of all: Money.

What if Manny wasn't nearly as rich as he claimed to be? What if his private plane was rented? What if the imported pastrami was from a cousin in the deli business?

Maybe that's why the third floor of the mansion was never completed, and why he served us discount airline food.

Maybe he'd bet his life savings on *Some Day My Prince Will Come* and when he realized he had a dud on his hands, decided to stop production for a two-million-dollar insurance payoff.

And there was no more certain way to stop production than to kill off his Number One bachelorette. Without Hope, the show was dead.

And just like that, Manny catapulted to the top of my suspect list.

I was heading up to my room for that much-needed shower when I heard the unmistakable lilt of Spencer's British accent coming from the living room.

"Oh, darling," he was cooing, "you're such a beauty. Did you know that? Did you?"

I stopped dead in my tracks. Spencer was supposed to be the bereaved fiancé, mourning Hope, and here he was, whispering sweet nothings to some other woman.

Who could it be? Brianna? One of the crew? A nubile native lass?

Burning with curiosity, I tiptoed into the living room, where I saw Spencer sitting on a sofa, his back to me, facing the window, with no sign of his paramour, who must have been stretched out on the sofa.

"You like it when I touch you like that?" he was now saying.

Now anyone with a sense of propriety would have turned right around and left the two lovebirds alone. But not moi. I simply had to know who he was talking to. As softly as possible, I crept closer to the sofa, eager to see who was sprawled out with Spencer Dalworth VII.

I didn't walk quite softly enough, though, because suddenly Spencer turned around and saw me.

"Hello, Jaine," he said, not a trace of embarrassment in his voice. "Look who I've been entertaining."

I took a step closer saw that his "lover" was none other than Prozac, the shameless hussy, who was writhing in ecstasy in Spencer's lap as he scratched her belly.

A little to the right. Now higher. Higher. To the left. Don't stop!

For crying out loud. She'd broken out of our room again!

"Prozac!" I cried.

She glared up at me, clearly irritated at the interruption.

The Countess of Swampshire, to you.

"She's such a little angel," Spencer was saying, making disgusting kitchy-koo noises.

"Appearances can be deceiving," I replied, slipping into a nearby armchair. I figured as long as I was there, I might as well question him about the murder.

As I settled into the chair, Prozac shot me a filthy look.

Hey, this is a private party. So beat it. Unless you want to find a little surprise in your slipper tonight.

At which point, Spencer wrinkled his nose in distaste.

"Do you smell something rancid?" he asked.

Prozac lifted her little pink nose and sniffed.

PU. Someone stinks worse than Manny's cigars.

"I'm afraid that would be me," I said. "I was just harpoon fishing and fell into the water."

An imperious thump of Prozac's tail.

Okay then, run along and take a shower. Come back for me in about five hours.

"Such a shame about Hope, isn't it?" I said, ignoring her evil eye.

For once, I was certain Spencer's response wouldn't be, "Brilliant!"

And indeed, at the mention of Hope's name, his eyes misted over with what looked like genuine tears.

"I still can't quite believe it," he said, shaking his head. "Hope was so vibrant and full of life. In those last few minutes on the plane, she threw her arms around me and told me how much she loved me. Then I jumped, and that's the last I saw of her."

By now, tears were running down his cheeks.

"So sorry," he said, taking out an immaculate hankie from his shirt pocket and wiping his eyes. "Shouldn't cry. Bad form. Makes everyone so uncomfortable."

"No, no," I said. "Cry all you want. It's only natural."

I reached out to give him a comforting pat but was met with a menacing hiss from Prozac.

Hands off, sister. He's mine.

"I hope you don't mind my asking," I said, when Spencer had dried his tears, "but is it true what Dallas said, that you'd promised to marry her?"

"I'm afraid I did," he sighed, "but my heart wasn't in it. The only reason I agreed to do the show was because Mummy was pressuring me to find a rich wife and save our estate. We owe a fortune in taxes, and Dallas seemed like the answer to our prayers. Her father practically owns the state of Texas. So I followed Mummy's instructions and asked her to marry me. But all the while, I couldn't help being attracted to Hope. She was so upbeat and positive."

I'd call it cloying and annoying, but to each his own.

"Dallas was used to having her own way. And I felt certain that she'd be the kind of woman who'd lead me around by the nose, just like Mummy. But I knew Hope wouldn't be that way, that she'd encourage my dreams and let me be free to be me."

Frankly, I wasn't so sure about that. Hope seemed like quite the manipulator. If Spencer was like most other men on the planet, chances were he was just hot for her cute little bod and had rationalized this whole "free to be me" thing to get at her underlovelies.

"And so for once in my life," he was saying, "I defied my mother. And look what happened. It got poor Hope killed."

Another batch of tears erupted from his usually vacant blue eyes.

He seemed to be truly grieving, and for what it's worth, I believed him. He was way too bad an actor to be faking it.

On his lap, Prozac wriggled her torso.

Yeah, yeah. It's a tragedy and all that. Boo hoo. Now rub my belly.

"I don't suppose you happened to see anybody heading off to the prop shed the morning of the murder?" I asked.

"No, I was busy chatting with the crew and trying to get Kirk to sober up. He must have gone on quite a bender the night before. He was really out of it."

I remembered seeing Spencer chatting with Kirk, but of course, either one of them could have wandered off to the prop shed when the other wasn't around.

"Do you think Dallas did it?" I asked.

"No, actually, I don't. She's a bit of a diva, but I don't think she has the psychological makeup to be a killer."

Whaddaya know? Who woulda thunk Mr. "Brilliant!" capable of psychological insights? (Or even the word "psychological"?)

"Any idea who the killer might be?"

He paused as if deciding whether or not to speak.

Finally, he said:

"I hate to say it because I'm very fond of him, but I think it could be Kirk. Hope told me she'd been his girlfriend, and that he was devastated when she broke up with him. I think in a moment of madness, he may have cut those cords. He had more access to the chutes than anyone else."

Made sense to me.

I made a mental note to chat with the hunky propmaster ASAP.

In the meanwhile, I really had to get back to Sauna Central and take that shower.

"Well, I'd best be pushing off," I said. "So very sorry for your loss."

"Thank you," he replied, offering up a wan smile.

"C'mon, Prozac," I said, scooping her up from Spencer's lap.

The way she was wailing, you would've thought I'd just spayed her without anesthesia.

Wait a minute! He hasn't finished my belly rub! We're in love! Nothing can come between us, I tell you. Nothing!

"Here," I said, holding out a piece of ham I'd nabbed from Manny's fridge. "If I give you this piece of ham, will you please stop wailing about Spencer?"

Her little pink nose twitched in excitement.

Spencer? Spencer who?

What can I say? When it comes to food, she's easily distracted.

She takes after me that way.

Chapter 21

Back in my room, I didn't even have the energy to read Prozac the riot act. Frankly, I didn't blame her for breaking out of Sauna Central. I just wished I could figure out how she was doing it.

The outside bolt had been locked. And the window screens securely fastened. I looked in the closet for a possible escape route I might have missed, like a trap door leading to the room next door, but found nada.

"What's your secret, Pro?" I asked, as she lay sprawled out on my bed, soaking up the breezes from the fan. "How'd you get to be such a smart cat?"

She graced me with a mighty yawn.

No exercise and plenty of naps.

With a sigh, I stripped off my stinky clothes and put them in the bathroom sink to soak. Then I headed for the shower, where I opened the stall door and gasped to find Godzilla taking a leisurely stroll around the tiles.

After my heart stopped fibrillating, I turned on the water, hoping to blast him down the drain. But alas, my shower in Sauna Central had zero water pressure, and the trickle that came out of the faucet didn't even touch my slimy friend.

Instead of being swept away to oblivion, Godzilla scuttled to safety, disappearing into a crack in the grout.

Now what to do?

I absolutely had to wash the stink of snotfish off my body, but I was terrified that once I stepped in the shower, Godzilla would pop back out from the grout to join me.

Taking one good whiff of myself, I realized I had no choice.

I simply had to get clean.

Ready to bolt at the first sign of Godzilla, I stepped into the shower and began scrubbing myself. It wasn't easy under the tepid trickle of water, but eventually, my eyes glued to the tiles for signs of Godzilla, I managed to clean myself off and scoot out of the shower to safety.

Although stink-free, I felt about as refreshed as a lettuce leaf on a hibachi.

How nice it would be, I thought, to go for a swim in the pool. But going for a swim would mean me and my thighs being seen in public in a bathing suit.

Never a happy scenario in the screenplay of my life.

But within minutes I was sweating like a dock-worker, so I figured what the heck. I'd go for it. After foraging around in my suitcase, I wiggled into my Day-Glo orange tankini with industrial-strength tummy tuck panels, a Home Shopping Club gift from my mom—from their Golda Meir swimsuit collection.

With any luck, the pool would be deserted when I got there, and I'd be able to go for a lovely dip.

Throwing on clean capris and a T-shirt as a cover-up, I grabbed the key to Sauna Central, along with the key to the Jeep, which—in all the excitement of finding Manny's two-million-dollar insurance policy—I'd forgotten to return.

Leaving Prozac snoring under the fan, I headed out into the hallway, where I bolted the door shut.

Then I made my way down to the pool, pray-ing I wouldn't get there only to find Prozac stretched out on a chaise, sipping a piña colada.

The good news was that the pool was 100 per-cent Prozac-free when I showed up. The bad news was that it was jammed with crew mem-bers—mostly burly guys with big guts, glugging down beers at an alarming rate.

Isn't it amazing how men can strut around with their bellies hanging out and not give it a second thought, while women obsess over the tiniest speck of cellulite on their thighs?

In spite of Gloria Steinem whispering in my ear, urging me to cast off my insecurities and take pride in my female body in all its glorious imperfections, I wimped out and kept my imperfect bod hidden under my capris and tee. Of course, I had more than a tiny speck of cellulite frolicking on my thighs, especially compared to the other gals at the pool—among them, the babe-alicious Brianna and Polly, who was stretched out on a chaise next to Kirk, looking Audrey Hepburn adorable in a tiny wisp of a bikini.

"Hi, guys," I said, wandering over to where Polly and Kirk were sitting. "How's it going?"

"Super!" Polly grinned, while Kirk gazed up at me with the same glazed look in his eyes he'd had ever since the murder. "Manny went off to the airport to check on his pastrami, so I'm finally getting some time off!"

She rolled her eyes over at Kirk and shot me a conspiratorial smile. At last Polly was getting a chance to cozy up to her heartthrob. Who, in his current condition, certainly didn't look like much of a heartthrob to me.

I took in his bloodshot eyes, ashen complexion, and greasy clumps of surfer blond hair and remembered what Spencer said, about how Kirk might have cut the cords on Hope's chute in a moment of passion.

Did that glazed look in his eyes mean he'd simply had too much to drink—or was it the look of a man filled with remorse over a murder he'd just committed?

I definitely wanted to question him, but now was not the time, not with Polly at his side, in seventh heaven, eager to win him over.

I just hoped she wasn't flirting with a killer.

"I think I'll go sit at the pool for a while," I said, "and leave you two alone."

Polly shot me a grateful smile as I wandered off to the pool.

Kicking off my flip-flops, I sat on the edge of the pool and dipped my feet in the water.

Nearby two guys I recognized as cameramen were leaning up against the edge of the pool, water up to their hairy chests, glugging down beers.

They both looked like mountain men, the kind of guys you'd expect to see building log cabins in Alaska or playing banjos in *Deliverance*.

One had a bushy red beard; the other, a bushy black beard.

I figured it was time to play PI again and ask some questions about the murder.

"Hello, there," I said to them, smiling brightly. "I don't think we've met. I'm Jaine Austen."

"Yeah, we know," said Redbeard. "You're Spencer's writer."

"Brilliant!" guffawed Blackbeard.

"What a shame about Hope," I said, easing into my interrogation.

"Yeah, I guess," Redbeard replied.

Blackbeard just shrugged, not exactly over-come with grief.

"I don't suppose either of you saw anyone heading over to the prop shed the morning of the murder."

"Nah," said Blackbeard. "All of us in the crew were hanging around, waiting for Dallas's hissy fit to be over and for shooting to start. Most of the guys were playing poker. Nobody went any-where, except maybe to use the Porta-Potties."

"I still can't believe Manny won't let us use the bathrooms in the mansion," Redbeard grum-bled. "What a jerk."

"Do you know he charges us ten bucks a beer?" Blackbeard said, waving his can of beer in my face. "Docks it from our pay."

"We have to go down to the general store in town to buy it on our own," Redbeard explained.

"And what about the factory-reject food he serves?" Blackbeard snorted, indignant.

"Yeah," said Redbeard. "Close your eyes and you're eating in Calcutta."

"Do you know anyone in the crew who might have had a motive to kill Hope?" I asked, wrench-ing the topic back to Hope's murder.

They shook their heads.

"Aside from Kirk, none of us even knew her," said Blackbeard. "She was real standoffish. Never gave any of us the time of day. She only had eyes for Prince Charming."

After bidding my bearded buddies good-bye, I circulated around for a bit, chatting with as many people as I could. I got the same story from everyone:

Nobody saw anyone going to the prop shed. Nobody much liked Hope, but nobody seemed to have a motive to kill her.

Everyone had been hanging around the pool the morning of the murder except for Frederico and Maria, the hair and makeup people, who were in their cabin most of the morning, having tantric sex.

The one thing everyone agreed on: Manny's food was the pits.

I looked around at the beer-swilling crew. It was possible one of them was the killer. But highly unlikely.

The only one they really wanted to kill was Manny.

By now the pool was a bit of a zoo, with frisbees (and beer cans) flying.

Polly was still valiantly trying to chat it up with Kirk, who was stretched out in his chaise in a glazed stupor, but all she seemed to be getting for her efforts were a few half-hearted nods.

I decided to wander over to the gazebo where Dallas and Spencer shot their picnic scene. Maybe I'd find a little privacy there, enough to take off my capris and tee and feel some breezes waft over my body.

I headed over to the thatched wooden structure, but as I got closer I saw that someone was already there, sitting in one of two wicker chairs inside the gazebo.

It was Justin, the wunderkind director, furiously tapping notes on his iPad.

He looked up at the sound of my approaching footsteps.

"What the hell do you want?"

Okay, so what he really said was, "Hello, Jaine," but I could tell he didn't appreciate being interrupted.

"Hi, Justin," I said. "What's up?"

"Just going over my movie script," he replied, his eyes lighting up. "It's going to be fantastic! A remake of *All About Eve*. I'm thinking Bradley Cooper and Helen Mirren for the leads. Or Jane Fonda and Ryan Gosling. Or JLo and Regis Philbin. I'm known for my unorthodox casting choices."

Known for his unorthodox casting choices? Was he kidding? Three months ago, he was eating pita wraps in the USC film school cafeteria.

"Want some mango?" he asked, grabbing a plump, golden red mango from an end table beside him. "I pick 'em off Manny's tree. Only fresh food around this stinking joint."

He took out his Swiss Army knife—the same knife, I now remembered, that he used to whack away an offending palm frond in the picnic scene—and began to cut the mango into wedges.

"Here," he said, handing me a slice. "Have some."

I bit into it, and it was dee-lish. But I couldn't think about the joys of fresh fruit now. I had a murder to solve.

Taking advantage of the momentary distraction from his movie project, I asked Justin if he'd seen anyone near the prop shed the morning of the murder.

"Nope. I was too busy talking Dallas out of her temper tantrum to pay attention to the rest of the crew."

"Any idea who the killer is?" I asked.

"Dallas, of course," he said without a second thought. "Why else would she be in jail?"

"A tragedy, isn't it?" I sighed.

"It sure is. Dallas would make the perfect conniving roommate for Eve Harrington in the rooming house scene."

"Not about Dallas. About Hope. Plummeting to her death the way she did."

"Right. Of course. Absolute tragedy."

But he was barely looking at me, back to making notes on his iPad.

He wasn't about to get off that easy.

"Hope's death sure was a break for you, huh?" I said.

"What's that supposed to mean?" he asked, looking up from his notes, suddenly on guard.

"Nothing," I said airily. "Just that with *Some Day My Prince Will Come* canceled, you're free to direct your major motion picture."

His boyish cheeks flushed red as his mango.

"What are you trying to say? That I'm the one who tampered with Hope's chute?"

"Oh, no!" I lied. "I'm just making a casual observation."

"Is that so?" he said, his eyes narrowed into angry slits. "Well, here's a casual observation for you: Mind your own business, bitch—if you know what's good for you."

With that, he picked up his Swiss Army knife and slashed into his mango.

And I couldn't help but wonder if, in a desperate effort to get out of his contract, he'd used that same Swiss Army knife to cut the cords on Hope's parachute.

Chapter 22

I walked away from Justin, feeling his eyes boring into my back, no love lost between us.

Our little encounter had left me hotter and sweatier than ever, my orange tankini a Spandex furnace under my clothes. I'd hoped the crowd at the pool would have thinned out by now, but it was still clogged with crew members. I simply could not bring myself to unveil my thighs in front of all these people.

And although late in the afternoon, the day showed no signs of cooling off, still beastly hot and humid. I'd never really recovered from that ghastly harpoon fishing expedition, and I was aching for a refreshing dip in the water.

But all I'd be dipping into here at the mansion pool would be floating beer cans.

Then suddenly I remembered the beautiful waterfall where Spencer and Brianna had shot their scene the other day. The pool of water at its base had been deep and crystal clear, surrounded by a thicket of tall shade trees.

How lovely it would be to dive into its cooling depths.

I felt around in my pocket for the key to the Jeep, grateful I hadn't returned it to Manny. Then, waving good-bye to Polly, who was still yakking at Kirk, I left the gang at the pool and made my way over to the garage.

Minutes later, I was grinding gears in the Jeep, trying to remember the way to Paratito Falls.

It wasn't easy, but after a few frustrating detours, I finally found it.

Stepping out onto the lush grass, I gazed up at the water rushing down the craggy falls and into the sparkling pool below.

Best of all, there wasn't a soul in sight. Just me and a few birds cawing in the trees.

Making my way over to the crystal clear basin, I saw that the water was surrounded by a border of sharp-edged, jagged rocks. I walked around the circumference, looking for a place to get into the water, one that wouldn't tear the soles of my feet to shreds. At last, I found a large smooth rock. This was the spot, I now remembered, where Spencer and Brianna had taken off their robes and jumped in.

Like a stripper in heat, I tore off my tee and

capris, leaving them in a sloppy pile at the shore. Then I made my way into the water.

Oh, joy! For the first time since I'd stepped off the plane at Paratito Island, I felt cool.

What bliss it was to dive under the water and get my head wet. Suddenly all the stress of Hope's murder ebbed from my body.

I was a kid at the beach again, having the time of my life. Splashing and kicking, floating on my back and swimming over to the falls, relishing the spray of the water on my face.

Thank heavens for my swim lessons at the Hermosa Beach YMCA. I did the crawl, the breast stroke, the side stroke, and even the back stroke (always tricky for me). I dove underwater, where the water was even cooler than on the surface.

(Note to Jan Wallis, my swim teacher at the Hermosa Y: If you're reading this, you would have been very proud of me.)

And then I did the unthinkable. The water felt so good against my body, I couldn't resist. I wriggled out of my ghastly tankini and tossed it over by my other clothing.

How marvelous it felt to swim free and unfettered by that miserable lump of orange spandex.

I don't know how long I was frolicking in the water; I soon lost all track of time. But then a strange thing happened. As I was doing the back stroke, I got the feeling I was being watched. I looked around, but saw no one.

I told myself I was being foolish, that I was still stressed out by Hope's murder, that the whole affair had affected my nerves. I tried to shake off the feeling of being spied on, but it wouldn't leave me. And then, when I was coming up from one of my underwater dives, I could swear I saw something flitting off into the thicket of trees.

Was it a living creature? A shadow? Or just my imagination?

By now, it was almost dark. I really needed to get back to the mansion. I didn't want to be driving on Paratito's pitted roads in the pitch dark.

I scrambled over to where I'd left my clothes.

But when I tried to climb out of the water, there was no sign of the smooth rock I'd used to get in the pool. The rocks near my clothes were jagged and slick with algae. I tried to grab hold of them, but my hands kept sliding, algae slime clinging under my fingernails. As much as I tried, I couldn't even begin to get a grip.

Panic setting in, I began to thrash around, frantically looking for the flat rock, but couldn't find it anywhere.

By now the sun was almost gone. Oh, God. What if I was trapped here overnight?

The water was no longer refreshingly cool, but chillingly cold; goosebumps were sponging up all over my body.

How ironic. What if I died of hypothermia in the hottest, muggiest place on earth?

And then finally, just when I was verging on advanced hysteria, I saw it: the smooth rock I'd used to get in the pool.

I swam to it as fast as I could and scurried out of the water to safety.

I looked over at my clothing several yards away and realized that my imagination had not been playing tricks on me. Someone had been at the waterfall, watching me. That person had moved my clothes, making my exit from the pool a daunting feat.

I hurried over to where my clothes were piled, wondering if my saboteur was still in the woods spying on me.

I cringed at the thought of my secret stalker seeing me naked right now.

Frantic to cover myself, I reached for my T-shirt. Then I screamed in terror. For there, slithering out from the sleeve, was a distressingly long snake, its scales glistening in the dusk.

I watched, trembling, as its slid onto the ground.

If I thought I was scared before, I was terrified now. What if it was a rattlesnake? Or some other venomous critter, just waiting to pounce and take a bite out of my ankle?

I remembered an article I once read about what to do when confronted with a rattlesnake.

Whatever you do, they'd said, don't run. Just stand still.

Very sensible advice. Which I promptly proceeded to ignore.

I grabbed my T-shirt and capris, leaving my tankini for the snake, and raced back to the Jeep, my heart pounding.

Someone had been out to scare me, all right.

And that someone, I was certain, was Hope's killer.

Chapter 23

That night at dinner, I was still so spooked by the scene at the waterfall, my food tasted like cardboard. Of course, here at the mansion, the food always tasted like cardboard, but that night, it was particularly choke-worthy.

Fear sat like a leaden weight in the pit of my stomach.

Meanwhile, next to me, Polly was moping over Kirk.

"I spent all afternoon turning on the charm," she was saying, "and got nothing in return. The guy just sat there like a lump.

"Oh, well," she said, trying to saw her way into her hockey puck of a pork chop, "I guess I'll just have to throw in the towel and wait for the next Mr. Wrong to come along. I don't know what it is about me," she sighed. "Somehow I keep picking the unavailable ones."

Frankly, I was only half listening to her, wondering who the heck had been stalking me at the waterfall. Word had clearly gotten out that I'd been poking around asking questions about the murder, and the killer had decided to put the fear of God in me.

I looked around the table, certain I'd been breaking bread (or what passed for it here at the mansion) with a cold-blooded killer.

At the head of the table, Manny was digging into a filet mignon, drinking a fine Cabernet, and still looking pretty chipper for a guy whose show had just bitten the dust.

I thought of that two-million-dollar insurance policy and wondered once again if he'd killed Hope to cash in on it. Polly said he'd been out at the airport this afternoon. What if he'd driven back just in time to see me heading off to the falls? What if he'd followed me? I'd been so involved trying to work the damn clutch, a troop of Marines could have been on my tail and I wouldn't have noticed.

Had Manny somehow discovered I knew about the insurance policy? What if he had a security camera in his office? What if he saw footage of me riffling through the papers on his desk and discovering the policy? What if he put two and two together and came after me with a slithering snake?

And there was Justin, whose expertise with a Swiss Army knife made him a prime suspect in my book. I'd clearly angered him with my questions in the gazebo. Had he been angry enough to follow me to the waterfall to scare the stuffing out of me?

Next to Justin sat Brianna, smiling and cooing, trying to score points with the up-and-coming director. She'd certainly benefited from Hope's death with a windfall of publicity. What's more, she'd seen me leave the pool that day and could have easily followed me over to Paratito Falls.

But somehow, looking at her gabbing animatedly with Justin, I couldn't picture her as my stalker. Frankly, I didn't think she'd have the guts to pick up a snake.

But who knew? I'd been wrong before. Maybe beneath that Double-D bra beat the heart of a raging sociopath.

Spencer, the would-be prince, sat at the foot of the table, subdued and barely talking, unable to muster up a single "brilliant."

As with Brianna, I had a hard time picturing him as the killer—not unless his "mummy" was calling the shots from behind the scenes.

Then my eyes slid over to where Kirk was sitting, aimlessly shoving the food around on his plate. Once again I wondered if that stricken look in his eyes wasn't grief, but guilt from having cut the cords on Hope's parachute.

And as I sat there watching him, I suddenly noticed a leaf trapped in the tangle of his wild hair.

I couldn't swear to it, but it looked like the same kind of leaf I'd seen on the shade trees at Paratito Falls.

Was it possible Kirk had been my swim stalker?

It was at that moment that Manny took a swig of his Cabernet and said, "By the way, Jaine, Dallas called. She wants to see you down at the jail tomorrow. She says you're doing some sort of private investigation for her."

Great. If the killer had any lingering doubts about my involvement in the case, they were gone now.

Damn that Manny. He might just as well have painted a bull's-eye on my back.

YOU'VE GOT MAIL!

To: Jausten
From: Shoptillyoudrop
Subject: Heaven, Sheer Heaven!

You know how much I love your daddy, darling, and I don't want to sound disloyal, but I must confess that dancing with Alonzo has been heaven, sheer heaven—gliding around the room, light as air, our steps in perfect harmony!

Meanwhile, poor Daddy seems to be having a bit of a problem with Lydia. They keep smashing into each other, like two bumper cars at an amusement park. Only neither one of them seems very amused.

Oh, well. I'm sure with enough practice, they'll be just fine.

XOXO,
Mom

To: Jausten
From: DaddyO
Subject: Hell, Sheer Hell!

I swear, Lambchop, it's been hell, sheer hell, dancing with The Battleaxe. She insists on lead-ing, and now my toes have been stepped on more often than a welcome mat at an open house. I swear, the woman has all the natural rhythm of a beheaded chicken!

And what's worse is watching your mom dance with that creep Alonzo. He calls himself a dancer? Hah! I've seen better dancing on "Stupid Pet Tricks." I can't believe I ever took him seriously. The man works as a clown, for crying out loud! We're taking dancing lessons from Ronald McDonald!

And I've been watching him very closely. I've seen the way he's been holding your mom and staring into her eyes. Did you know he calls her his "Spanish butterfly"? If you ask me, I think he's got a crush on her!

Love 'n' kisses
From your
Utterly miserable
DaddyO

To: Jausten
From: Shoptillyoudrop
Subject: Now I've Heard Everything!

Now I've heard everything! Daddy actually thinks dear, sweet Alonzo has a crush on me! Of all the ridiculous notions. For one thing, Alonzo's young enough to be my son. And for another, he's got a fiancé named Gary!

Time to hit the Oreos.

XOXO,
Mom

To: Jausten
From: Shoptillyoudrop
Subject: Guess What Showed Up?

Guess what showed up just as I was finishing
my Oreos? My gorgeous robin's-egg-blue
sequined evening gown from the Home Shopping Club! Now if only I could convince Daddy
to rent a tux. But he's bound and determined to
wear the moth-eaten rag he wore to our
wedding. Oh, dear. I just know a button will go
flying and poke somebody's
eye out!

Must run and start dinner. I was going to serve
leftover meatloaf, but Daddy's been so
depressed about dancing with Lydia, I'm making
him a rack of lamb. Hope that will cheer him up.

XOXO,
Mom

PS. Needless to say, Daddy's been ignoring any
and all hints about the trip to Colonial Williamsburg. He's clearly had his fill of Lydia for the
foreseeable future.

To: Jausten
From: DaddyO

Dearest Lambchop—Here I am, sitting in the den, soaking my feet in Epsom salts, my poor toes groaning in protest. Mom's making rack of lamb for dinner. It smells wonderful. But even your mom's fabulous cooking can't make up for the horrors of dancing with The Battleaxe.

I simply cannot let this travesty continue. Somehow, someway, I'm going to think of a plan to get your mom back in my arms!

Love 'n' snuggles from
Your determined
DaddyO

To: Jausten
From: SirLancelot
Subject: Nippy Weather

While the upholsterer is busy sewing up your passenger seat, guess where I am? Skiing, in Mammoth! It was Brett's day off, so we drove up for the day. You should see that man on the slopes. His form was impeccable. And his skiing wasn't bad either. Après-ski we sat around the fire sipping hot toddies, followed by the most fabulous dinner—Chateaubriand and a bottle of the most divine Cabernet. Then we took a walk outside, with snowflakes falling and Jack Frost nipping at our noses. I just love nippy weather, don't you?

Chapter 24

"**I** know what you did, Jaine!"

I was in Manny's office the next morning, summoned there after breakfast.

Now I stood facing him as he sat behind his desk, chomping on a smelly cigar, glaring at me, fury in his eyes.

Darn it. I was right. There *was* a hidden camera in the room, and he'd seen me reading his insurance policy. Now he knew that I knew he had a motive to kill Hope. Which gave him a brand new motive—to kill me.

I looked around the room for signs of the camera but saw nothing. It must have been hidden somewhere. Maybe even in his fish tank.

"I'm so sorry, Manny. I—"

"You damn well should be sorry!" he shouted, grinding out his cigar with a vengeance. "You snuck into my office the other day and stole an Eskimo Pie!"

Wait. What? Huh???

"I keep track of these things, Jaine. There were five Eskimo Pies when I left the office and only four when I got back. Brianna told me she saw you eating one."

Why, that Double-D double crosser, ratting me out like that. And she was the one who ate most of it, anyway. Of all the nerve!

And then a wave of relief washed over me when I realized Manny wasn't talking about the insurance policy.

"Plus I seem to be missing a couple of Dove Bars and an onion bagel."

"I'm really sorry, Manny. I was just so hungry, I couldn't help myself."

"You know the rules, Jaine," he replied, his unibrow furrowed in reproach. "Snacks are always available for a nominal fee from the basement vending machine."

"Yes, of course. Absolutely. Totally understood."

I started to sprint for the door, but I didn't get far when I heard:

"Don't go. Not yet. I need you to take notes for a pilot idea I've come up with. It's destined to be a ratings blockbuster."

The less said about Manny's "blockbuster" pilot, the better.

(For those of you masochists out there who insist on hearing the gruesome details: It was called *The Real Mothers-in-Law of Miami Beach*,

about a bunch of backstabbing biddies in a
Miami condo fighting over mah-jongg, bingo,
and the three available men in the building.)

I spent the rest of the morning taking notes
on his idiotic show.

Every once in a while, I looked up and caught
Manny staring at me with a strange, contempla-
tive look in his eyes. And I couldn't help thinking that maybe he knew the truth about the
insurance policy, after all. Maybe there really was
a camera in the room. Maybe it was Manny spying on me at the waterfall yesterday. Maybe he
was just stringing me along now, dictating notes
on his silly show, all the while setting a trap, waiting for his chance to grind me out like a used
cigar.

Eventually I escaped from Manny's clutches
and made my way over to visit Dallas in jail.

She'd been stuck in that hellhole for three
whole days. Poor kid. I just hoped she managed
to survive seventy-two hours without a deep
pore facial mask.

On my way over to the garage to pick up the
Jeep, I checked my emails. Never a wise move in
times of stress. I shuddered to think of what
plan Daddy might hatch to worm his way back
into Mom's arms on the dance floor. And needless to say, I quickly deleted that irritating note
from Lance, who had the nerve to be frolicking
in nippy weather while I was stuck here in Paratito, roasting like a human rotisserie chicken.

After I'd dashed off a text, reminding Mr. Ski Bunny to water my Boston fern, I hopped in the Jeep and took off.

When I pulled into town, I saw that once again Paratito's main street was deserted—except for a lone native guy sitting outside Starbucks with a Frappuccino and a harpoon.

I got out of the Jeep and headed for the jailhouse.

When I walked inside, I blinked in disbelief.

In just three days, Dallas's jail cell had gone from hovel to haven.

Dallas was stretched out in a hammock, basking in the cooling breezes of an oscillating fan.

A small TV had been set up in the corner of her cell; stacks of magazines piled high on a table beside the hammock. The mattress on her cot, formerly a skinny slab of straw, was now pillow-top-thick, covered in gazillion-thread count sheets and a hibiscus print duvet. Bunches of pink and green throw pillows dotted the bed, one of which read THE PRINCESS SLEEPS HERE.

The princess in question was sipping on a frothy coconut shell cocktail.

And at her feet sat Ari, the assistant chief of police, giving her a foot massage.

"Hi, Jaine!" Dallas called out as I walked in the door. "C'mon in!"

She waved me into her open cell.

"You remember Ari, don't you?"

"So nice to see you again," he said, wiping foot cream from his hands before shaking mine.

"Ari, sweetheart," Dallas said, fluttering her lush brown lashes at him. "Be a darling and make

Jaine and me some lunch. One of your yummy
tuna niçoise salads?"

"Of course," he said, gazing at her like a lovestruck puppy.

"And a coconut rum drink for Jaine, if you
don't mind."

"My pleasure," he beamed.

Any minute now, I expected him to salaam at
her feet.

Leaving the jail cell wide open, he trotted off
to a tiny room at the other end of the jail—apparently the jailhouse kitchen.

"Ari's such an angel," Dallas said when he'd
gone. "Frankly, I think he has a bit of a crush
on me."

A bit of a crush? Was she kidding? The guy
made Romeo look like Homer Simpson.

"I can't get over the change in your cell," I
said, looking around at her new décor.

"Ari had everything flown in from Tahiti. The
poor dear used up his life savings. Naturally, I'll
have Daddy reimburse him.

"Here," she said, thrusting her coconut shell
cocktail at me. "Have a taste. It's divine."

I took a sip, and indeed it was.

"Jail is ever so much nicer than I thought it
would be," Dallas said, wriggling her freshly
massaged toes.

Tell me about it. The only thing missing was a
Jacuzzi and a wet bar.

"So," she asked eagerly, "what's going on with
your investigation? Have you found the killer
yet?"

"No," I admitted, "not exactly. But I've got several suspects."

I proceeded to give her the dirt on everything I'd learned so far—about Manny's insurance policy, Kirk's affair with Hope, and the newly revived careers of Brianna and Justin.

"Wow!" she said when I was through. "You've got to tell Tonga everything!"

"Where is Tonga, anyway?" I asked.

"He said he was going to investigate the murder scene, but frankly, I think he's out fishing."

She rolled her eyes in disgust.

"You know," she said, "in between foot massages and *Cosmo* quizzes, I've had a lot of time to think these past few days, and my gut keeps coming back to Brianna."

"Brianna?"

I was miffed at the Double-D bachelorette for ratting me out to Manny about my Eskimo Pie heist, but frankly, she seemed the least likely of my suspects.

"I can't stop thinking about something that happened early on in the show," Dallas said, "back when all the bachelorettes were still on the island. Hope and Brianna were sharing a room. One day, we had to stop shooting because of rain, and I happened to walk by their room as they were playing a game of Monopoly.

"I heard Hope say, 'You'd better pay up.'

"And then Brianna got real mad and said, 'Like hell I will.'

"At the time, I thought they were talking about the Monopoly game, but now I'm not so sure. They weren't even looking at the board."

"You think Hope was blackmailing Brianna?"

"It's possible," Dallas nodded. "After that day, I'd see Brianna staring at Hope in a funny way. Sort of cold and calculating. The same way my dog Fluffernut looks at his chew toy just before he's about to pounce."

At which point, Ari returned with our salads and rum drinks.

I'm not exactly what you'd call a salad fan (my idea of a salad is usually the pickle on my Quarter Pounder), but I must admit Ari's tuna niçoise salad was dee-lish. Thick chunks of tuna and potatoes, with juicy tomatoes and skinny string beans, all tossed in a heavenly dressing.

I swan-dived into mine with gusto.

Dallas began to babble about *Cosmo*'s "Ten Biggest Mistakes a Gal Can Make in the Boudoir" (and trust me, I'd dated all ten of them), but I hardly heard a word she said.

My mind was riveted on the idea of Brianna as the killer.

In fact, I was so darn distracted, I barely managed to polish off seconds on my tuna niçoise salad.

I stepped outside into the blazing sun just in time to see Tonga pulling up in a dirty white pickup truck, his hair wet and slicked back, his truck reeking of fish.

I had no doubt whatsoever that Dallas had been right; instead of tracking down Hope's killer, Paratito's chief law enforcement officer had been off somewhere harpoon fishing.

In the trunk of his car I spotted a cooler, no doubt filled with snotfish.

"Ah, beloved future sister-in-law," he said, beaming at the sight of me. "My brother told me of the miraculous turtle you gave him. Blessings are sure to follow in your path for years to come."

Yeah, right. The only blessing I wanted right then was to get away from that stinky truck of his.

But, remembering my mission, I filled him in on everything I'd discovered about the murder—my damning theories about Manny, Kirk, Justin, and Brianna. Not to mention Hope's possible attempts to blackmail Brianna.

When I was through with my recitation, Tonga smiled at me benevolently.

"Ah, dearly beloved future sister-in-law. You mustn't fill your sweet head with such unpleasant thoughts."

With that, he actually had the nerve to pat me on the noggin like a toy poodle.

"When you are Konga's wife, you will learn to leave the thinking to the men. And you will fill your days with women's work.

"Which reminds me," he said, reaching into his pocket of his khaki shirt, whose armhole sweat stains were the size of pu pu platters. "Here's that recipe for fricasseed octopus glands! And another for sautéed chicken necks!"

He handed me recipe cards written in what I hoped wasn't the blood of some poor strangled chicken.

"Yes, when you are Konga's wife, you will learn to be a true woman. Now if you'll excuse me, I've got work to do."

With that, he grabbed the cooler from his truck and trotted off to jail, no doubt to spend the rest of his afternoon gutting snotfish.

As for me, I stormed into my Jeep and sped off, a string of four-letter words flowing like coconut rum from my womanly lips.

Chapter 25

B ack at the mansion, I made a beeline for Brianna's room, hoping to question her about Dallas's blackmail theory.

But her room was empty when I got there, and I figured she was out at the pool, airing her Double D's.

Taking advantage of her absence, I decided to do a little snooping.

Clearly not a neat freak, Brianna had left her bed unmade in a tangled mass of sheets, her pillow squished from where she'd been sleeping.

A night table next to her bed was crammed with makeup—an artillery of lipsticks, mascara, bronzers, and blushers—along with a cuticle pusher, nail clipper, eyelash curler, and other instruments of cosmetic torture.

Then I noticed a book poking out from

among the rumpled sheets. I pulled it out and saw it was a copy of *The 7 Habits of Highly Effective People.*

I have to admit, I was a bit surprised. I had Brianna pegged as the type who moved her lips while reading the *National Enquirer.*

And I was about to get a whole lot more surprised when, in the course of my snooping, I opened the drawers to Brianna's night table and found them crammed with even more books. Brainbenders like *The Prince,* by Machiavelli. *Das Kapital,* by Karl Marx. And *No Exit,* by Jean Paul Sartre.

True, I also found a *Buns of Steel* video along with a hot pink vibrator, but the rest was all advanced smartie stuff.

Whaddaya know? It seemed Brianna was not half the bubblebrain she appeared to be.

On the contrary, from the looks of her reading material, she was a very smart cookie, fully capable of plotting and pulling off a cold-blooded murder.

If Hope had been blackmailing her, Brianna may well have been the one who cut the cords on her parachute.

I was wracking my brains, trying to figure out what hold Hope might have had over Brianna, when I happened to glance down at the floor and saw another book peeking out from under the bed.

When I reached down and pulled it out, I recognized it right away. It was Hope's yearbook, the one she showed me my first day at the mansion. I remembered how proud Hope had been as she'd pointed out pictures of her teenage self.

Sitting at the edge of Brianna's bed, I began leafing through the book, gazing at Class President Hope, Class Treasurer Hope, and finally, Hope, the Girl Most Likely to Succeed.

How irrevocably that last prediction had been dashed.

I was idly turning the pages, glancing at the head shots of Hope's classmates when I came across a picture that made me stop dead in my tracks.

Smiling up at me from the glossy yearbook page was a handsome young man with full lips, delicate features, and bright red hair. His name? Brian Scott. There was no mistaking his resemblance to Brianna, whose last name, I now remembered, also happened to be Scott.

Good heavens. Was it possible? Had Double-D Brianna started out as a guy?

When Hope warned Brianna to "pay up" at that Monopoly game, had she been blackmailing her former classmate, threatening to expose her past life as a man?

I didn't have time to ponder this train of thought, because just then I looked up and saw Brianna herself standing in the doorway, clad in a string bikini, all five feet, eleven inches of her. Why had I never noticed she was so tall, her arms so muscular, her hands so large?

"So," she said, eyeing the yearbook in my lap, "you've discovered my little secret."

Then she sailed across the room and plopped

down on the bed beside me. Reaching across me, she grabbed a cuticle pusher from the night table and began pushing back her cuticles, totally unfazed.

"Yes," she said, gazing at the pretty young man in the yearbook, "once upon a time I was Brian Scott. A girl trapped in a boy's body. But that's all behind me now. Thanks to some marvelous doctors in Denmark, I'm one hundred percent female."

"And Hope was blackmailing you," I said, going for the jugular.

"Through the nose," she nodded. "I had no idea when I showed up for the show that Hope would be one of the other contestants. She recognized me right away and, calculating bitch that she was, threatened to tell the world the truth about me unless I coughed up ten grand."

"Is that why you sneaked off to the prop shed and cut the cords on her parachute?" I asked, hoping to prompt a confession.

"Don't be ridiculous," she said, with a toss of her flaming red mane. "I didn't kill Hope. I didn't care if she blabbed. I'm not ashamed of starting out as a man. And I don't give a flying frisbee if word gets out. It'll probably get me a whole lot of publicity.

"You know," she said, pointing to the copy of *The 7 Habits of Highly Successful People*, "this guy has a lot of good tips for getting ahead in the world, tips I plan to use to become a star in Hollywood."

And from the look of sheer determination in her eyes, I had no doubt that she and her boobs would make their way straight to the top in Tinseltown.

"Sorry to disappoint you, hon," she was saying, "but I didn't kill Hope. Her threats didn't scare me a bit. If you want to talk to someone who was out at the prop shed the morning of the murder, go see Akela."

"Akela?" I asked. "The maid?"

"I'd forgotten all about it when we talked the other day, but afterward I remembered seeing Akela scurrying out to the prop shed. I didn't think much of it at the time. Akela's always scurrying somewhere, scared as a mouse. I figured she was on an errand doing her housework. But now," she added, "I'm not so sure. Maybe she's not as mousy as I thought. Maybe she's the killer."

Maybe so.

It was definitely time to pay my skittish maid a little visit.

In the meanwhile, I bid Brianna farewell.

"See ya," she said, barely glancing up from her cuticles, still totally unflustered.

But when I looked down at her hands, I saw a drop of blood where she'd shoved her cuticle pusher just a bit too hard.

For all I knew, Brianna was faking this whole cool as a cucumber thing. Maybe she was deeply ashamed of her transsexual identity. And maybe, just maybe, she'd killed Hope to keep her secret safe.

* * *

Happy to get away from Brianna and her cuticle pusher, I returned to Sauna Central to give Prozac a hunk of ahi tuna I'd saved from my lunch.

I found her sprawled on the bed, watching Godzilla, our resident waterbug, pushing something across the floor.

Upon closer inspection, I saw that the object being pushed was one of my favorite earrings— a delicate seed pearl dangler I'd been foolish enough to leave on top of my dresser.

I should have known nothing was safe from Godzilla's slimy grasp.

Prozac eyed him, utterly rapt, as he made his way across the room with my precious cargo.

Wow! What a bug! He ought to be on America's Got Talent*!*

Determined to put an end to this nonsense and kill Godzilla once and for all, I marched over to where he was nudging my beautiful pearl earring across the floor.

But as I approached, instead of skittering away like any normal insect in danger, the sneaky devil slithered up and sat on top of my earring.

No way could I stomp on him now, not without ruining my earring.

I could practically hear him chortling in triumph.

Heaven only knew what ghastly gook he was secreting onto my beautiful pearl, and I stood there helpless to stop him.

Utterly disgusted, I tossed Prozac her tuna

chunk (she certainly didn't deserve it!) and stormed out of the room.

Good grief. I'd been outsmarted by a water-bug.

And I actually thought I stood a chance at solving Hope's murder?

Chapter 26

Next stop: Akela, the maid.

According to Brianna, she'd been heading to the prop shed the morning of the murder.

At last, I'd found a suspect at the scene of the crime!

Leaving my humiliating encounter with Godzilla behind me, I made my way downstairs to the mansion's kitchen—a huge room with two hulking stainless-steel refrigerators, a massive granite island, and enough cabinets to stock a small grocery store.

The room was deserted when I got there, and the lure of those refrigerators was just too great to resist. I opened one and discovered it was a freezer, jammed to the gills with trays of airline food.

Well, that sure was no fun.

The good stuff had to have been in the other fridge. I trotted over to it, my salivary glands on alert, wondering what treasures I might unearth.

But as I approached, I groaned to see a padlock on the stainless-steel door.

"Manny keeps all the good stuff under lock and key."

I turned and saw Polly coming in the kitchen, her boyish bod clad in capris and a tee.

"How infuriating," I said, fuming at the thought of Manny eating royally while the rest of us ate cardboard.

"I've got a splitting headache," Polly said, taking an aspirin tin from her pocket. Then she reached for a glass from one of the cabinets and filled it from the tap at the sink. "Manny's been driving me crazy, dictating notes on some idiotic new show about mothers-in-law in Miami."

"I feel your pain," I said. "I was the designated note-taker this morning."

"If you ask me," Polly said, gulping down two aspirin, "the wrong person got murdered on this island."

Amen to that.

"Do you have any idea where Akela is?" I asked.

"She's on her break this time of day—probably in her cabin. It's the first one on the left as you head down the path to the main road. Is there anything I can help you with?"

"No, I need to talk to Akela in person. Brianna says she saw her heading to the prop shed the morning of the murder."

"Really?" Polly asked, wide-eyed. "Do you actually think Akela had something to do with Hope's murder? The woman's scared of her own shadow."

"I know it seems unlikely, but I can't rule anyone out."

"So how's it going with the murder investigation?"

"Lots of suspects, no real evidence."

"Try and pin it on Manny if you can," she said, rinsing out her water glass. "The man deserves to do some time in prison, for cruel and inhuman treatment of his staff, if nothing else."

"How true."

Then she put her hands on my shoulders, her brow furrowed in concern.

"Just be careful, okay? Whoever killed Hope is dangerous. If he killed once, he can kill again."

"Don't worry," I assured her. "I'm a trained professional."

Okay, so I've never received any actual training. But I have watched umpteen seasons of *Law & Order*. That must count for something, right?

I sure as heck hoped so.

Minutes later, I was knocking at the door of Akela's one-room cabin.

"Come in," I heard her say, her timid voice barely audible through the door.

I walked into the cabin, a no-frills room with a cot, a dresser, and little else.

A short, squat gal with a round moon face and enormous brown eyes, Akela was stretched out on the cot, still in her maid's uniform. Her hair, normally caught up in a bun, now lay loose and flowing down her back.

As I walked into the room, she sat up straight and slipped something under her pillow, something she clearly didn't want me to see.

"I hope I didn't wake you," I said.

"No, no," she assured me. "I was just resting."

"Do you mind if we have a little chat about Hope's murder?" I asked.

Suddenly her moon face froze.

"No." She shook her head firmly. "No talk about the murder."

Then she hunkered back down on the bed and closed her eyes, dismissing me.

If she thought she was getting rid of me that easily, she was sadly mistaken.

"Look, Akela. We can do this the easy way, and you talk to me. Or," I added, in my best Bad Cop voice, "we do this the hard way, and I get my cat."

At the mention of Prozac, Akela's eyes sprang open, wide with panic.

"No kitty!" she cried, bolting up in bed. "No kitty!"

Who says a PI in a Cuckoo for Cocoa Puffs T-shirt can't play hardball?

"Thanks for being so understanding," I said, gracing her with a victor's smile.

Looking around the room and seeing no chairs, I plopped my fanny at the edge of her bed and got down to business.

"Brianna said she saw you heading to the prop shed the morning of the murder. Is that true?"

Her eyes grew big as Oreos, alive with fear.

"Yes, I went to the prop shed. But I didn't go near the parachutes. I went to get Mop & Glo."

Mop & Glo? Were the bachelorettes going to compete for Spencer's hand with a cleaning competition?

"Manny keeps cleaning supplies in the prop shed. We were out of Mop & Glo, and so I went to get some. I swear on the name of Wahili."

"Wha-who?"

"Wahili. The Paratitan God of Truth."

"So that's all you did? You picked up some Mop & Glo?"

She squirmed uneasily, her eyes darting around her rustic cabin, refusing to meet mine.

"No," she finally admitted, red-faced. "I did something else."

"What was that?" I asked in my most confession-inducing voice.

"I hid a cheesecake."

"A cheesecake?"

"Sara Lee," she nodded. "Manny keeps them in his freezer for his dessert. But every once in a while, I take one and hide it in the prop shed. Then, at the end of the day, I bring it back to my cabin. Manny, he is a selfish man. Keeps all the good food for himself."

"So you sneaked off with Sara Lee, huh?"

"You're not going to have him punish me, are you?"

"Punish you?" I grinned. "Are you kidding? You ought to get a royal lei for that."

A shy smile broke out on her face. "You want some?"

She obviously did not know me very well. The only possible answer to that question was, "Bring on the forks!"

"Why, yes," I said. "That would be lovely."

Akela jumped off her cot and went to her dresser, where she opened the top drawer and pulled out a cheesecake, along with two plastic forks.

We spent the next several minutes sitting cross-legged on her cot, chowing down on cheesecake and trashing Manny, both of which were immensely satisfying.

Surely this darling woman willing to share a Sara Lee cheesecake couldn't possibly be a killer, could she?

So engrossed was I in the yummy goodness of Sara Lee that I totally forgot the reason for my visit. It wasn't until I was scraping the last morsels of cheesecake from the tin that I remembered my investigation and asked Akela if she'd seen anyone near the prop shed when she was there.

"No one," she shook her head.

"Do you have any idea who might have wanted to kill Hope?"

"Could be anyone," she said. "Miss Hope was a bad lady. She would not have been good for Mr. Spencer. He is a good man. So sweet. So kind."

Her eyes lit up with what I can only describe as love. Either that, or a cheesecake high.

"Look what he gave me."

She reached behind her and pulled out what I'd seen her shove under her pillow when I first came in the cabin.

It was a photo, an 8x10 glossy of Spencer Dalworth VII, Earl of Swampshire. Signed "To Akela—All my best wishes, Spence."

And adorned, I could not help but notice, with a large ♥.

Suddenly a scenario started unfolding in my brain.

Was it possible Akela had developed a psychotic crush on Spencer? Had she mistaken his casual kindnesses for love? Was it possible he was even diddling with her on the side? What about that ♥? And what about the two forks in her dresser? Clearly, she'd been sharing her cheesecakes with someone. Had that someone been Spencer?

What if Akela had fallen deeply in love with Spencer and then, learning he was about to marry Hope, had tiptoed out to the prop shed and cut the cords on her rival's parachute?

I licked the last morsels of cheesecake from my fork, wondering if I'd just shared a Sara Lee with a killer.

Still in a cheesecake glow, I didn't even mind the particle board ravioli at dinner that night. I barely nibbled at them while, at the head of the table, Manny scarfed down a beautiful salmon filet.

He really was a most insufferable man.

I watched Akela as she ran around passing out food trays, darting lovestruck glances at Spencer. At one point, I thought I even saw him wink at her.

Good heavens. Had the royal Brit been carrying on an affair with the Paratitan maid, after all?

Meanwhile, Polly sat next to me, a troubled look in her eyes. Like me, she barely touched her food. But unlike me, I was quite certain she didn't have half a cheesecake tumbling around in her tummy.

"What's wrong?" I asked, as she poked at one of her ravioli.

"I'm worried about Kirk."

Glancing around the table, I realized he wasn't there.

"I stopped by his cabin on my way to dinner," she said, "and he looked terrible. Sitting in his chair, just staring off into space. I'm no doctor, but I think he's seriously depressed. He said something about how life didn't seem worth living anymore."

"You think he'd try to kill himself?"

"I'm afraid he might." Under her shaggy bangs, her eyes were wide with concern.

"Did you tell Manny?"

"Yes, I told Mr. Empathy. All he had to say was, 'Not my problemo.'"

I made up my mind to pay Kirk a visit right after dinner. He was the one suspect I still hadn't questioned—the one suspect with unbridled access to Hope's parachute.

I was asking Polly directions to his cabin when I looked up and saw Akela bringing in Manny's dessert—a big bowl of strawberry ice cream.

She was heading for our table when suddenly she looked down at her feet, horrified.

I followed her glance and groaned to see Prozac, prancing around her ankles.

Good lord! My feline Houdini had staged another Escape from Sauna Central!

Akela stifled a gasp, plopped the ice cream down on a sideboard and dashed back into the mansion.

And like a flash, Prozac hopped up on said sideboard and began lapping up Manny's strawberry ice cream, a little pink mustache clinging to her whiskers.

"Excuse me," I said, jumping up from my chair. "I'm not feeling very well."

Which was no lie.

Manny's seat at the head of the table faced away from the house, so he was mercifully unaware of Prozac's antics behind him.

But everyone else was staring at her, wide-eyed.

I quickly raced over and scooped Prozac away from her strawberry treat.

Only to be met by an indignant glare.

Wait a minute! I was just getting to a chunk of strawberry!

Wasting no time, I dashed inside, and as I did, I heard Manny asking: "Hey, where's my dessert?"

"Here it is," I heard Polly say. "Akela added a special ingredient tonight. Just for you."

I peeked out to the patio and saw her handing him the bowl of strawberry ice cream.

Manny dug into it with gusto.

"Mmm," he said, lapping up Prozac's cat spit. "Delicious!"

At last. A chapter with a happy ending.

Chapter 27

I couldn't stay mad at Prozac. That clever cat put cat spit in Manny's ice cream, a treat for one and all.

I was still, however, beyond baffled by how she kept escaping from our room. After once again securing her behind our bolted door, I made my way over to Kirk's cabin.

His door was open when I got there. Peeking inside, I saw Kirk slumped in a chair, a bottle of bourbon on the floor at his feet.

"Kirk?" I said, as I slipped into the room. "Are you okay?"

"Never better," he said, looking up at me with bloodshot eyes, red-rimmed with tears.

His thick mop of hair was still clotted in greasy clumps, his bare feet crusted with dirt, his face covered in stubble. I could only imagine when he'd last showered and shaved.

Nearby on a makeshift desk sat a laptop and a framed photo of Kirk and Hope in happier days, his arm around her tiny waist, both of them smiling into the camera—his eyes filled with love, hers as calculating as an Excel spreadsheet.

Once again I remembered the scene outside the mansion when Hope told Kirk she was dumping him for Spencer. Had he been so blinded by rage and rejection that he'd sent the woman he loved hurtling to her death?

"Want some?" he asked, picking up the bottle of bourbon from the floor and holding it out to me.

I shuddered to think how many of Godzilla's cousins had been scampering over it.

"No thanks. I'm good."

"All the more for me then," he said, taking a swig.

Then his eyes wandered over to the picture on his desk, the one of him and Hope. He stared at it longingly, lost in memories.

"Hope was the best thing that ever happened to me," he said, a faraway look in his eyes. "Like a dream come true. I couldn't believe a girl as wonderful as Hope would be interested in a blue-collar guy like me. I never made it past high school. But she liked me. That was the miracle."

He shook his head in wonder, then let out a deep sigh.

"I should've known it was too good to last.

She was bound to dump me sooner or later. She was so ambitious, determined to make a name for herself. Me, all I wanted was her."

Another slug of his bourbon.

"Underneath it all, I always knew it was going to happen. But still, it was like a sucker punch to my gut when she dumped me. My stomach hasn't stopped hurting since."

I thought perhaps his tummy problems might have something to do with that bourbon he was knocking back with alarming speed, but I deemed it wise to keep my mouth shut.

"But what I don't understand," he said, scratching his head, "is Spencer. I thought for sure he was in love with Dallas. Although I shouldn't be surprised he wound up choosing Hope. She was so damn special."

Hope? Special? On what alternate universe?

By now tears were streaming down his face. I offered him a few futile pats on his arm, knowing I was wasting my time, that nothing I could say or do would be of any comfort.

And besides, I had to stop this stroll down memory lane and get him to focus on the murder. That's why I was there. Even if he wasn't the killer, maybe he could give me a valuable lead.

"Hey, Kirk," I said, as gently as I could. "I know it's painful, but I need to talk to you about Hope's death."

"Hope's death? All my fault," he said, his words slurred by booze.

Good heavens. Sounded like the start of a confession to me.

"Hope's death is all your fault?"

"Yes," he nodded, his chin sinking deep into his chest. "All my fault."

"What do you mean?" I asked, wondering if I could whip out my cell phone and turn on my voice recorder app in time to catch his confession.

But I never did get a confession, because just then, his head lolled back in his chair, eyes shut.

Seconds later, he was snoring.

I tried to gently nudge him awake, but it was no good. The guy was out like a light, dead to the world.

YOU'VE GOT MAIL!

**To: Jausten
From: DaddyO
Subject: The Mastermind**

Well, Lambchop. I told you I'd think of a way to get back in your mother's arms for the Evening in Paris waltz. And I did it! Not only that, I managed to bump The Battleaxe from the program, too!

Oh, happy day!

All it took was a bit of careful strategizing. And I am nothing if not a master strategist. (Some day I really ought to take up chess. With my brain power, I know I'd be great at it.)

But back to my plan. It was a bit of genius, if I do say so myself. I called Alonzo, blocking my phone number and disguising my voice, and pretended to be a producer from *Dancing with the Stars*. I told him I'd heard about what a wonderful dancer he was, and that I was over at Disney World in Orlando conducting auditions for the show. I said I wanted him to come over and audition, but the only time slot I had available was at 7 o'clock tonight. (Exactly when he's scheduled to perform at the Evening in Paris gala.) And without missing a beat, he bailed on the gala and said he'd love to come to the audition.

There was only one problem, though. He was in the middle of a Ronald McDonald gig, and his car was in the shop. He'd been planning on taking the bus to Tampa Vistas tonight, but no way could he take a bus all the way to Orlando. Now at that point a lesser man than your Daddy would have been stymied. But not me. In a flash, I knew exactly what to do. I told him I'd send a driver to pick him up. And the minute we hung up, I called Ed Nivens and told him I needed him to pick up Alonzo from McDonald's and drive him to Disney World.

Ed balked at first, but then I threatened to show Lydia pictures of Ed playing golf when he was supposed to be laid up with a bad back. (Of course, I had no such pictures, but your Daddy is nothing if not a great bluffer). And so, weaving my masterly web, I got Ed to agree to pick up Alonzo and drive him to Disney World, ensuring that the waltzing wonder would be nowhere near the Evening in Paris gala in time to dance with your mom.

Seconds after I hung up, Alonzo called your mom, as I knew he would. I'd carefully timed my call when your mom was in the tub, primping for her dancing debut.

So I answered her cell phone and listened as he apologized for not being able to attend the gala. I assured him I'd give your mom the message. Which I did. Only I added a few extra details. I said that Alonzo insisted that Mom dance with me. And that Lydia be booted from the show.

Your mom was aghast.

"Lydia, not perform?" she cried.

"Yep," I nodded gleefully. "Alonzo said she'd just have to sit it out. For the good of the show."

So I did it, Lambchop!
I get to dance with your mom! And even better, The Battleaxe has been grounded.

Victory is mine!

Love 'n' snuggles from
DaddyO
(aka The Mastermind)

To: Jausten
From: SirLancelot
Subject: Newsflash!

Fasten your seatbelt, hon! Potential earth-shattering news: Brett and I are meeting again for dinner tonight, and he says he has something very important he wants to tell me. I smell a Significant Other in my future!

Ciao for now!
Lance

PS. Another weensy glitch with the Corolla. It seems that when they replaced the windshield, they had to open the hood to remove the windshield wipers and some of the highly flammable glass sealant fell onto the engine. And wouldn't you know, it was at that exact moment that one of the workers chose to light up a cigarette. There was a teensy fire, and you may need a new engine, but don't worry. I'm sure Senor Picasso will pay for it.

Chapter 28

I was sitting out on the patio the next morning, sawing into my breakfast waffle—trying not to think of my Corolla's "teensy" engine fire and Daddy's plot to keep Alonzo from the Evening in Paris gala—when Blackbeard, one of the camera guys I'd chatted with at the pool, came huffing up to Manny.

"Kirk's dead!" Blackbeard announced, ashen under his bushy beard.

"What?" Manny cried, looking up from the fluffy ham omelet he'd been busy inhaling.

"I went to his cabin to wake him, and he was cold as ice. No pulse. With an empty bottle of sleeping pills in his lap. Looks like he may have offed himself."

Next to me, Polly gasped.

"I was afraid something like this was going to

happen," she said, glaring at Manny. "I told you Kirk was seriously depressed."

"What am I—a psychiatrist?" he shot back. "How was I to know the fool was going to kill himself?"

Fishing his cell phone from his pocket, he put in a call to the police, after which he promptly returned to his breakfast.

Not even death was going to come between Manny and his ham omelet.

Ten minutes later, the two-man Paratito Police Department—Tonga and his sidekick, Ari— were riding up to the mansion in the official police Jeep.

Manny and Polly accompanied them to Kirk's cabin, where, according to Polly, they found Kirk slumped over in his seat, an empty bottle of Ambien in his lap. Along with an empty bottle of bourbon on the floor.

On his computer, he'd left the following note:

Forgive me for what I have done to my beloved Hope. I was the one who cut the cords on her parachute. I can no longer live with the guilt.

So Kirk was the killer after all.

The case of Hope's death, Tonga informed us, was closed.

The cast and crew of *Some Day My Prince Will Come* stood on the front lawn of the mansion as Kirk's body was carted away, whispering among themselves, stunned and relieved that the killer was no longer among them.

"I suspected it was him all along," Spencer said.

And it was true. I remembered when I questioned him, Spencer said he thought Kirk was the killer.

"Poor chap clearly went bonkers after Hope rejected him."

Others, too, chimed in that they'd suspected Kirk.

"It makes perfect sense," said Blackbeard. "After all, he had unlimited access to the chutes."

Yes, everyone was convinced Kirk was the killer.

But I had my doubts. Something about that suicide note bothered me. When last I saw Kirk, he'd been totally comatose. How had he worked up the energy to go over to his computer and type out a coherent suicide note? And when I'd left him, he was barely capable of opening a bottle of pills. Which, by the way, I had absolutely no memory of seeing in his cabin. It certainly hadn't been on his desk. Or on the rickety night table beside his bed.

Then again, it was entirely possible Kirk had woken from his stupor in the middle of the night, summoned the energy to type out that suicide note and gulp down a bottle of sleeping pills. Maybe the pills were in a dresser drawer. Or in his backpack.

I really had to stop playing amateur PI. The case was closed.

It probably all happened just like Tonga said.

And yet, something in the pit of my stomach didn't feel right. I tried to tell myself it was

Manny's godawful waffles, but my doubts lingered on.

Later that afternoon, I was lounging at the pool with a bunch of crew members. Most of the others were busy working their phones—texting, sexting, and updating their résumés.

But I just lay there, daydreaming about the first meal I'd eat when I got back home. I was debating between pepperoni pizza and chicken lo mein when Polly came racing outside.

"Guess what?" she cried. "Dallas is back! She's driving up to the mansion now."

Along with several of the others, I jumped up and hurried to the front lawn just in time to see Dallas emerging from the PPD Jeep.

Unlike the rest of us, depleted by cardboard food and unrelenting heat, Dallas stepped down from the Jeep looking fresh as a daisy, clad in shorts and a halter top, her chestnut hair gleaming, her tanned skin glowing. Nary a bead of perspiration dared show itself on her brow.

In one hand, she clutched her down pillow; in the other, an icy coconut rum drink.

Tonga leaped out of the Jeep and followed her as she made her way up to the mansion, dripping apologies for having arrested her.

"A most grievous error," he was saying. "I pray that you will find it in your heart to forgive us. For I can assure you it has been an honor to have you stay in our humble prison. And please be sure to pass on my best regards to your revered father."

It looked like someone was trying to tap dance his way out of a lawsuit.

Meanwhile, Ari trailed behind Dallas, toting her pink and green hibiscus bedding, a lovestruck look in his eyes.

Soon Manny was huffing to her side, leaving a trail of cigar ashes behind him.

"Welcome back, Dallas, darling! I knew all along you were innocent!"

"Me, too!" said Justin, rushing to join them.

What a couple of hypocrites.

Just two days ago, they were ready to see her rot in jail.

I followed Dallas and her entourage into the mansion, where Brianna was sashaying down the stairs to greet her.

"Wow, Dallas!" she gushed. "You look fab. I can't believe you just did time in the slammer. You're positively glowing."

"I know," Dallas said with a toss of her chestnut tresses. "Ari gives the best facials ever! And you should taste his coconut rum drinks."

Ari, still toting her hibiscus bedding, blushed a deep red.

"Ari, sweetheart," Dallas said, turning to grace him with a sparkling smile. "You've been a perfect angel. I don't know what I'm going to do without you."

He gazed back at her, adoration oozing from every pore.

Poor guy.

While Dallas would soon be jetting back to Texas, Ari undoubtedly would be checking in at Heartbreak Hotel.

Oh, well. At least he'd have his coconut rum drinks to console him.

When the excitement of Dallas's return had died down, Manny gathered us all in the living room.

With a proud flourish of his cigar, he announced that once Tonga filed the required paperwork with the authorities in Tahiti, we'd all be free to leave the island. Which, he guessed, would probably be the day after tomorrow.

A collective groan, as we all thought about having to hang around Waterbug World for even one extra day.

"We've suffered so many deaths," Manny intoned, pasting a pained look on his face. "First, our beloved Hope. Then poor, tortured Kirk. And finally, the death of *Some Day My Prince Will Come*. A groundbreaking show, certain to have been a ratings blockbuster."

I simply could not believe the bilge coming from his mouth, knowing as I did how the show was rejected by virtually every TV outlet known to man.

"Finally," Manny was blathering on, "I want to thank you all for your hard work on the show. And as a gesture of my appreciation, all beer will be half price for the remainder of your stay on the island."

What a sport, huh?

We were all getting up to leave when he called out, "Jaine. Stay a minute. I need to talk to you."

Oh, hell. I hoped he didn't expect me to take more notes on *The Real Mothers-in-Law of Miami Beach*.

I approached him hesitantly, prepared to fake a migraine if necessary.

"Jaine, I got a message from King Konga. They're having a celebration at the tribal village tomorrow night, and he wants you to come."

"Forget it, Manny," I said, my mind flooded with images of Suma and her Spear of Death. "No way am I going back there. His number one wife threatened to kill me if I ever went near him again."

"Nonsense," Manny replied. "Nobody's going to hurt you. You'll be with Konga all night."

A prospect almost as frightening as Suma's Spear of Death.

"Sorry, Manny. No can do. There's no way I'm spending another night with that toothless wonder."

I started to walk away when Manny said, "Okay. Fine with me. If you don't mind having your cat spend six months in quarantine."

I stopped dead in my tracks and whirled around.

"What do you mean?"

Manny's eyes were narrowed into sly little slits.

"Remember how I pulled some strings so your cat didn't have to go through quarantine in Tahiti?"

"Yes."

"Well, all it takes is one quick phone call and the Tahitian animal control authorities will be on your four-footed monster faster than mustard on pastrami."

"Are you telling me that if I don't go on another date with Konga, Prozac will be locked up in quarantine?"

"For six whole months," he replied with a genial smile.

Can you believe it? The low-down cigar-chomping cheapskate was actually blackmailing me!

"Okay, I'll go," I snapped.

Then I stomped out of the room, muttering a stream of X-rated curses.

Where was Suma and her Spear of Death when I needed her?

Chapter 29

Not content with pimping me out to Konga, after lunch Manny actually expected me to work on his idiotic mothers-in-law show. Refusing to lift even a pinkie to help him, I faked a migraine and spent the rest of the day holed up with Prozac in Sauna Central.

Which, I might add, was almost as bad as a migraine.

Prozac insisted that the fan be aimed directly at her, and every time I tried to adjust it to get some of the air, too, she began yowling like a banshee.

And so I lay next to her in bed, beads of sweat spronging all over my body, making do with Prozac's leftover breezes. So hot and lethargic was I, I didn't even bat an eye when I saw Godzilla strolling around the room, no doubt looking for some trinket to filch.

Eventually I drifted off to sleep and dreamed I was swimming in a sea of Chunky Monkey, nibbling on stray banana bits as I swam.

Really most delightful.

Needless to say, it was quite a letdown to wake up back in Sauna Central, awash in sweat, Prozac's tail draped over my nose.

Checking my watch, I saw that I was late for dinner, so I stumbled into my bathroom, splashed some tepid water on my face, and headed down to join the others on the patio.

As I grabbed a seat, I saw Manny and Dallas, feasting on filet mignon, while the rest of us peasants were saddled with rubberized chicken.

Dallas was the center of attention, talking about her time in jail.

"I'm thinking about writing my memoirs: *Unjustly Accused: My Four Days in a Third World Prison.*

"It was quite an ordeal," she added with a deep sigh, "but somehow I found a core of inner strength that kept me going."

An ordeal? What a crock! I almost choked on my rubber chicken when I thought about how pampered she'd been, with her hammock and foot rubs and coconut rum drinks.

As Dallas yakked away, Spencer stared down at his plate, avoiding all eye contact with her, probably embarrassed about the way he'd so unceremoniously dumped her for Hope.

But the others at the table seemed mesmerized by her tale, no doubt hoping to get hired if her memoirs were made into a major motion picture.

Next to me, Polly had the splitting headache I'd been faking all day. It seems she'd spent the entire afternoon tracking down Manny's shipment of pastrami, which was still lost somewhere over the Pacific.

"My God," she said. "The fuss that man is making over that pastrami. You'd think the Titanic had just sunk."

"He's impossible," I agreed.

Then I told her how Manny was blackmailing me into going to Konga's tribal ceremony.

"You poor thing," she tsked.

"Would you mind driving me there and waiting for me to make sure I'm okay?" I asked. "Konga's wife threatened to kill me if I ever went near him again."

"Of course, honey," she said. "Not a problem."

After dinner, Polly went to her cabin to nurse her headache, while I headed down to the basement for my nightly round of Vending Machine Roulette. That night I scored a particularly stale Three Musketeers bar, no doubt manufactured sometime during the Carter administration.

I took a bite, eager to get rid of the taste of rubber chicken in my mouth, but the stuff was like granite, and, refusing to risk losing a tooth, gave up and tossed it in the trash.

Unable to face the prospect of returning to Sauna Central, I began strolling around the grounds of the mansion. It was a balmy night, with actual breezes wafting through the air. I breathed in the heady aroma of gardenias and gazed up at the night sky ablaze with stars.

For once, Paratito Island really did seem like a bit of paradise.

I was walking along, thinking about the glories of nature, the mysteries of the universe, and how I'd sell my soul for a decent dessert, when I approached the gazebo and saw two people locked in a steamy embrace.

You know what a snoop I am. I simply couldn't resist creeping closer to the gazebo and hiding behind a hibiscus bush to get a better look at the lovers.

I almost bust a gut when I saw who they were—Spencer and Dallas!

What the *what?*

What happened to the brokenhearted lover I'd spoken to the other day, moaning about losing his precious Hope, the love of his life?

Right now Hope was the last thing on his mind as he held Dallas in his arms, his lips locked on hers. When they finally came up for air, Spencer said: "It's you I loved all along, Dallas. It's you I wanted to marry."

"Then why did you choose Hope?" Dallas asked.

Good question.

"Manny forced me to," Spencer said. "He insisted that marrying Hope would be good for the ratings and threatened to sue me if I didn't go along with his plans. Said I'd be in breach of my contract."

Are you buying any of this? I sure wasn't.

Never once did I hear Manny talk about wanting Spencer to choose Hope. Why would Manny care who Spencer chose when he already knew his show was dead in the water? And what about all that bilge Spencer had fed me, about how he'd been head over heels in love with Hope, and that he dumped Dallas because he feared she'd be a bossy shrew like his mom?

None of this was making sense.

But apparently Dallas was buying it, because soon they were sealed in another lip-lock, sucking face with wild abandon.

Having had enough of this mushfest, I tiptoed away, heading back to the mansion, my brain abuzz with questions.

If Spencer truly loved Dallas, why had he chosen Hope to be his bride?

And suddenly I remembered how Hope had been bribing Brianna, threatening to tell the world about her past as a man. If Hope had been blackmailing Brianna, who's to say she wasn't blackmailing Spencer, too?

Did Hope have some hold on Spencer? Was that why she'd been so certain he was going to choose her as his bride? Had she unearthed some deep, dark royal secret and used it as leverage to get him to marry her?

And had the desperate nobleman killed her to shut her up?

These were the thoughts buzzing in my brain when I heard someone call my name.

I looked up and saw Tai getting out of his Jeep and hurrying toward me.

"Wait up, Jaine!" he called out as I headed up the steps to the verandah. "I need to talk to you."

I watched as he ran across the lawn, his muscles rippling in the moonlight. There was a time when those muscles would have reduced me to a puddle of goo, but not anymore. Now he was just a doofus with a hot bod.

"I've come to apologize," he said, looking down, abashed, at the wooden decking. "I realize you may have thought I was asking you out on a date that night I asked you to dinner at my village."

Ya think?

"I should have told you it was a set up to introduce you to my father."

Damn straight he should have.

I was all set to give him a stern lecture on the ethics of dating Do's and Don'ts when I happened to glance into Manny's office window and groaned in dismay. There was Prozac, perched on top of Manny's fish tank, her paw in the water, trolling for an exotic snack.

The little minx had broken out of Sauna Central again!

"Can't talk now," I said. "Gotta run."

With that, I made a frantic dash for the front door.

"But wait!" Tai cried. "There's something I've got to tell you about the ceremony tomorrow night!"

But I couldn't stand there blabbing about tribal ceremonies.

Abandoning Tai, I scurried into the mansion and made a beeline for Manny's fish tank, where Prozac was *thisclose* to nabbing a spectacular rainbow-colored beauty.

With a bounding leap across the room, I managed to snatch her away from her colorful prey.

Prozac wriggled in my arms, indignant.

What a buzzkill! I swear, one of these days I'm going to put you up for adoption.

Prozac could sulk all she wanted. No way was I about to allow her to snack on one of Manny's tropical fish.

On the other hand, I saw no reason why she couldn't snack on Manny's tuna salad, a tub of which I grabbed from his mini-fridge on my way out the door.

PS. It was dee-lish. And so was the Dove Bar I'd snatched for dessert.

YOU'VE GOT MAIL!

TAMPA VISTAS GAZETTE.COM

Eiffel Tower Collapses; Ronald McDonald Hijacked to Orlando

During a freak accident at the Tampa Vistas Evening in Paris gala, a seven-foot-tall papier-mâché Eiffel Tower collapsed onto Edna Lindstrom's magnificent egg salad replica of the Arch of Triumph. Details are sketchy, but witnesses say it all started when the button on Hank Austen's tuxedo popped off his jacket, almost poking a fellow dancer's eye out.

In related news, Alonzo Vega, dance instructor and part-time Ronald McDonald, who was supposed to dance at last night's gala, was instead driven to Disney World, lured by the promise of a job from a man pretending to be a producer on Dancing with the Stars.

To: Jausten
From: Shoptillyoudrop
Subject: So Mad I Could Spit!

I'm so mad I could spit! The Evening in Paris gala was ruined, and all because of Daddy!

Daddy actually had the gall to lure Alonzo away from the gala, pretending to be a producer from *Dancing with the Stars*, and roping in poor Ed Nivens to drive Alonzo all the way to Disney World so he'd miss the gala. Daddy said he only did it because he wanted to dance with me. Which, I must admit, melts my heart just a tad. But I simply can't forgive him for what happened at the gala.

Daddy lied and said Alonzo banned Lydia from performing. But Lydia wasn't about to bow out from the show. Luckily, she was able to recruit her brother, Lester, who was in town for the gala, to be her partner. Lester happens to be a marvelous dancer. And with the right partner guiding her, Lydia did a terrific job. She and Lester were sailing along like true pros, while I was struggling with Daddy, trying to keep him from stomping all over my beautiful new baby blue satin pumps (only $69.82, plus expedited shipping and handling). At first, everything was going along fine. (Except for the shoe stomping thing.)

All of us were doing the waltz just as Alonzo taught us, dancing in a circle: Edna and Roger, Stan and Audrey Rothman, Lydia and her brother, me and Daddy, and Nick and Gina Roulakis. There we were, whirling around beneath the Eiffel Tower in three-quarter time.

Then, just as the dance was almost over, when the men were supposed to swing their arms back in a graceful arc, Daddy hurled his arm back with all the force of an Olympic discus thrower.

And just as I feared all along, the stress on his poor tux was too much. The button on his tummy popped right off and went flying in the air, bonking Lydia's brother Lester on his forehead, *thisclose* to his eye! Thank God Lester wasn't seriously hurt. But he was so taken aback, he stumbled onto Edna and Roger, who stumbled onto the Rothmans, who stumbled onto Gina and Nick, like a bunch of dancing dominos, until finally Nick, the former linebacker, went hurtling into the papier-mâché Eiffel Tower and sent it crashing down onto Edna's egg salad Arch of Triumph. The gala was a shambles. All because Daddy refused to rent a tux!

I may never speak to him again.

Can't write any more. In desperate need of Oreo Therapy—

XOXO,
Mom

PS. Alonzo is threatening to sue Daddy for unlawful abduction.

To: Jausten
From: DaddyO
Subject: In the Doghouse

I suppose Mom told you what happened at the gala. I can't understand why everybody's blaming *me* for what happened. After all, I wasn't the one who crashed into that silly papier-mâché Eiffel Tower. Nick Roulakis did.

True, I never should have made that call to Alonzo, but I was so sick at the thought of him dancing with your mother, I couldn't stop myself. Can I help it if I love her so much, I want to be the only one to hold her in my arms?

Now I've been banned from the clubhouse for six months, and Mom's serving Lean Cuisine for dinner tonight.

There's only one way out of this mess. It'll be hell on wheels, but I'm going to have to do it.

Wish me luck, Lambchop!

Love 'n' snuggles from your
shunned by one and all,
DaddyO

To: Jausten
From: Shoptillyoudrop
Subject: Change of Heart

You know I can't stay mad at your daddy for long. After all, when you think about it, he went to an awful lot of trouble just to dance with me.

Today he bought me the most beautiful bouquet of roses, and tonight he's taking me to dinner at Tampa Vistas' most elegant restaurant, Le Chateaubriand.

And most important, sweetheart, he's agreed to go on Lydia's tour of Colonial Williamsburg! Isn't that marvelous?

XOXO,
Mom

PS. More good news: One of the real producers of *Dancing with the Stars* read about what happened to Alonzo and has invited him to audition for the show. Alonzo's so happy, he's agreed not to press charges against Daddy.

WWW.TAMPA VISTAS GAZETTE.COM

Most Graceful Couple

Before the collapse of the Eiffel Tower at the Evening in Paris gala, attendees were

*asked to vote on the Most Graceful Couple
in the Gala Waltz. The results are in and the
winners are Lydia Pinkus and her brother,
Lester.*

**To: Jausten
From: DaddyO
Subject: Arggggh!**

Dearest Lambchop—

Please see attached story from the *Tampa Vistas
Gazette*.

Life's just not fair, is it?

Take care, love bug. I'm off to find where your
mom hides her Oreos.

Love 'n' hugs
From
DaddyO

**To: Jausten
From: SirLancelot
Subject: Utter Tragedy!**

Tragedy. Utter tragedy. Brett did not ask me to
marry him. On the contrary, he took me to dinner to tell me he'd fallen for one of the mechanics at Senor Picasso's, the idiot who set fire to

your engine. It seems the mechanic is an aspiring actor, and Brett wants him to star in his stupid play.

And it turns out Senor Picasso made a big fuss when I told him I expected him to buy you a new engine. But as you well know, I can be pretty darn intimidating when I want to be, and so I threatened to call my attorney, Raoul ("No Case Too Big or Too Small") Duvernois. I guess Senor Picasso must have heard of Raoul's reputation (he's got ads on buses all over town), because eventually Picasso agreed to replace your engine for free, and he's not even charging you the original $39.95 for the paint job. All you've got to do is drive around town with Senor Picasso's One-Day Auto Paint Job logo on the sides of your car. What fun, right? You should see the way it pops against the sunshine yellow background. Even better, they're still going to throw in those free floor mats!

Ciao for now!
Lance

Chapter 30

Those of you who have been biting your nails, wondering if Manny's pastrami ever made it safely across the Pacific, will be pleased to know that it showed up the next afternoon. Manny picked it up himself from the Paratito Airport and brought it back to the mansion, cradling the package in his arms like a proud papa carrying home his newborn from the hospital.

Honestly, the way he was gazing at the package, you'd think it was the Hope Diamond. Or a crate of Chunky Monkey.

While Manny had been off at the airport pastrami-wrangling, I'd foolishly read the latest batch of emails from back home. (You'd think that by now, in the interests of my psychic well-being, I'd be smart enough to ignore them.)

Leave it to Daddy to single-handedly ruin the Tampa Vistas' Evening in Paris gala! And how on earth was I going to drive around town with Senor Picasso's logo plastered all over my car?

With thumbs flying, I zapped Lance a scathing text, venting my fury at being stuck with Senor Picasso's logo and reminding him to mist my Boston fern.

But upset as I was, it was hard to stay focused on my email horror stories.

My mind kept drifting back to Spencer and Dallas and their smoochfest at the gazebo last night.

Spencer claimed Manny had forced him to choose Hope as his bride-to-be. But I wasn't buying it. I felt certain Hope had been blackmailing Spencer, just as she'd blackmailed Brianna.

But about what?

I wracked my brains, trying to figure out what sort of hold Hope had over Spencer.

But the vocabulary-challenged Brit seemed like the poster boy for bland behavior. Was it possible that Spencer had been telling the truth, after all—that Manny had forced him to choose Hope?

I decided to pay Manny a visit and find out.

Soon after his return from the airport, I strolled over to his office, where I found him snacking on a plate of his beloved pastrami. Several slices had been rolled up into meaty little tubes, each skewered with a toothpick, and Manny was busy chomping into one as I came into the room.

"Delicious!" he cried, waving it in front of my face. "Hardly a speck of fat."

Indeed, it did look pretty darn tasty.

Now a normal person would have offered me one of the skewers, but not Manny. He just kept on eating, in spite of the drool practically oozing out of my mouth.

"This is just a snack," he said. "I'm saving my appetite for the triple-decker pastrami sandwich I'm having Akela make me later on."

I guess he must have noticed the pastrami lust in my eyes, because then he said, "I'd offer you a slice, but I figure you're probably still full after the tuna salad and Dove Bar you filched from my mini-fridge last night."

Ouch. Busted again.

I blushed a deep crimson.

"I told you, Jaine. I keep track of what's in my mini-fridge at all times. And when I saw that missing Dove Bar, I figured it had to be you," he said, staring most pointedly at my hips.

The nerve of that man! Eyeing my hips when he was sporting a pot belly the size of a beer keg.

"If you weren't such a cheapskate and served your employees edible food, I wouldn't have been so desperate for a Dove Bar!"

Okay, so that's what I should've said. The words that reluctantly tumbled from my cowardly lips were:

"I'm so sorry, Manny."

"You should be, young lady. I was going to ask you to come back and work for me on *The Real*

Mothers-in-Law of Miami Beach, but now that's out of the question."

Good news indeed. Nevertheless, I tried to paste a disappointed look on my face.

"I don't blame you, Manny," I said. "Not one bit."

"Well, now that I see you're contrite, I might change my mind."

Yuck, no!

"Listen, Manny," I said quickly, before he could offer me the job. "There's something important I need to ask you."

He looked up from his pastrami, curious.

"Did you ever tell Spencer he had to choose Hope as the final bachelorette?"

He blinked in surprise. "No. In fact, I was sure he was going to go after the big bucks and choose Dallas."

So I was right! Spencer had lied. Manny hadn't made him choose Hope. My blackmail theory was alive and well!

"Speaking of Hope," Manny said, "I need you to go to her room and pack up her belongings to send to her parents."

"Absolutely. I'd be more than happy to do it."

And I meant it. I couldn't wait to go through Hope's things. Maybe somewhere among her possessions I'd find the blackmail threat I was desperately seeking.

"That's the attitude I like to see," Manny beamed. "There just may be room for you on *Mothers-in-Law*, after all."

And before he could whip out a contract, I hustled upstairs to Hope's room.

* * *

I found Hope's suitcase on the top shelf of her closet—a hot pink number with bright yellow daisies. So typical of the perky bachelorette.

And suddenly I felt a pang of pity. Hope may have been a calculating opportunist, but she certainly didn't deserve to die. After all, if every calculating opportunist in Hollywood dropped dead tomorrow, there'd be nobody left to run the studios.

I began emptying her drawers of her T-shirts and lace panties, all smelling faintly of jasmine. I marveled at her tiny shorts and halter tops, her size 2 sundresses with their teeny waists.

As I packed, I searched her pockets, looking for a clue to her relationship with Spencer, but came up empty-handed.

I emptied her night table drawer, hoping to find a diary with a full confession of her blackmail plot, but all I found was a dog-eared copy of *Fifty Shades of Gray*.

Checking under her mattress was an equal waste of time.

And then, in the bottom of her dresser, I found Hope's purse—a pink and white gingham tote. Inside were several lipsticks, a comb, a hankie embroidered with the letter *H*, a tampon, her wallet, and her cell phone. I went through her wallet, but all it yielded was twenty-six dollars in cash, some credit cards, and a Sephora Beauty Insider Card.

Finally, I picked up her cell phone. Like her luggage, its case was decorated with bright yellow daisies.

I was staring at the daisies when suddenly I flashed back to my first day with Spencer, sitting at the pool, going over his lines. He'd just gotten off the phone with his mummy when his phone had pinged with a text. One look at it, and he'd gone ashen with fear. He'd looked over at the cast and crew. And there was Hope in one of her perky sundresses, waving and grinning at Spencer. Could she possibly have been acknowledging a text she'd just sent him?

"Hey, what's up?"

I looked over and saw Polly standing in the doorway.

"Manny said you were packing Hope's things, and he asked me to give you a hand."

"You're not going to believe this," I said, "but I think Spencer's the one who killed Hope."

"Spencer?" Polly shook her head in disbelief. "No way. He's too dumb to kill anyone and get away with it."

I quickly filled her in on what I'd learned so far, about Spencer's tryst with Dallas and how he lied about Manny forcing him to choose Hope. I told her about that day at the pool when he'd gotten the alarming text and how Hope had been waving to him when he got it, with a smug smile on her face.

"So you think she was blackmailing him?"

"I'd bet my bottom Pop-Tart. I just need to get into her phone and check her texts."

"Okay," Polly grinned. "Let's give it a shot. I never really believed Kirk was the killer. He was much too sweet a guy to ever hurt anyone."

"First thing we need to do is crack Hope's passcode," I said, turning on the phone.

We tried the obvious combinations: 1234. Her birthday and her street address. (Both of which we'd picked up from her driver's license.) But none of it worked.

Then Polly had an idea.

"I bet I know what it is," she said. Quickly she typed in the numbers for "Hope" (4673), and the main screen opened up.

"Bingo!" she cried. "I knew the little egomaniac would choose her own name."

We scanned her texts, searching for something to or from Spencer. But we came up with zero. Zip. Nada.

Then we checked her photos. Same thing. Just lots of selfies of Hope and her smug smile.

"So much for my blackmail theory," I sighed.

"Oh, well," Polly said. "At least we tried."

"I bet Spencer already got to the phone and deleted every incriminating text and photo."

And then, as I idly scrolled through Hope's pictures, I saw something that made me stop dead in my tracks. It was the picture Hope had taken the day of Dallas's picnic scene with Spencer, when they'd found Dallas's missing hair extensions in the picnic basket. I remembered how, after Dallas had marched over and deleted the picture, Hope had shown me how to retrieve recently deleted photos.

Maybe there was an incriminating picture in the phone, after all.

Quickly I went back to the main screen and

clicked on PHOTO ALBUMS. Then I saw the magical words, RECENTLY DELETED PHOTOS.

One click, and I hit the jackpot.

There it was: A photo of Spencer, wearing nothing but a smile and a dog collar, holding a can of Reddi-wip. In the corner of the picture, a woman's leg appeared in fishnet stockings and stiletto heels.

"Omigod!" I gasped. "Look at this!"

I showed the picture to Polly.

"It looks like Spencer Dalworth's not exactly the country bumpkin he seems to me."

"No, indeed," said Polly, her eyes wide as saucers. "He's been a very naughty boy."

"If a picture like that were ever leaked to the press, it would be a crushing blow to his noble family name."

"Mummy would have a cow!" Polly agreed. "And heaven knows what hell she'd put him through."

"So I was right all along!" I beamed. "Hope was blackmailing Spencer. And Spencer killed her to shut her up. He undoubtedly snuck off to the prop shed the morning of the murder and snipped the cords on Hope's chute. Somehow he managed to plant the wire cutter in Dallas's room and delete the incriminating photo from Hope's phone. But he didn't realize the photo was still stored there.

"Maybe Kirk saw him sneaking over to the prop shed and was threatening to go to the police. So Spencer forced a fatal dose of sleeping pills down Kirk's throat and tapped out a convenient note on his laptop."

"My gosh, Jaine," Polly gasped. "It all makes sense. Spencer's the killer."

"I've got to tell Tonga," I said. "C'mon, let's go down to police headquarters."

"But don't you have to be at that tribal ceremony?"

Oh, crud. The ceremony. I'd forgotten all about it. I checked my watch and saw that it was starting in less than a half hour.

"You're right," I said. "I'll take the phone with me and show it to him there."

Polly came with me to Sauna Central to help me pick out an outfit to wear to Konga's big do.

"Guess what, Pro?" I cried, as we came bursting into the room. "We found Hope's killer!"

Prozac looked up at me, irritated, from where she was perched on the bed.

Do you mind? I was in the middle of a very important gynecological exam.

I leaped into the shower while Polly picked through my closet to find an outfit suitable for mixing and mingling in Paratitan society. Fifteen minutes later, I was clad in capris and a black tee, my hair frizzy from the shower, Konga's tooth necklace stinking up my neck. I didn't even bother with makeup. No need getting Konga all hot and bothered.

Bidding adieu to Prozac and locking the door securely behind us, Polly and I made our way downstairs and over to the garage to get one of the production company Jeeps. We were just about to climb in when we heard a giant bellow coming from the mansion.

And then, like a beer-bellied tornado, Manny

came stomping out the front door with Prozac in his arms.

Storming over to us, his face an alarming shade of red, he shouted:

"This little monster just attacked my triple-decker pastrami sandwich!"

Indeed, a chunk of pastrami was lodged in her whiskers.

Prozac preened proudly.

It was dee-lish.

Good lord. Another escape from Sauna Central! And we'd just locked her in. How the heck was she doing it?

"I'm so sorry, Manny," I said.

"Take her with you!" he said, shoving her in my arms. "I won't have this feline garbage disposal roaming around unsupervised while you're gone."

And off he stomped back to the mansion.

Polly and I got in the Jeep, Prozac purring contentedly in my arms.

Oh, goodie. A road trip.

"Do you mind awfully watching her while I'm at the ceremony?" I asked Polly.

"Not a problem, hon. Any cat who can aggravate Manny is A-OK in my book."

Prozac looked up and preened.

At last! Someone who appreciates my talents!

"And you won't mind waiting till the ceremony is over, just to make sure Suma doesn't impale me with her spear?"

"Don't worry," she assured me. "I'll be here for you."

Which was all very well and good, but I didn't see how Polly, a gal only slightly bigger than Hope, would be able to quell the mighty wrath of Suma.

And so I set off for the ceremony with Prozac in my lap, thrilled the murder was solved, and praying that I'd live to tell about it.

Chapter 31

When I hustled into Konga's village that night, I felt like I'd stepped straight into a *National Geographic* centerfold.

Native tribesmen in loincloths and spears, their faces painted with red and yellow stripes, stood in a circle around a giant fire pit under glowing tiki torches. Seated among them were Konga's wives, all of them wearing floral sarongs and sour expressions.

And roasting in the fire pit was the ugliest fish I'd ever seen. The thing was as big as a satellite dish, with ghastly tentacles splayed out on the grill. And what a stink! I'd been in gas station restrooms that smelled better than that fish.

Konga sat on what looked like a throne at the far end of the circle, his three hairs and six teeth polished to perfection, a giant tassel loincloth hanging from his gut. He waved at the sight of me, flashing me all six of his teeth. I was just grateful that's all he flashed.

Next to Konga stood a large man with what looked like a ginormous hypodermic needle. I figured it was one of those flavor injectors chefs use to shoot marinades into their food.

I was standing there, trying to spot Tonga in the crowd, when suddenly Suma appeared at my side, clad in a copious muumuu and bristling with annoyance.

"You're late," she hissed.

"So sorry. A little mishap with my cat."

"We don't have time to talk. You've got to change into your outfit."

"Change? What's wrong with what I'm wearing?"

"You can't possibly wear this tonight," she said, looking at me as if I'd lost my mind.

Then she hustled me over to a nearby hut, a one-room shack not much bigger than a closet where a hammock, a tiny wooden table, and rickety dinette chair jostled for space. Spread out on the hammock was a white silk version of Suma's muumuu, trimmed with what looked like animal bones.

I just hoped no one from PETA was on the guest list.

"You'll wear this," she said, holding it up. "Now quick. Get dressed."

I clambered out of my capris and tee and stood there awkwardly as Suma surveyed my body in my panties and bra.

"Hard work will get rid of thigh flab in no time," she said.

Thigh flab? Look who was talking! The woman had enough blubber on her thighs to feed the state of Alaska.

Gulping back my annoyance, I slipped into my animal-boned muumuu which, I'm happy to report, was too big.

(The last time I got to say that, I was seven.)

Then Suma spun me around to inspect me.

"How's my hair?" I asked, regretting that I hadn't bothered to blow it out.

"Awful, but we've got no time to fix it now. No one has ever been late for a Male 'Ana ceremony before."

"What exactly is a Male 'Ana ceremony?"

"A wedding."

"How nice. Who's getting married?"

"You are."

Omigod. She had to be kidding.

"In the Paratitan culture, when the king offers you his tooth necklace, he's asking you to be his bride."

I fingered Konga's decayed teeth hanging from my neck.

"When you accepted Konga's necklace, you gave your consent to marry him."

"Hell, no, I didn't! I had no idea it was an engagement present."

"I never dreamed he'd actually go ahead and marry you," Suma said with a rueful sigh. "He's always giving away the necklace and then changing his mind and asking for it back. Frankly, he's what you Americans would call a 'nutcase.'"

"But," she added, with a possessive glint in her eye, "he's *my* nutcase, and I don't like sharing. I used all my feminine wiles to talk him out of marrying you, but nothing worked."

Feminine wiles?

With her linebacker shoulders and unmistakable mustache, the only male I saw her working her wiles on was Sasquatch.

"I tried to warn you. I sent Tai to the mansion last night to explain everything and tell you not to come tonight."

Oh, crud. So that's what Tai had been trying to tell me on the verandah. If only I'd stuck around to listen!

"Now it's too late," she snapped.

With that, she picked up a giant broach of brightly colored feathers and pinned it to my bosom.

"These," she explained, as she clamped the feathers in place, "are the Paratitan holy matrimonial feathers. They've been in our tribe for generations.

"Hurry!" she said. "You're about to become Konga's Wife Number Twelve. And," she added, with unmistakable malice in her eyes, "I'm about to make your life a living hell."

"But honestly," I protested, "I don't want to marry Konga."

"Well, you're going to, like it or not. Konga cannot lose face in front of his tribe."

With her linebacker grip, she grabbed me by the elbow and yanked me out the door and into the waiting crowd.

Konga beamed at the sight of me in my wedding gown, the ceremonial wedding feathers plastered on my chest.

The others chanted to a native drumbeat as I walked around the fire pit toward my future hubby, who waited for me with a leering grin and an unsettling rustle of the tassels on his loincloth.

I considered making a break for it and running off, but I didn't have the courage—not with all those guys standing there, brandishing spears.

I could feel the other wives' eyes boring into me as I made my way toward Konga. Together with Suma, they would indeed make my life a living hell.

I cursed the day I set foot on this stupid island.

By now I'd reached my fiancé. He welcomed me with open (and ever so hairy) arms.

His gap-toothed grin, along with the smell of the stinkfish grilling on the fire pit, filled me with waves of nausea.

Konga, apparently acting as both groom and minister, began to yammer:

"Jaine, my beloved, my most groovy bride-to-be, you are about to enter the blessed state of matrimony, where you will promise to love, honor, and obey me; wash my fish and my feet; cook my meals; and perform your wifely duties in the matrimonial bed."

(The latter accompanied by a most nauseating wink.)

"You shall promise to wash my hair, floss my

teeth, polish my harpoon, and minister to the needs of my pet pig, Ava Gardner."

My God, I was being sold into slavery! Damn that Manny for making me come here tonight!

"And now," Konga continued, "before our nuptials are sealed, it is time for the most revered of Paratitan tribal traditions. The bridal tattoo."

The guy beside him, brandishing the hypodermic needle, nodded with a happy grin.

Oh, lord. Suddenly I remembered that tattoo of Konga on Suma's shoulder—the one I'd noticed the day we went harpoon fishing.

Criminy. That hypo was for me! I was about to get a tattoo of the toothless wonder etched on my arm forever.

By now, of course, I was ready to trade places with the stinkfish roasting on the fire. I wanted to run, but once again, the sight of all those guys with spears scared me silly.

I kept praying I'd wake up and that this would all be a bad dream, but no. The guy with the hypo plodded closer and closer.

And just when I'd given up hope, I saw a tawny flash of fur come tearing through the village. It was Prozac! Lured no doubt by the smell of the roasting stinkfish.

But then she spotted me, standing there in my wedding dress, my bridal feathers pinned to my chest.

At the sight of that bright plume of feathers, she lit up like a Christmas tree.

Oh, look! A birdie! For moi*!*

And with a single leap, she jumped onto to my bosom, clawing the feathers to pieces.

By now the villagers were aghast. Prozac had destroyed the holy feathers of their tribe. But instead of being mad, they cringed in fear, backing away, terror in their eyes. Even Konga had retreated, cowering behind Suma.

"No kitty! No kitty!" they cried. Just like Akela at the mansion.

Wow, these people were seriously afraid of cats.

Tai stepped forward. Even he looked scared.

"Remember the first day you came to the island?" he said. "I told you cats played an important part in our culture. Some are good. And some are evil. I couldn't see Prozac clearly that first day because she was in her carrier. But now I realize your cat is the spitting image of our Evil God, Nokiti."

He pointed to a totem pole at the far end of the circle.

Sure enough, at the top of the pole, was the face of a cat with an uncanny resemblance to Prozac.

Omigosh. Akela hadn't been saying, "No kitty!" when she saw Prozac, she'd been invoking the name of Nokiti, the Evil God of Paratito.

"Go!" Konga now commanded, his voice trembling. "And never return to our village again."

"Not a problem," I assured him. "It's been lovely meeting you. Too bad we weren't a match, but I'm sure you'll find the twelfth soulmate of your dreams out there somewhere."

"Just go!" he screamed.

"Begone, Mainland Trash!" Suma chimed in.

Ever happy to oblige, I raced to the hut where I'd changed, grabbed my capris and tee, along with my purse, and skedaddled out of there faster than a speeding stinkfish.

Chapter 32

"I'm so sorry Prozac got loose!" Polly said as I hurled myself into the waiting Jeep. "She wriggled out of the car before I could stop her. I ran after her, and the next thing I knew, I saw her jumping into your arms at the fire pit.

"What was going on there, anyway?" she asked, starting up the Jeep. "And what on earth are you wearing? Are those real animal bones?"

"It's my wedding dress," I said, collapsing into my seat.

"Your what?"

"I was supposed to marry Konga and become his twelfth wife. They were going to tattoo a picture of him on my shoulder!"

"You poor thing!" Polly tsked, as she took off down the road.

"But thank heavens for Prozac, my rescuing

angel. She raced right in to save the day!" I said, nuzzling my angel's neck and showering her with baby kisses. "How am I ever going to thank you?"

Prozac looked up at me with calculating eyes.
Don't worry. I'll think of something.

"You're not going to believe this," I jabbered on to Polly, "but that beer-bellied bozo expected me to wash his feet and feed his pet pig, Ava Gardner! And all he was wearing was a tassel loincloth. Oh, gaak! I shudder to think what was under those tassels—Hey," I said, interrupting my own horror story. "Where are we going? This isn't the way back to the mansion."

Indeed, as I looked around, I realized we were on an unfamiliar dirt road.

"Change of plan," Polly said. "We're not going to the mansion."

With that, she pulled up to a clearing in the woods, where another Jeep was parked.

And standing there, looking dapper as ever in white linen, was the very last person I expected to see—Spencer Dalworth VII.

"Omigod!" I whispered. "It's Spencer. He knows we're on to him. Somehow he must have found out about that undeleted photo in Hope's phone."

"Of course he did," Polly said. "I told him all about it. Right after I deleted it permanently while you were in the shower getting ready for your date with Konga."

I looked over at Polly, and all traces of the warmhearted gal who'd befriended me were gone. The perky bestie with the shaggy bangs and friendly smile had morphed into the kind of steely-eyed piranha you see manning the make-up counters at Bloomie's.

"Hi, sweetie!" she called out to Spencer.

My God, she was on his side!

And before I knew what was happening, she'd whipped a gun from the Jeep's glove compartment and aimed it straight at me.

"Get out," she said, poking me in the ribs with the butt of her revolver.

I climbed out of the car, Prozac clutched in my arms.

"Look who's here, darling!" Polly said, shoving me toward Spencer. "Right on schedule. I kept an eye on her at the ceremony. She didn't have a chance to talk to the cops."

"Brilliant!" Spencer said, nodding his approval, his eyes as vacant as ever.

"So you knew Spencer was the killer all along," I gasped.

"Oh, but Spencer's not the killer," Polly chirped with pride. "I am!"

"You cut the cords on Hope's chute? But that's impossible. You were with me all morning the day of the murder."

"That's where we fooled everyone, right, darling?"

"Absolutely, sweetpea," Spencer concurred.

"I didn't cut the cords that morning. I did it the night before. It was so easy. Pretending to comfort Kirk after Hope dumped him, I went back with him to his cabin to get him drunk. More than drunk, thanks to the heavy sedative I slipped into one of his beers. It left him pretty much zonked out until well into the next day.

"As soon as he passed out, I zipped over to the prop shed and cut the cords on Hope's chute. Then over to the mansion to plant the wire cutter in Dallas's closet. I felt bad about framing her, but I had no other choice. She seemed like the best bet as a suspect, after the way she'd practically threatened to kill Hope in front of the cast and crew.

"The next day, Kirk was still so zonked out from the sedative he was barely able to function, let alone check the cords on the parachutes before the jump. After the murder, I convinced him to lie and tell the police he'd checked the cords. I put the fear of God into him, telling him he could be arrested for criminal negligence if he admitted the truth.

"I was careful to stay by your side the entire morning of the murder, Jaine."

"And I hung around Kirk," Spencer added, "making sure he went nowhere near the chutes."

"With Kirk swearing he'd checked the chutes that morning, we both had airtight alibis."

"Absolutely airtight!" Spencer echoed happily.

"Time to get moving, hon." With her gun firmly planted in my ribs, Polly started shoving me forward into a thicket of trees, Spencer lighting our way with a flashlight.

In the distance, I could hear a muffled roar, like thunder or a railroad train. But I knew that was impossible. There were no trains in Paratito.

"You were right about Hope," Polly said, the butt of her gun prodding me from behind. "She was blackmailing Spencer. Threatening to go public with his dog-collar fetish if he didn't marry her. Would you believe the little creep snuck into his bedroom suite to make a pass at him, and when he rebuffed her, she followed him to my cabin and stood outside taking pictures of us? The girl had no ethics whatsoever."

"Most unsportsmanlike," Spencer piped up.

"So that was *you* in the picture," I said, remembering the woman's leg in the fishnet stocking.

"Of course it was," Polly replied. "Spencer's definitely a leg man, aren't you, honeybun?"

"Absolutely, pumpkin."

Oh, gaak. I couldn't decide which was making me more nauseous: the gun in my back or their treacly love chat.

By now we'd wended our way through more trees, and the sound in the distance had grown louder. I recognized it now. It was rushing water.

"Spencer and I are in love," Polly said proudly. "We were from the moment we met. And we're going to be really rich some day. As soon as Spencer marries Dallas, of course."

"Wait. What? So Spencer wasn't lying when he told Dallas he wanted to marry her?"

"We figured he'd stick it out for a year or two," Polly said, "and then walk away with a bundle in a divorce settlement. Either that, or knock Dallas off for the insurance money. We hadn't decided for sure. All we knew was that Hope was standing in our way and we had to get rid of her. Just like we're going to have to get rid of you."

We now came to a clearing in the trees, and I saw the source of the rushing water. We'd reached the cliffs of Paratito's Grand Waterfall.

"I followed you that day when you went swimming in the waterfall pool," Polly said. "I tried to scare you, but you kept nosing around, asking questions.

"So here we are," she said with a sigh. "Sad to say, you're going to walk just a little too close to the ledge of the falls and plummet to your death."

She prodded me closer to the falls. Pelted by the spray, I looked down—way down—and felt my knees go weak at the sight of the water thundering down onto the rocks below.

In my arms, Prozac bristled at the water splashing her face. Assuming, no doubt, that she was about to get a bath, she broke into her patented "No Bath!" yowl, screeching at the top of her lungs.

How many times do I have to tell you? No baths! No showers! No water of any kind!

"Time to say good-bye, Jaine," Polly said, with a jaunty wave. "Go ahead, Spencer. You do it this time. I already killed Hope and Kirk."

"You killed Kirk, too?" I asked, furious with myself for not suspecting that my Paratitan BFF had been a two-time murderer.

"I had no choice," Polly replied. "The blubbering idiot was about to go to the police and confess that he'd never checked the cords that morning. Then our alibis would be out the window."

"And besides," Spencer added, "we needed someone to confess to the murder to get Dallas out of jail."

"So I force-fed Kirk a lethal dose of sedatives and wrote that pathetic suicide note," Polly said, beaming with pride.

Good lord, how could someone who just this morning was so darn likeable be such a roaring psychopath now?

"Really, Spencer," Polly was saying. "Time to do your share. You kill Jaine."

"Don't do it, Spencer!" I cried, in a desperate attempt to save my life. "If you wind up with Polly, she'll be every bit as bossy as your mother and have you under her thumb for the rest of your life. Don't you see? You're just trading one manipulative bitch for another."

He blinked, confused, and for a minute I thought I had him.

But then Prozac started wailing again, which seemed to snap him out of his stupor.

"Go ahead!" Polly cried, her face flushed with excitement. "Kill her!"

She was actually getting off on this.

"If you say so, darling," Spencer replied, back under her spell.

"Okay, kill me. But don't hurt Prozac," I pleaded. "Take her. She's a darling cat, no trouble whatsoever."

"Are you kidding?" Polly snorted. "I've seen the little monster in action. She's toast."

At that, tears began streaming down my

cheeks. I was terrified at the prospect of dying, of course, but simply could not bear the thought of Prozac's furry little body being hurled to oblivion.

"Cheer up, sweetheart," Polly said. "Maybe she'll survive the jump. Nine lives and all that. Go ahead, Spencer. Give her a push."

He stepped toward me. I stepped back. By now, I was perilously close to the edge, Prozac yowling at the top of her lungs.

They had me cornered. There was no place to go but over the cliff.

Then, just as Spencer stepped forward to do me in once and for all, he screamed out in pain.

I gasped to see a spear piercing his thigh, blood gushing from his leg.

"My God!" Polly cried, rushing to his side. "What the hell happened?"

It was then that I turned and saw Suma, still in her muumuu, taking another spear from a holster she had slung over her shoulder. She took aim, and this time, she zinged Polly, who crumpled to the ground, moaning.

Dear, sweet, darling Suma. This blubbery mountain of a woman had just saved my life!

After grabbing Polly's gun from where she'd dropped it on the ground, I hurried over to Suma. I would have thrown my arms around her in gratitude had I not been holding Prozac and had she not said, "Keep that evil monster away from me."

"Suma, how did you know I was here?"

"I've been following you ever since you drove away from the ceremony. I saw the Jeep turn down the road to the waterfall and followed the path. I wasn't sure exactly where you were—not until I heard your monster cat wailing."

Prozac flicked her tail, a tad peeved.

I wish everybody would stop calling me a monster. A cat's got feelings, you know.

"Lucky for you, I don't go anywhere in the woods without my spears. One never knows what dangerous animals one may come across," she said, eyeing Spencer and Polly, gushing blood at the edge of the falls.

"You care about me!" I said, my eyes welling with tears. "You sensed I was in danger and came to my rescue."

"Don't be silly. I came for my necklace."

She pointed to Konga's teeth still strung around my neck.

"Oh. Right."

I happily returned Konga's teeth to his Number One Wife.

"May they rot on your neck forever," I said.

"And the muumuu. I need that back, too. You can send it to me tomorrow. Along with your capris and T-shirt. They're just my size."

Her size? On what planet?

"Although I may have to take them in a little," she added.

Okay, now she was beginning to get on my nerves.

Suma stood guard while I took the Jeep and returned to the village to summon Tonga and Ari. Spencer and Polly were quickly arrested and hauled off to the criminal wing of Paratito's General Hospital, which was little more than a shack with a couple of stethoscopes. I just hoped they were out of antiseptic. And anesthesia.

Back at the mansion, Manny was stunned to learn of this latest turn of events.

"But Polly seemed like such a sweet kid," he said.

"Tell me about it."

Uncharacteristically touched by our ordeal, Manny had Akela make me a double-decker pastrami sandwich on rye. With an extra side of pastrami for Prozac.

Which I gratefully toted to Sauna Central.

Near brushes with death can sure whet a gal's appetite. This gal, anyway. Absolutely starving, I threw myself on my bed and began wolfing down my pastrami sandwich with gusto. On the floor next to my bed, Prozac was swan-diving into her pastrami with equal abandon.

Our chowfest was interrupted just then, however, when Godzilla came zapping out from under the baseboard. In nanoseconds, he'd snatched a pastrami shard that had fallen from Pro's plate.

Never one to share, Prozac hissed in outrage as the giant waterbug shifted into high gear and scooted off with his prize.

Let me tell you, that waterbug could move. Before I knew it, he'd zipped across the room and under my bed, Prozac hot on his heels.

I followed the chase, getting down on my knees to lift the bottom of the bedspread and watch the action.

And then I blinked, amazed, as Godzilla scooted out through a gaping hole in the wall behind my bed. Probably an opening for one of the electrical outlets that had never been installed.

Like a shot, Prozac squeezed herself through the hole and was gone.

I raced out to the hallway to find Prozac still chasing Godzilla.

So that's how she'd been making her Great Escapes from Sauna Central!

If only I'd bothered to look under my own bed!

Scooping Prozac up in my arms, I let Godzilla run off with his prize. After all, he'd helped me solve the Case of the Getaway Kitty.

Back in my room, I finished my pastrami sandwich, thrilled that this whole mess was over. Then, exhausted from all I'd been through, I flopped back in bed and fell into a deep sleep— joy in my heart, pastrami on my breath, and Prozac's tail draped ever so thoughtfully across my nose.

So all's well that ends well.

Or as Spencer would say:

Brilliant. Absolutely brilliant.

YOU'VE GOT MAIL!

To: Jausten
From: SirLancelot
Subject: Oops!

With all the hooha of Brett and my broken heart
and the paint job on your Corolla, I'm afraid I
forgot to mist your Boston fern.

It looks a wee bit dead to me.

Epilogue

Justice seekers will be pleased to note that Polly and Spencer, former lovebirds, are awaiting trial in Tahiti. Spencer, the spineless wonder, apparently cut a deal with the prosecutors and agreed to testify against Polly for a reduced sentence.

In happier news, Spencer's mummy, the Countess of Swampshire, has been dating a fabulously wealthy cement manufacturer from New Jersey, so the Swampshire family fortune will be resuscitated after all.

I still can't believe I'd been so fooled by Polly. She'd seemed like such a sweetie, didn't she? And by the way, that gun she threatened me with at the waterfall? A prop she'd taken from the prop shed. Minus any bullets! All that heart-stopping terror at the edge of the falls, when I could have just made a run for it!

It turns out Manny decided not to shoot *The Real Mothers-in-Law of Miami Beach*. Instead, he went with *The Real Housewives of Paratito*—all about Konga and his eleven wives. Which turned out to be the surprise hit of the season. And the most popular character on the show? Suma! Standing before the camera, Suma let her true self come shining through, and now that trash-talking, harpoon-wielding mama is a reality TV sensation! Flush with her newfound success, she divorced Konga, moved to L.A., and last I heard, was dating a wrestler named The Undertaker.

Konga, although having lost his first wife (along with another tooth), has found himself two delightful new brides, Svetlana and Olga, from an online Russian dating service.

And you'll be happy to know that Akela the maid moved all the way from Paratito to Downers Grove, Illinois, and is now working her dream job as a taste tester at Sara Lee.

Here in Hollywood, Justin, the wunderkind director, got fired from the remake of *All About Eve* (his unorthodox casting choices turned out to be a bit too unorthodox for the studio) and is now maneuvering his way through the mean streets of Tinseltown as an Uber driver.

In the strange bedfellows department, you'll never guess who Dallas wound up marrying. Ari, her lovestruck jailer! Ari moved to Texas, sold the recipe for his coconut rum drink on *Shark Tank*, and is now worth millions.

As promised, Dallas wrote a book about her days in captivity, which is now being made into a TV movie. And guess who's starring as Dallas? None other than our guy-turned-gal Brianna! Who, rumor has it, is dating Blackbeard, the cameraman.

As for me, never in my life was I happier to return to my beloved apartment. I spent my first day home soaking in a cool tub, scarfing down Chunky Monkey and chilled Chardonnay.

I stayed furious with Lance for a good two weeks for killing my Boston fern and ruining my Corolla, but he finally wormed his way back into my good graces with a series of heartfelt apologies, emoticon valentines, and daily boxes of Krispy Kreme donuts.

And good news about the Corolla. Suma, who, as I mentioned, has moved to L.A. to be near The Undertaker, thundered over to Senor Picasso's and had a word with the good senor on my behalf. (Now that she no longer sees me as a threat, she's actually been quite nice to me.) Anyhow, after three minutes with Suma, Senor Picasso caved like a wet noodle. The Corolla's been painted white again. No charge.

As for Prozac, she's thrilled to be home, lolling in the breezes from my open window. And yet, every once in a while, I catch her staring down at the floor wistfully.

I think she misses Godzilla.

Well, gotta run. Her royal highness needs her back scratched.

And I need a Krispy Kreme.

Catch you next time.

Freelance writer Jaine Austen is feeling festive about spending Christmas house-sitting at a posh Bel Air mansion, accompanied by her friend Lance and her cat, Prozac. But when a grumpy neighbor gets himself iced, she'll have to find the culprit or she may spend the New Year in jail . . .

Scotty Parker is a former child star who once played Tiny Tim, but now he's grown up into the role of neighborhood Scrooge. He cuts the wires on his neighbors' Christmas lights and tells local kids that Santa had a stroke. And his miserly, bah-humbug attitude lasts year-round—a fact known all too well by his current wife, his ex-wife, his maid, and many more.

Scotty thinks he can stage a comeback with the screenplay he's working on (*The Return of Tiny Tim: Vengeance Is Mine!*), and Jaine's been reluctantly helping him edit it. So when Scotty is bludgeoned with a frozen chocolate yule log and the police start making a list of suspects and checking it twice, Jaine's name is unfortunately included. True, she's been under some stress, with Lance trying to set her up on dates and her fickle feline taking a sudden liking to someone else—but she's not guilty of murder. Now she just has to prove it, by using her gift for detection and figuring out who committed this holiday homicide.

Please turn the page for an exciting sneak peek of Laura Levine's next Jaine Austen mystery DEATH OF A NEIGHBORHOOD SCROOGE coming soon wherever print and e-books are sold!

Prologue

I blame Connie Van Hooten for everything. If she hadn't packed up her staff and gone yachting in the Mediterranean, I would've never spent that cursed Christmas as a murder suspect. At first, it had all seemed like a dream come true.

I remember the exact moment my neighbor, Lance Venable, came rushing into my apartment with the good news.

"Guess what we're going to be doing this holiday season?" he gushed, excitement oozing from every pore.

"Binge watching *30 Rock*? That was my plan."

"No! We're going to be spending two glorious weeks in Bel Air. One of my customers at Neiman's has hired us to housesit her fabulous home over the holidays!"

The Neiman's to which Lance was referring was, of course, the famed department store, where Lance works as a shoe salesman, fondling the tootsies of the rich and famous.

"Not only that," Lance was babbling, "Connie's paying us each a thousand bucks!"

Good news, indeed. Not only would we get to stay at a ritzy estate in Bel Air, we'd be getting paid for the privilege—money that would come in especially handy during the holiday season when my writing assignments usually dry up like a snow cone in the Sahara.

"Lance, that's wonderful!"

"You should see the place. It's got so many valuables, it's practically a museum!"

Lance went on to explain that because of the museum-quality trinkets in her mansion, Connie Van Hooten had a strict No Pet policy. Instead, that generous woman had offered to put up my cat, Prozac, along with Lance's adorable pooch, Mamie, at the Fur Seasons Pet Hotel, a five-star getaway for LA's most pampered furballs.

Like I said, it all seemed like a dream come true.

Except for one pesky fly in the ointment.

My cat, Prozac.

She knew something was afoot the minute she saw me start to pack.

In spite of the gobs of praise I'd been heaping on the Fur Seasons, yakking about their luxurious accommodations, I could tell Prozac was not a happy camper. Tiny little clues. Like the way she hissed whenever I went near my suitcase. Or the damp surprises I was finding in my slippers in the morning. But I kept telling myself that once she got settled in her new digs, she'd be fine.

Then came the day of our departure.

Lance had already dropped off Mamie at the pet hotel and was en route to Casa Van Hooten. I, however, was running late, due to a tiny temper tantrum from my beloved kitty as I tried to get her into her cat carrier.

Trust me, Daniel had an easier time in the lion's den.

At last I'd managed to get her in the carrier and set off for the hotel, Prozac wailing nonstop all the way.

Once inside the Fur Seasons—a bubble gum pink building in one of the trendier sections of West Hollywood—Prozac grudgingly settled down in my arms, glaring at Kathy, the perky concierge who was showing us around the joint.

"Here's our pet spa," Kathy said, as we passed a lavender-scented room filled with pampered pets on grooming tables, getting haircuts triple the cost of mine.

"And our media center," she said, leading us into a room with a ginormous theater-sized screen and a showroom's worth of overstuffed armchairs. Pets were sprawled everywhere—some snoozing, some playing with squeaky toys, others gazing at a nature video on the screen, no doubt dreaming of their future directorial debuts.

"And finally," Kathy said, leading us down a pristine hallway, "here's Prozac's bedroom."

She pointed to a cute little haven of a room,

its twin bed covered in a downy duvet, with matching drapes and 60" flat screen TV.

"So what do you think?" Kathy asked.

"I think I want that TV," I said.

Nestled in my arms, Prozac gave a disdainful sniff.

Smells like Cat Chow and Mr. Clean to me.

"I'm sure your darling Prozac will adore it here," Kathy gushed. "Won't you, Pwozie-Wozie?

A menacing hiss from Prozac.

You call me Pwozie-Wozie one more time, lady, and your pinkie is history.

Well, this was it. Time to say goodbye.

Giving her one last hug, I plopped Prozac on her downy bed.

"Bye, darling. I promise I'll stop by on Christmas Day and bring you a great big present."

She shot me one of her pitiful Little Orphan Annie looks.

Go ahead. Leave me all alone in the hands of perfect strangers. Break my heart. Desert me in my hour of need—Hey, do I smell salmon?

Indeed, she did.

For at that moment a Fur Seasons attendant came hustling into the room with a bowl of char-broiled salmon.

"Bye, Pro!" I called out, as she swan dived into the stuff.

She glanced up at me vacantly.

Yeah, right. Whatever.

So much for broken hearts.

Chapter 1

"**W**hat a palace!" I said, surveying Connie Van Hooten's hangar-sized living room, with its limestone fireplace, triple crown moldings, and cathedral-quality stained glass windows.

"Isn't it fab?" Lance gushed. "And check this out!"

He gestured to a wall-length étagère filled with Lalique crystal, Faberge eggs, and scads of other priceless doodads.

"Good Lord. It's like I'm standing in a branch of the Louvre."

"This vase," Lance said, picking up a blue and white porcelain beauty, "is Ming Dynasty. Fourteen grand."

"Holy Cow!" I cried. "No wonder Mrs. Van Hooten didn't want any pets around."

I shuddered to think what havoc Prozac would have wrecked on that étagère.

"I'm thinking we'll put up a Christmas tree right here," Lance said, pointing to a space between the limestone fireplace and what looked like a Rodin sculpture.

"We can't put up a tree, Lance. What if we spill pine needles on the rug?"

I pointed to the heirloom Persian rug beneath our feet.

"Don't be silly," Lance said. "We'll put a lining under the tree and be super careful. You know how meticulous I am."

He was right about that. From his headful of perfectly groomed blond curls down to his spotless white Reeboks, Lance was the poster boy for meticulous. I mean, this was a guy who ironed his undies.

"I brought all my favorite Christmas ornaments," he was saying, "and I found a fabulous article in *Martha Stewart Living* about ornaments we can make by hand. Pine cone Santas. Acorn garlands. Pipe cleaner elves. Won't that be fun?"

Oh, groan. There's nothing more exhausting than Lance in the throes of one of his creative jags.

"C'mon, let me show you to your room," he said, grabbing my suitcase and leading me up a flight of stairs straight out of *Gone with the Wind*. I followed him up the steps, desperately trying to figure out how to weasel my way out of any future arts and crafts projects.

Upstairs, he ushered me down a hallway past a massive master suite to my room.

"Isn't it stunning?" Lance asked, gesturing around the room.

Indeed it was: Sumptuous down bedding, quilted silk headboard, thick-as-a-cloud carpeting, all done up in pale peach and dotted with antiques.

"That chair over there," Lance said, pointing to a delicately carved beauty, "is an authentic Queen Anne. And so is the matching dressing table."

I looked at the slender legs of the chair and thought how much Prozac would have loved using them as scratching posts.

Yes, it was all for the best that I'd brought Pro to the Fur Seasons.

And yet, I still couldn't help but feel a tad guilty about leaving her there.

True, she'd seemed perfectly content when I'd last seen her chowing down on her char-broiled salmon.

But what would happen tonight at bedtime? I suddenly pictured her all alone on her Fur Seasons bed. Her big green eyes wide with fear. How would she ever drift off to sleep without my neck to nuzzle into?

How would I drift off to sleep, for that matter?

"Get your stuff unpacked," Lance said, "while I go downstairs to whip up a batch of hot mulled cider. Won't that be nice? Warming up with a glass of mulled cider on a nippy December day?"

"Lance, this is LA. The Santa Anas are blowing in from the desert. It's 81 degrees."

"Oh, well. I'll just pump up the A/C and soon we'll have Jack Frost nipping at our noses!"

And off he dashed to run up Connie Van Hooten's electricity bill.

After stashing my things in my walk-in closet (bigger than my bedroom at home), I headed back downstairs, where Lance was waiting for me in the living room with the promised mulled cider.

"I just know this is going to be the most fantabulous Christmas ever!" Lance said, as we settled across from each other on two down-filled sofas flanking the fireplace.

"By the time our stay here is over, I'll forget that Justin ever existed. Yes, indeed," he said, sipping at his cider, "this is the perfect place to mend a broken heart."

"Lance, if I remember correctly, you and this Justin guy were dating for a grand total of three weeks."

"Yes, Jaine, but a lot of strong emotional ties can develop in three weeks, something you'd know if you'd had even a scrap of a love life of your own."

"Wait a minute," I protested. "I've had my share of boyfriends."

"A pitiful few, but you've never experienced the depth of true love as I have," he sighed, plastering a soulful expression on his face, Romeo in Reeboks.

And he was off and running, yammering about his love affair gone awry.

As I often do when Lance goes rambling down romance lane, I quickly tuned out, my thoughts drifting back to Prozac, alone and lonely in her room at the Fur Seasons.

"Hey, what's with you?" Lance said after a while, busting into my reverie. "You forgot the world revolves around me, me, me—and haven't been listening to a word I've said."

Okay, so he didn't say the part about the world revolving around him, but I bet my bottom Pop Tart he was thinking it.

"I'm worried about Prozac," I confessed. "I'm afraid she's going to be miserable without me."

"Nonsense!" Lance said. "I'm sure Pro has made a million kitty friends by now. If I know that cat, she's probably leading them in a Conga line."

Lance continued to assure me that Prozac would be absolutely fine and ordered me to stop worrying. And somewhere in the middle of my second mulled cider, I did.

Lance was right. Prozac would survive perfectly well without me.

She was probably having the time of her life letting Mamie sniff her tush as she watched *My Cat From Hell* on her 60" TV.

I was finally beginning to relax, imagining Prozac sprawled out on her fluffy duvet, when the sonorous chimes of Mrs. Van H's doorbell filled the air.

"I'll get it," Lance said, springing up to answer the door.

"Jaine!" he called out after a few seconds. "It's for you."

I walked out into the grand foyer and saw the attendant from the Fur Seasons, the one who'd brought Prozac her char-broiled salmon, standing in the doorway holding Prozac's carrier.

Inside the cage, Pro was wailing like a banshee.

"I'm sorry, Ms. Austen," the attendant said, "but we cannot keep your pet any longer."

"Why on earth not?" Lance asked, as I scooped Pro out of the carrier and put an end to her wails.

"I'm afraid she attacked Kathy, our concierge."

"Oh, no!" I gasped.

"In fact, Kathy's in the emergency room right now, having surgery on her pinky finger."

Lolling in my arms, not the least bit ashamed of what she'd done, Prozac gave a complacent thump of her tale.

I warned her not to call me Pwozie-Wozie.

"Prozac, how could you?" I cried, after the Fur Seasons gal had gone.

The little devil looked up from where she was nestled in my arms.

It was easy. I just chomped down on her pinky and took a bite.

"Well, we certainly can't keep Prozac here," I said, thinking of the Ming vase and the Persian carpet and the Queen Anne furniture. "She's bound to break, scratch or tinkle on something."

In my arms, Prozac began to squirm.

Lemme go! I wanna see all the stuff I can break!

"Let's put her in the kitchen for now," Lance said. "She can't do much harm in there."

I wasn't so sure about that, once I got a look at Mrs. Van H's stainless steel and marble-countered kitchen, eyeing the fine stemware in glass-fronted cabinets.

"We'd better give her something to eat," I said. "That should distract her for a while."

And indeed, in spite of the char-broiled salmon she'd recently scarfed down, Prozac dived into the dish of caviar Lance had unearthed from the Van Hooten pantry with Olympian gusto.

Leaving her inhaling fish eggs, we headed back out to the living room to figure out what to do next.

"I know!" Lance said. "We'll just keep her in the kitchen all the time."

"Forget it, Lance. Prozac's the Houdini of cats. She'll figure out a way to escape before we've even shut the door."

"Okay, then," Lance said. "We'll box up everything valuable in the house and stow it away."

"Are you kidding? Everything in this house is valuable. By the time we box it all up, it'll be time to go home. Look, there's no way out of it. I'm simply going to have to take Pro and go back to my apartment."

"But you can't!" Lance moaned. "Not now, with my heart smashed to tiny pieces. I simply can't bear the thought of spending Christmas alone."

He slumped down into the sofa, all traces of his holiday high leeched out of him.

"Maybe I can call the Fur Seasons and beg them to take Prozac back."

I realized there was exactly zero chance of this happening, but I reached for my cell anyway.

And just as I did, it rang.

I didn't recognize the name on my caller ID, but I answered it anyway, hoping it wasn't one of the army of robocallers who seem to be tailing me these days like particularly hungry bloodhounds.

"Hi!" A woman's voice came chirping over my speaker.

Oh, hell. I just knew it was going to be someone trying to sell me solar paneling.

"Is this Jaine Austen?" the chirpy woman asked.

"Yes," I replied warily, waiting for her sales spiel to begin.

"Do you have a cat name Prozac?"

Thanks heavens! No sales spiel. I was off the hook for solar paneling.

"Yes, I have a cat named Prozac."

"I got your name and number from her collar," the chirpy woman said. "The adorable little thing just wandered into our house from our terrace."

"See?" I whispered to Lance. "I told you she's a world class escape artist." And then, to the chirpy woman, I said, "I'll come right over and pick her up."

When she gave me her address, I realized she was on the same street as Mrs. Van Hooten. I told her where I was staying, and she told me she was right next door.

"We're the big beige house, just south of Mrs. Van Hooten's."

After hanging up, I charged into the kitchen with Lance and sure enough, one of the windows was slightly ajar. Obviously Prozac's means of escape.

"I'll go get her," I said, scurrying out of the house, down the front path and over to the house next door.

Like Mrs.Van Hooten's, it was a magnificent piece of architecture. But I could see from the patchy lawn, overgrown bushes, and the water stains on the exterior paint that the house had seen better days.

Heading up the front steps, I spotted a large plastic Rudolph reindeer, lying on a patch of fake snow, fake blood oozing from its head.

Wow. Nothing says "Bah! Humbug!" like a dead Rudolph on your front lawn.

Across the path on the other side of the lawn a menacing mechanical snowman glared at me with beady black eyes.

I rang the doorbell, trying not to stare at my creepy companions.

Seconds later, the door was opened by a leggy blond beauty in baby blue sweats, her lush mane of hair cascading like a blond waterfall, a Victoria's Secret model come to life.

In her arms, she held Prozac, who was gazing up at her worshipfully, nuzzling her neck, purring in delight.

"You must be Jaine," the blonde said. "Are you staying with Connie for the holidays?"

"No, my friend Lance and I are housesitting for Mrs. Van Hooten while she's away in the Mediterranean."

"Well, it's super to meet you!" she exclaimed, gracing me with a blindingly white smile. "I'm

Missy Parker. Excuse the gruesome Christmas decorations," she added, gesturing to Rudolph and the snowman. "My husband thinks they're funny. C'mon in and meet him."

She ushered me into a living room which had many of the same spectacular features of Mrs. Van H's manse—triple molded ceilings, ornate fireplace, wide planked hardwood floors.

But here the walls were dingy, riddled with settling cracks, dusty drapes hanging from unwashed windows.

"Scotty, say hello to Jaine Austen."

I got my first glimpse of Scotty Parker as he sat in a cracked recliner—a middle aged guy at least twenty years older than his wife—his eyes riveted on a 1970's era TV hulking in the corner, watching the Dow Jones ticker crawl across the bottom of the screen on CNBC.

When he finally tore himself away from the Industrial Average to look up at me, I was surprised to see—in spite of his burgeoning pot belly and thinning red hair—the freckled face of an impish teenager.

Think Huckleberry Finn after years of too much booze and not enough exercise.

"Jaine and her friend are housesitting for Mrs. Van Hooten next door," Missy explained. "Connie's such a doll," she added, grinning at me.

"The woman's a royal bitch," Scotty snapped. "Had her face lifted so many times, her kneecaps are where her chin used to be."

"Oh, Scotty!" Missy said, rolling her eyes. "Don't be that way. He doesn't really mean it," she assured me.

"Yeah, I do," he grumbled.

"I'm surprised Connie's letting you keep a cat in her house," Missy said, eager to change the subject. "She's so fussy about her collectibles."

"That's just it," I said. "Prozac was supposed to be staying at a pet hotel, but things didn't work out."

I shot Prozac a look of rebuke, but she was too busy rubbing up against Missy's cascading curls to notice.

"That's too bad," Missy said.

"I'm afraid I'm going to have to take Prozac and go back to my apartment. I can't possibly risk having her break something at Mrs. Van Hooten's house."

"And leave your friend to housesit all alone?" Missy exclaimed. "What a pity."

Her silken brow wrinkled in dismay.

"I know! Why don't you have Prozac stay here! I've always wanted a kitty. And we don't have any valuables for her to break."

This spoken, I couldn't help but notice, with a tinge of regret.

And she sure wasn't lying about the paucity of valuables, I thought, eyeing the room full of mismatched furniture, decades old, each piece looking like it had been rescued from a second-rate thrift shop.

"I keep my valuables locked up," Scotty said. "Can't trust the help these days."

That last bit shouted at a tiny slip of a Hispanic maid walking by in the foyer, carrying a load of laundry.

Hearing Scotty's zinger, the maid stopped in

her tracks just long enough to lob him a death ray glare.

"So, how about it, Scotty?" Missy was saying, scratching Prozac behind her ears. "Can Prozac stay with us?"

Scotty looked up, assessing me and Prozac, and from the disgruntled look on his face, I was guessing he found us both wanting. Which is why I was so surprised when he shrugged and said, "Sure. Why not?"

"That's wonderful!" I said. "Thank you so much!"

"And why don't you bring your friend and stop by for dinner tomorrow night?" he added.

Wow. I'd totally misjudged the guy. I had him down as a grouchypants extraordinaire, and here he was turning out to be a real sweetie.

"We'd love to," I said.

"Good," he said. "It's pot luck. You two bring the entrée. Dinner for six."

Whoa. An entrée for *six*? As they say on the Champs Elysees, *quel chutzpah*!

But he was, after all, taking care of Prozac, and I guess dinner for six was the least I could do to repay him.

"Bye, honey," I said to Prozac as I turned to go. "I'll see you tomorrow."

Wrenching herself away from where she'd been nuzzling Missy's neck, Prozac shot me a blank stare.

And you are. . . ?

What can I say? Loyalty's not one of her strong points.

Missy walked me to the door, assuring me I could come visit Pro whenever I wanted.

And then, just as I was about to leave, Scotty shouted out, "Don't forget that entrée! Steaks would be great! Preferably filet mignon."

Filet mignon for six? He had to be kidding! No way was this guy a sweetie. On the contrary, I thought, as I made my way past dead Rudolph and the malevolent snowman.

Ebenezer Scrooge was alive and well and living in Bel Air.

Connect with

Us

Visit us online at
KensingtonBooks.com
to read more from your favorite authors, see books
by series, view reading group guides, and more.

Join us on social media

for sneak peeks, chances to win books and prize packs,
and to share your thoughts with other readers.

**facebook.com/kensingtonpublishing
twitter.com/kensingtonbooks**

Tell us what you think!

To share your thoughts, submit a review,
or sign up for our eNewsletters, please visit:
KensingtonBooks.com/TellUs.